W9-AVL-359

AN UNNATURAL
SELECTION

A Nature Station Mystery

by

Jannifer Powelson

RISING PHOENIX PRESS

ISBN: 978-1-940834-67-2

Published by Progressive Rising Phoenix Press.
www.progressiverisingphoenix.com

Book Design/Layout and Book Cover design by Kalpart.
Visit www.kalpart.com

Editor: Mary Welk

Cover photos by: Jannifer Powelson
Front cover photo: Butterfly Milkweed
Back cover photo: Spiderwort

Printed in the U.S.A.

DEDICATION

To my little book nerds, Alexandra

and Brenna.

CHAPTER 1

An early June breeze drifted lazily through Kristen Matthews' bedroom windows, causing the curtains to sway
ghost-like in the hazy light of a beautiful Saturday evening.
Such lovely weather usually had a good effect on Kristen's
mood, but tonight she was at her wits' end as she grabbed a
red knit shirt from her closet; her bed was already strewn
with discarded clothing choices.

"What do you think about this one?" she asked her
long-time friend and co-worker, Hope Johnson.

Hope struggled to remain diplomatic and chose her
words carefully. "Red is definitely your color, but don't you
want to wear something a little snazzier?"

Kristen tucked a strand of long, blond hair behind her
ear, looking perplexed. "I suppose I could wear my newer
jeans, the ones with the glittery swirls on the pockets."

"Those jeans are very flattering, and they're a step
above your normal workday jeans, but you're finally going
out to dinner with Brett to celebrate solving Johnny's murder
case. You should wear something special."

Kristen sighed and tried to calm the nervous flutter in
her stomach. She had first met Brett Stevenson while employed as a biologist for the Illinois Department of Natural

Resources. After several years with the department, she'd been downsized out of her job when the state budget hit rock bottom.

Brett had been luckier. He continued to serve as an IDNR forester, though his territory had increased due to vacant positions remaining unfilled. He and Kristen met occasionally for business purposes after she opened the Nature Station on land she'd bought near the small Illinois town of Eklund. Brett was preparing a forestry management plan for the Station's timber acreage when the two of them discovered Johnny Thomas' dead body sprawled across a path near Kristen's north property line. That had occurred in April. They'd gotten together casually a few times while working to solve the gruesome murder, but had yet to go out on an official date; their schedules had been too hectic. Brett being out of town recently for two weeks of training hadn't helped matters.

"Yeah, so what are you getting at?"

Hope was seated with her petite legs delicately hanging over the arm of a cozy chair next to a large window, one of Kristen's favorite spots to read. She rose now, walked over to where Kristen was standing, and patted her arm affectionately.

"I know it's been awhile since you've been on a real date. I'm afraid you've gotten stuck in a bit of a rut." She strode over to the closet and retrieved a simple black sheath dress. "Why don't you wear this?"

Kristen blinked her sapphire eyes in astonishment. Instead of answering, she merely raised her eyebrows.

Hope took Kristen's silence as encouragement and pulled a sparkly scarf off a hook. She draped it gracefully around the dress' neckline.

"See, this is simple but elegant, just right for your date with Brett."

"You do realize we are only going to dinner at Barney's Supper Club right here in town. Even though it's Eklund's finest restaurant, it's not exactly a five-star establishment."

"A little black dress is never too much. Besides, the dress was hanging in your closet, so you must have worn it at some point." Hope knelt down to view possible shoe options and chose a pair of black strappy sandals. "These are just right."

"They aren't just right, they're uncomfortable."

"I know they aren't as comfortable as your work boots." Hope wrinkled her snub nose in their direction, despite the fact that she herself was wearing similar boots in a more modest size six. "But you have to admit they're darling."

Kristen glanced at her bedside clock; a look of alarm crossed her face. "Okay, I give up. I need to figure out something fast because Brett is due to arrive in just a few minutes."

"Trust me. You can't go wrong with this outfit."

"All right, you win. Besides, I don't have time to argue." Kristen rolled her eyes as she started to gather her stuff. "Maybe if we had indulged in a glass of wine while you were helping me decide what to wear, things would have gone more smoothly."

"If I had any idea this would be such an ordeal, I would have welcomed a glass." Hope sighed dramatically, though her soft, brown eyes were twinkling with amusement. Her brunette bob swung forward as she sat down again in the comfortable chair and considered Kristen. The two had been best buddies since grade school, and their friendship continued to grow as they worked together to operate and provide educational programs at the Nature Station.

"Go help yourself while I finish getting ready."

Hope shook her head. "No, that's okay. I'm meeting Todd later for dinner."

Todd and Hope had been dating for well over a year, and Kristen suspected the relationship between her best friend and the handsome county deputy was getting serious. She was sincerely happy for them and hoped they'd decide to take the plunge soon.

As for herself, she'd spent enough time with Brett to want to build a relationship as strong as she'd witnessed with Hope and Todd. She'd been on her own for years, but he seemed the right person with whom to settle down.

And if truth be told, she knew she wasn't getting any younger, nor was Hope; both women were thirty-two.

Kristen threw the dress over her arm, picked up the shoes by their tiny straps, and went around the corner into the bathroom to throw herself together. Luckily, she'd taken a shower before they'd started the clothing selection process. She only needed to put on her dress, apply makeup, and tame her wavy locks. She'd wait until the last possible moment to strap on her sandals, afraid she'd twist her ankle in her haste to get dressed before Brett arrived.

When she was finished, she sprayed on a light floral scent, then hobbled into the bedroom where Hope waited.

"What do you think?"

Hope had used the time while Kristen was in the bathroom to rummage through her jewelry box to choose some silver dangly earrings and a bangle bracelet. She brought them over to Kristen, nodding in approval.

"You look fabulous!"

Kristen glanced at herself in the mirror hanging on her closet door. *Not bad*, she thought, eyeing the figure-slimming, sleeveless dress that hit her knees. The weather had been perfect lately for nightly runs, and in combination with the work she did at the Nature Station, Kristen's naturally sturdy figure was held in check. Since she'd hit her thirties, she had to work harder to maintain her weight, but the effort was worth it.

"Thanks for your help. I couldn't have done it without you." She hugged her friend.

"My pleasure. You'd better get downstairs before Brett arrives," Hope said and winked.

Just then the doorbell rang.

"Right on time," Kristen said with a grin. The women headed toward the stairs where Kristen picked her way carefully down the bare wooden steps.

"I'll scoot out as soon as I say hello to Brett."

"You know you're welcome to stay longer."

"I need to get myself ready for my evening with Todd. He'll be done with his shift soon," Hope said ruefully. "Getting myself dressed shouldn't be quite the production this turned out to be."

"Oh, stop it." Kristen opened the door, a huge smile on her face.

"Hi," said Brett. His hazel eyes gleamed with appreciation as he checked out Kristen's dress. "You look terrific."

Kristen normally felt uncomfortable under a man's scrutiny, but she didn't mind it in Brett's case. She checked out Brett and noticed he had also cleaned up his act. He was wearing casual khaki slacks and a plaid short-sleeved shirt, a different look than his usual work jeans and IDNR shirt.

"I guess I'll be leaving now," said Hope with a grin. "Have a great time."

"Bye," said Kristen, feeling slightly guilty for momentarily forgetting her friend. Brett waved as Hope slipped out the door, then he turned to Kristen.

"Wow," he stammered. "I can't believe how beautiful you look."

"Thanks," said Kristen, all of a sudden feeling shy. The color rose on her face. She felt almost like a teenager, not a thirty-something independent woman.

Brett touched her cheek gently. "It's so cute when you blush."

Kristen's face went from pink to red. "I can't help it," she said, laughing. "My fair, sensitive skin is the downside of having blond hair and blue eyes.

"It's all part of your beauty." Brett couldn't seem to take his eyes off her face. He leaned in closer and gave her a lingering kiss.

Wow! Kristen felt the heat of his kiss and was thankful Hope had talked her into stepping outside of her safe zone to wear something dressier than she normally would for a night out in Eklund. "I'm ready to go whenever you are."

"Then let's get moving. I have reservations at Barney's for seven o'clock."

"Oh? I didn't realize they accepted reservations."

"I have the perfect evening planned. The nice lady I talked to on the phone was more than willing to accommodate my requests."

Kristen's nerves had calmed somewhat with Brett's arrival, but she still felt a tiny flutter in her stomach upon hearing his remark. A romantic dinner was just what they needed. She willed herself to relax and enjoy some light-hearted fun with Brett. They'd been through a lot together during the past few weeks.

"Well then, what are we waiting for?" They walked over to Brett's truck with Kristen's dog Peaches trailing alongside them, her tail wagging. Brett held the door for her as she tried to gracefully maneuver herself up onto the seat without experiencing any clothing malfunctions. Soon they were backing out of the driveway.

"The prairie seems to be thriving," said Brett, referring to the grassland acreage that was part of the Nature Station and flourished adjacent to Kristen's hundred-year-old four-square house.

Kristen glanced at the prairie, seeing it with fresh eyes. The warm season grasses were starting to prosper, and stunning early blooming wildflowers like Spiderwort, Butterfly Milkweed, and Foxglove Beardtongue dotted the landscape. Fresh trails had been mowed around the edge of the prairie, separating it from the timber acres. The oak, hickory, and other trees had leafed out, providing a full canopy of shade. With the sun still blazing in the west, the light hit the plants full blast, making them appear even lovelier. Kristen sighed in pleasure at the natural beauty of her property, as well as the prospect of an entertaining evening with a wonderful man.

Brett reached over and squeezed her hand as they drove the short distance into the charming little town of Eklund. With a population of only a few thousand, everyone who lived there knew each other, which meant that even though all the businesses in town were small, local patronage helped them prosper. As they pulled into Barney's crowded parking lot, Kristen was relieved Brett had thought to reserve them a table.

Being an old fashioned kind of guy, he came around to give Kristen a hand as she climbed out of the truck. Normally she wouldn't require a man's assistance. She'd been hopping in and out of pick-up trucks all her life—in fact, she drove one of her own, a much clunkier truck than this newer model—but she wasn't normally wearing a little black dress and spike heels. Brett gave her another kiss, this one a friendly peck on her cheek, before offering her his arm. Kristen accepted it gratefully, pleased to be able to lean on him as she hobbled across the parking lot. Besides that, he smelled great; she'd be crazy not to want to snuggle a little closer.

There were several people waiting in line to be seated, Brett spoke to one of Barney's employees, whose nametag read "Patricia." Holding two large menus under her arm, she promptly led them away from the hostess station to a quiet booth in the back corner of the large dining room. Along the way, Kristen noticed a few people she knew, including Nancy Meyers, a retired nurse and a regular helper at Nature Station events. They stopped briefly at her table, where Nancy sipped a glass of red wine while she perused the menu with a man Kristen assumed was her husband.

"Kristen, you look gorgeous in that dress, much different than when I saw you earlier this week after working outdoors all day! Of course, t-shirts and jeans suit you well too," Nancy added with a wink.

Nancy looked awfully nice herself, wearing a fashionable turquoise blouse and jewelry of a matching hue. The vivid colors complemented her bright blue eyes while providing contrast for her perfectly styled, snow white hair.

"Thanks, Nancy. You look incredible!" Kristen leaned in closer to the older woman, so Brett couldn't hear. "Hope talked me into this outfit."

"Evidently she knows her stuff." Nancy glanced meaningfully at Brett. "Enjoy your dinner!"

"You, too!" said Kristen. "I'll see you when you volunteer next week."

They arrived at their booth and ordered drinks, a beer for Brett and a glass of pinot grigio for Kristen. They chatted while studying their menus. Kristen hadn't eaten at Barney's for some time; her budget limited her visits to once or twice a year for special occasions. She decided on chicken cordon bleu, while Brett selected ribeye steak. The business of ordering complete, Kristen examined the small vase of wildflowers on the table. The cluster of hourglass-shaped orange butterfly milkweed along with tri-petaled periwinkle spiderwort and white tubular foxglove beardtongue stood out strikingly against the crisp white linen tablecloths.

Brett noticed her look. "Did Barney's purchase the flowers from you?"

In order to ensure the Nation Station remained profitable, Kristen strove to find ways to increase attendance at organized events at the Station's Red Barn and surrounding natural areas. To supplement the revenue generated by their programs, a small gift shop carried a variety of earth-friendly items, many crafted by local artisans. The prairie contributed to the operating budget too; they harvested grass and wildflower seed to sell and saved the rest to grow new seedlings, which they also sold at the shop. Barney had contracted with the Nature Station to purchase fresh-cut flowers after he'd become enamored with their unique beauty during a prairie walk event.

"Yes, during the summer months we supply them with wildflowers, and sometimes even prairie grasses for the weekend crowd."

"They're gorgeous." He looked at her with appreciation. "You've really built quite a business at the Nature Station."

Kristen smiled, remembering the hard work that had gone into making her business successful. "We've built it slowly but surely over the past four years, and the help I've received from IDNR to establish the prairie and improve the timber has been invaluable, as you well know."

"Yeah, working on your forestry plan was one of my favorite jobs."

"Except for stumbling over a dead body and being questioned for a murder while in the midst of a timber analysis."

"To be honest, I could have done without that part."

"I feel the same way. At least being thrown into those unpleasant circumstances helped us get to know each other more quickly."

"You're right about that." Brett took a drink from the glass of beer that had just been delivered by their waiter. "So was there any excitement at the Station today?"

"Nothing as shocking as a murder, thank goodness. We held our first Prairie Walk of the season this morning. We had an excellent turnout, which wasn't surprising, given the warm, sunny weather and all the interesting plants in bloom."

"What's on deck for tomorrow?"

"We're open from noon until five o'clock to the general public, but we have a Family Nature Hike planned too. We started those in April, and it was such a great success that we decided to continue holding them one Sunday afternoon a month." Kristen frowned, remembering their first one in April. She had questioned a few Nature Station volunteers during that event about Johnny Thomas's murder, including Lisa McLeod, who had actually been the one to strangle him. Kristen had not even remotely suspected the woman, but then she was trained as a biologist, not a detective.

"You look like you drifted off for a moment."

"Believe it or not, I was thinking about Johnny's murder."

"We're not supposed to be discussing Johnny's untimely death tonight. We should be celebrating that the murderer was caught." He lifted his glass in an impromptu toast. "The case is closed, thanks to you!"

Kristen raised her glass too. "I had some help from you too, so don't be so modest."

"Why don't we put it behind us for now?" he said, clinking his glass against hers.

"Sure." She was glad to think about something more positive. "How was your work week? I haven't seen much of you lately."

"I returned from training earlier in the week, and I spent a day or two trying to catch up on paperwork and returning phone calls and e-mails. Yesterday I had a meeting with a forestry landowner first thing in the morning. I went on two other field visits afterwards." He reached for Kristen's hand across the table. "I've missed you. It was lousy timing having to attend two weeks of training away from you. I'm glad it's finished."

Kristen remembered her years working for the state. She knew mandatory training sessions were seldom entertaining and not always productive.

"That's okay. You couldn't help it. At least we were able to talk on the phone most days. I hope the course was at least worthwhile."

"Surprisingly, it was for the most part." He paused and took another swig of his beer. "When I returned, my boss informed me I was going to be in charge of an intern for the summer."

"With any luck he'll be more of a help than a hindrance."

"Actually, the intern is a *she*."

Kristen's brows shot upward. "Really? I don't mean to be sexist, but most of the IDNR foresters I've met are men, so I assumed the intern was too."

"You're right, most of them are men."

Was it just her imagination, or did Brett seem a tad bit uncomfortable? "When does she start?" she asked, trying to act naturally.

"She began working with me this week. She had some training to complete in Springfield last week, and when I returned from my own training, she reported to my office. Her name's Cassie, by the way."

How sweet. "What type of work will she be doing?"

"Since I was trying to catch up on things after being away, I had her help with routine office duties. But when I got back to the field yesterday, she rode along with me."

Various uncharitable thoughts crowded Kristen's brain as she sipped her wine. "You're used to working alone, so I'm sure it's tough getting used to having someone work closely with you."

"Oh, Cassie's a lot of fun and picks up on things really quickly, so it's not too bad."

Perfect. I wonder what she looks like. Kristen told herself to stop being ridiculous. She refused to feel jealousy toward a woman she'd never met. Besides, Brett had seemed totally enthralled with her, until they started to discuss Cassie, she remembered.

The waiter picked that moment to deliver their salads, for which Kristen was grateful. Maybe diving into their food would dissipate the strange vibes she was feeling.

Kristen poured Italian salad dressing over her mixture of greens and chose a piece of warm whole wheat bread from the basket before passing it to Brett. "Would you like some butter?"

"Sure," said Brett, flashing a picture perfect smile.

The full effect of his good looks hit her. Between his black hair, hazel eyes, and suntanned skin, he was quite handsome, not to mention a nice guy. She felt the awkwardness of the moment pass.

Shortly after they devoured their salads, their entrees arrived and they chatted casually while they ate. Kristen took a bite of her chicken, savoring the rich flavor. "This tastes excellent! I only had time for an apple and a measly sandwich for lunch."

"My steak is delicious, but let's try to save room for dessert."

Kristen thought of her little black dress and wondered how much more it could hold. "Maybe I'll just have a bite of yours."

"That'll work, but I have to warn you—I'm in the mood for chocolate."

"Me, too!" Kristen had a weakness for milk chocolate herself, so that wouldn't be a problem. She glanced around the restaurant, which was still packed with diners. She spied another Nature Station volunteer, Robert Wellington, across the room and waved when she caught his eye.

"You seem to know half the people here tonight."

"That's how it is in small towns, everyone knows everyone." *And each other's business*, she thought to herself. "Besides, I've lived here since I was born, so I'm bound to see people I know. I'm sure it would be the same if we went out in your home town."

"Stanford is even smaller than Eklund, so it's not likely we'd be going on a date there," he said ruefully. "But if we did, the odds would be even greater we'd run into a friend or family member."

Kristen laughed. "The man I waved to is Robert Wellington. Do you remember him? He's retired from the State Bank of Eklund."

"Sure, I met him at the Red Barn after we discovered Johnny's body." He muttered something under his breath Kristen couldn't understand before speaking more clearly. "Darn it! We need to find something else to discuss."

"I agree, but you have to admit that not only was Johnny's death and investigation into his murder a big deal to us, but the entire town is still talking about it." She took another sip of her wine, enjoying the slightly tart taste. "As horrible as it was, eventually we'll get over it."

"Before we know it, another scandal will break out in the normally sleepy town of Eklund that will take over as our next dinner date topic of conversation."

"I suppose you're right," said Kristen, a feeling of discomfort suddenly washing over her that had nothing to do with the strappy sandals pinching her toes. She understood all too well the consequences of a scandal, though thankfully she and the Nature Station had managed to weather the recent one unscathed. She hoped she wouldn't have to endure another anytime soon.

CHAPTER 2

The waiter cleared away their dirty dishes and offered them the dessert menu. Stuffed from an excellent dinner, the couple still scanned the list of scrumptious sweets.

"If we want something chocolate, there's chocolate cake or cheesecake with homemade chocolate sauce. Which do you prefer?" asked Brett.

"Either one sounds yummy. I only want a tiny taste, so you choose."

Brett hemmed and hawed until the waiter returned. "Have you made your selection?" the waiter asked.

Naturally, Kristen giggled to herself.

Brett looked at her oddly but said, "We'll try the cheesecake. Two forks, please."

That sounds cozy, thought Kristen. The evening was turning out perfectly, just as Brett had planned it, despite her earlier misgivings.

"What was so funny?" Brett studied her face.

"Oh, nothing much. When the waiter asked about our dessert selection, I thought to myself, *naturally.*" She finished the sentence lamely, thinking he might not understand. *Maybe I've been out in the sun too much lately.*

Her eyes lit up when Brett snickered. "Oh, you mean like Charles Darwin's theory of Natural Selection."

Kristen laughed. "Why, naturally!" It was good to know she could be herself around Brett.

Brett looked thoughtful. "Isn't it wonderful how we have so much in common? It's amazing that we can find humor in biological principals that are decades old."

"I agree," she said. "Now if you'll excuse me, I need to use the ladies room. Maybe we can discuss Gregor Mendel and Carl Linnaeus when I return."

"Of course, though we need to save time for Aldo Leopold and Watson and Crick." Brett smiled engagingly. "You go ahead. If the cheesecake arrives, I promise not to get started until you return."

"No worries, I'll just be a minute." Kristen slid out of the booth as gracefully as possible. After having been seated for such a long period of time, her legs were stiff, and she felt like she was walking on stilts in her heels. Despite her hindrances, she breezed into the restroom, in a hurry to return to the table.

There were only two stalls in the small bathroom, and one of them looked to be occupied, though she couldn't hear any sounds coming from it. *Not always a bad thing*, she thought, grinning. She went into the vacant stall, conducted her business, and exited to wash her hands at the sink. She glanced at her appearance in the sink mirror and was relieved to see her hair and makeup were still in place. She reapplied her lipstick and noticed the stall was still closed; she had yet to hear a peep from anyone in it. Curious, she looked under the door and, sure enough, she saw a pair of shoes. *How strange*. Starting to feel uneasy again, she called out, "Hello! Is everything okay in there?"

Not one to normally make conversation with people behind closed doors in public restrooms, she felt awkward, but couldn't help starting to think something was dreadfully wrong. She tip-toed over and tapped lightly on the door. Hearing no response, she checked the door and, sure enough, it was locked. She bent down slightly to peer more closely at the shoes she'd seen earlier.

A sudden chill crept through her body. She jerked upright again, the tiny hairs on her bare arms rising in protest as she shivered. She stepped back and rubbed her arms, telling herself it was the air conditioning vent blowing too much cold air in a small space that caused her goose bumps.

But when she inhaled deeply in an attempt to fend off her uneasiness, she caught the sour stench of vomit coming from the stall. The odor worried Kristen, and she became increasingly concerned when she peeked once more beneath the stall's door and realized the shoes she saw there were resting at an odd angle.

Sure now that something was indeed not right, she knelt down for a better view. All she could see was a pair of stylish black dress shoes and the lower legs of a woman's black slacks. A jolt of fear ran through her when she noticed a turquoise earring lying on the floor. She remembered Nancy wearing turquoise jewelry when they'd visited earlier that evening.

Kristen willed herself to remain calm. After all, it needn't be Nancy behind the stall door; it could be any female patron of the restaurant. But if the beautiful earring *was* Nancy's, what then was it doing on the floor?

Kristen tried to think of a reasonable explanation. Before she called in help, she decided she should look inside the stall. There was no sense in causing a false alarm if the woman sitting inside was simply nauseated and in no mood to talk.

She carefully pulled herself to her feet, again feeling the effects of a form fitting dress and spike heels. *What next?* She tossed a few ideas around in her head and then knocked again on the stall, jangling the door. She called out one last time, "Hello! Are you all right?"

Again, no answer. She almost wished someone else would enter the restroom so she could ask for their input. When seconds passed and no one else arrived, she decided to take matters into her own hands. This time she prayed no one would walk into the bathroom or they'd see her peering into the stall through the gaps in the metal framework. How on earth would she explain her actions to a newcomer? She normally cursed the gap between the frame and the door and could never understand why the door couldn't be engineered differently to allow the bathroom user more privacy, not to mention making things less awkward for the women waiting in line.

She didn't have time to ponder the deficiencies in public bathroom design; she couldn't put the chore off any longer. Inching her face closer to the gray metal door, she looked through the crack, now thankful for the gap which would allow her to see if there really was a problem.

She squinted, half closing her right eye to see better, and then opened it wide in shock. Sure enough, it was Nancy sitting in the stall, and it appeared she had bigger problems than merely dropping an earring.

Kristen couldn't do anything to help Nancy until the door was open, so she ran out into the dining area, stopping by her own table first. Brett looked at her quizzically, probably wondering what had taken her so long. Sure enough, their cheesecake was sitting there, untouched. The delicious dessert didn't appeal to Kristen in the least at the moment. In fact, she felt her stomach cramp from her nervousness.

"There's a problem in the bathroom." Kristen blurted it out, not thinking of how Brett may interpret her remark.

"Did the toilet overflow?" he asked, looking puzzled.

"No, nothing like that," she said, looking around wildly. "We've got to find someone to help us."

He put his hand over Kristen's in an attempt to soothe her. "Please tell me what happened. You're starting to scare me."

She was sure she looked scary, with her hair most likely disarranged from checking under bathroom stalls. "It's Nancy. There's something wrong with her. I tried to get her to talk to me when I couldn't hear any sounds coming from her stall."

"Hold on, that's not so bad, is it?"

"No, you don't understand!" By now, Kristen was starting to have problems breathing. She managed to take a deep breath before continuing. "I noticed her feet were at an odd angle, then I saw an earring lying on the floor. I finally got a look inside the stall. Nancy is sitting on the toilet, slumped over, and she appears to be unconscious." By now growing frustrated, Kristen spoke loudly, "We've got to find help!"

"Okay, don't worry; we will." Brett stood up and together they walked briskly over to the hostess area where Patricia looked at them quizzically.

Kristen rushed to explain. "I found Nancy Meyers in the restroom. She's locked in her stall, and she's slouched over and not responding. I don't know what's happened to her, but she needs help!"

"How do you know it's Nancy if you couldn't open the door?" Patricia asked, then hurried to reassure Kristen. "Never mind; I'll have Barney take a look. He can take the door off the frame if need be."

Kristen wrung her hands, her anxiety showing. "I know it's Nancy because after I tried everything else, I finally looked through the gap between the doorframe and the door."

Patricia merely nodded and left the two of them standing there while she walked quickly back into the kitchen. A few seconds later, she emerged with Barney. They strode toward the ladies room, Kristen and Brett following close behind. By now, the other diners were starting to notice the commotion. Kristen felt sure Barney would want to clear up whatever had happened in the bathroom as soon as possible to avoid potential damage to his thriving business.

Kristen's anxiety lessened now that she had Brett at her side and Patricia and Barney along to get to the bottom of the situation. Though it felt like ages since she'd excused herself from the table to use the restroom, she supposed only a few minutes had elapsed. Still, they needed to figure out what had happened to Nancy quickly and what—if anything—could be done to aid her. Kristen gulped at that thought then took a deep breath to steady herself as they prepared to enter the bathroom.

Patricia went in first to make sure no other ladies were present before the entire group barged into the bathroom. On entering, Kristen inhaled the smell of vomit that had begun to carry into the rest of the room rather than linger inside the small stall. She almost gagged.

Barney carried a hammer, and now he used it to jar the door off its hinges. Kristen heard Patricia gasp aloud at the sight of Nancy drooped over in the stall, the contents of her stomach spread inelegantly over her blouse.

Kristen had seen Nancy drinking red wine, which would account for the purplish tinge to the vomit clinging to her chest. Was the answer that simple? Had Nancy drunk too much wine, gotten sick, and then passed out? Kristen shook her head. *No way, I'm feeling very negative vibes, not to mention nausea.*

Barney crept closer to check Nancy's pulse and determine if she was still breathing. Unfortunately, he didn't seem to be having much luck. Kristen felt panic wash over her as her mind flashed back to that day in April when she was the one searching for Johnny Thomas' pulse—and not finding it. She'd been alone when she discovered Johnny's body. At least she wasn't totally alone now since technically, she reasoned, she hadn't known Nancy was a goner back when she first attempted to help her. Not that she felt reassured by that thought. Odds were good Nancy was dead when Kristen entered the restroom earlier. She snapped back to reality, telling herself to quit worrying about herself and do something useful.

"I'm going to call 911."

The rest of the group was still staring at Nancy, their jaws dropped in disbelief. Kristen's practical words now seemed to revive them.

"Yes, you'd best do that right away," said Barney, his brow glistening with sweat.

Kristen stationed herself outside the bathroom door in an effort to detour other diners or staff from entering the room. She still had her purse with her from her initial trip to the bathroom, so she pulled out her phone and dialed the emergency number. The female dispatcher who answered was trained to deal with emergencies, and her soothing voice helped Kristen pull herself together. The woman promised to send help right away.

Kristen checked her watch. An ambulance would arrive shortly, so she poked her head inside the restroom to alert the rest of group and see if anything had changed. *Apparently not, from the look of things*, she thought glumly. Then she remembered the man who had been with Nancy, her husband, she guessed. He'd probably be worried by now, and she was surprised he hadn't come looking for her. Before she could act on that thought, Barney exited the restroom mumbling, "I need to make an announcement to the other diners."

What does one say at a time like this? Kristen wondered. "Do you think you should talk to Nancy's husband first?"

"Oh my goodness, of course!" He wrinkled his brow. "I have no idea what in the world to tell him."

"I would just inform him another diner discovered Nancy in the bathroom, unresponsive."

"Brilliant." Barney patted her arm. "Now why don't you come with me to help explain."

"Sure, I'll go along with you for moral support," stammered Kristen, though she hoped she wouldn't need to actually say anything. After all, she was still feeling the strain of finding Nancy's lifeless body and wasn't sure she'd be able to find the right words to console her dead friend's husband.

Maybe he doesn't need to be consoled, she thought as she gazed across the room and found Mr. Meyers sitting alone at his table nursing the tail end of a draft beer. He appeared totally relaxed. She recalled how Brett had looked at her quizzically when she returned to their table. He'd obviously been wondering what took her so long in the restroom. Wouldn't Mr. Meyers feel equally anxious about Nancy's long absence?

Not if she'd told him she wasn't feeling well, Kristen reasoned. She shrugged. He probably had no idea his wife was sick to the point of dying. It would be a shame to disturb him with such devastating news. He was sure to be shocked.

Then again, she thought coolly, *maybe not!*

CHAPTER 3

Kristen and Barney plodded over to the table where Mr. Meyers sat. Barney's complexion had paled considerably from when he initially came out of the kitchen, his face flushed from the heat of the ovens and probably also from the craziness of a hectic Saturday night. Kristen may have been the one to stumble across Nancy's corpse, but she had no intention of speaking to Mr. Meyers. That was Barney's job.

The restaurant owner cleared his throat before speaking, probably stalling until he decided how to approach Nancy's husband. "Mr. Meyers?"

"Yes?" The man turned toward them, smiling politely. "The dinner was superb."

"Well, thank you." Barney stood there, bumbling for the right words. "I hate to tell you this, but you wife has taken ill."

Meyers looked alarmed. "Where is she?"

Barney put his big hand gently on Meyers' shoulder. "No, you can't see her right now." He paused to steady his voice. "We've called 911, but I need to warn you that things don't look good. I couldn't find a pulse, and she wasn't breathing."

Kristen stood silently, closely watching Meyer's expression. His initial look of shock and then pain were real. Unless the man was an excellent actor, she could sense his anguish. Then again, why wouldn't Nancy's husband feel the normal emotions of grief? After all, they had been enjoying a night out to dinner at Eklund's posh restaurant. Maybe investigating Johnny's murder had made her paranoid and overly analytical.

Barney spoke quietly to Meyers, explaining the need to make a statement to the staff and other diners. He then cleared his throat and picked up a water glass from a neighboring table, banging a fork on the side of it to get everyone's attention.

"I have an announcement to make."

It didn't take long for the lingering crowd to quiet down. They'd probably noticed something was up from the behavior of Kristen and her crew.

"Another diner is ill in the restroom. Please do not go near that area, as emergency personnel will be arriving momentarily. We ask that everyone remain at their tables until we receive further instructions."

Did Barney sense something was amiss? Kristen was probably being paranoid again. Just then, she heard the wail of sirens. She looked toward the front windows and saw flashing lights. Soon EMTs plowed through the front door. Barney directed them toward the restroom. With one last look at Nancy's forlorn husband, Kristen started tottering back to her table where she saw Brett waiting for her. He'd left the restroom when the EMTs entered.

Just as she reached their booth, she heard the loud, authoritative voice of Sheriff Miller boom out to remind everyone to stay seated. She turned and saw Miller's eyes scanning the room. His gaze landed on Kristen; a stony expression crossed his face.

Oh great! She slid across the seat of the booth, ending up next to Brett and not caring that she'd previously been seated across from him. Ignoring convention, she kicked off her painful sandals and snuggled up to her date, needing to feel the warmth of his strong body next to hers. Brett put his arm around her bare shoulders and hugged her to him.

She grabbed her glass and swallowed the remainder of her wine, hoping to fortify herself against what was sure to be an interrogation from the sheriff. They'd crossed swords several times during the investigation into Johnny's murder, and she felt sure Miller would savor the opportunity to make her feel even more miserable than she already felt about Nancy's demise.

Hearing more voices and footsteps, she lifted her head from Brett's shoulder and saw Hope's boyfriend, Todd, stride toward the bathroom. He met Kristen's eyes and gave her a halfhearted smile. She was glad to see a friendly face, though she was disappointed he'd been called into an emergency situation right before his shift was due to end. The way things were going, he'd miss his date with Hope.

Diners at other tables, and the staff who had come out of the kitchen, were talking among themselves, trying to figure out what was happening. Even though Kristen had an idea of what was taking place, it didn't ease her mind. She sighed, suddenly exhausted. She leaned even closer to Brett, grateful he was there to provide emotional support the second time she had discovered a body. She wasn't optimistic anything could be done to save poor Nancy, so she needed to get a grip and accept her death.

"Are you okay?" asked Brett, squeezing her shoulder.

"All things considered, I guess so."

"Don't worry, I'm sure we'll learn what took place soon, and then we'll all be released to go home."

Though Kristen nodded in agreement, she felt there was something different about Nancy's illness and ultimate death. She couldn't explain her reasoning, but she didn't think this would be an open and shut case.

As if reading her thoughts, the sheriff strode out of the restroom, looking troubled. Kristen snapped to attention. *Oh no, this can't be good.*

"Ladies and gentlemen, thanks for your patience." He paused, measuring his words carefully. "I'm afraid I'm going to have to ask you to stick around for a while longer as we wrap up a few things. We may need to question some of you."

Kristen's ears perked up at the sheriff's remark. What had the authorities discovered that required them to question other diners? Just then the sheriff looked directly at her. "And we'll get started with you, Ms. Matthews."

The sheriff walked over to their booth and merely stood there. Even though he didn't say a word, Kristen felt a combination of intimidation and indignation. Why did he have to behave like such a jerk? She hadn't done anything wrong.

"Hello, Sheriff. I understand you'd like to speak with me?"

"Not really, but once again, it seems you're in the wrong place at the wrong time."

"With all due respect, that's hardly my fault. I was only trying to help Nancy." Kristen paused and then spoke quietly so the others in the now somber restaurant couldn't hear their conversation. "Is she...." She took a deep breath before continuing, "...dead?"

Miller nodded curtly, but his tone became more polite. "If you'll please come with me, I'd like to discuss a few things with you where we have more privacy."

Kristen wobbled to her feet then remembered she wasn't wearing any shoes. Though she was glad to cast off the annoying encumbrances, they really were cute, and besides, they added a solid four inches to her height. She could have used the extra height to measure up under the sheriff's scrutiny. "Sure," she said meekly.

Brett sprung to his feet. "Now hold on. Can't you talk to both of us at the same time?"

"It's my understanding it was Ms. Matthews who discovered Mrs. Meyers initially, alone. Is that true?"

"Well, yes, but—" Brett's words were cut off by the sheriff.

"Then we need to talk to her first, and alone!"

Kristen looked at Brett and shrugged. "Don't worry about me. I'll be fine. I've had prior experience with the sheriff's interrogation techniques."

Kristen shouldn't provoke the sheriff, especially when he was going to question her about Nancy's death, but she couldn't seem to stop herself. She knew from dealing with him previously that he brought out the worst in her.

Miller threw a glare in Kristen's direction, but beckoned her to follow him to what she assumed was Barney's office. He noticed her bare feet. "Don't you want to grab your shoes?"

"No, I just took them off, and after everything I've been through tonight, I can't imagine cramming my feet back into them right now." She glanced at her watch. Even though it felt like it was really late, she'd only left the table to use the ladies room about half an hour ago.

"I wouldn't complain. You're in better shape than Mrs. Meyers."

Kristen was taken aback at the sheriff's abruptness. "I just meant that my feet really hurt from wearing these very stylish, but extremely painful, shoes all evening."

The sheriff had the grace to look embarrassed. "I'm sorry. That was uncalled for. Now let's get down to business. Tell me what happened."

"Can you tell *me* what happened?"

"What do you mean? I'm the one who's supposed to be asking the questions."

"I realize that, but why is the sheriff's department starting to question other diners? If it's merely a matter of Nancy falling ill, it seems overkill to have you and your deputies investigating her death. What's *really* going on here?" She looked him squarely in the eye.

"Overkill is the key word." He paused. "We have reason to think Nancy may not have died from natural causes."

Kristen was shocked at this revelation. "No, it can't be!"

He held up a hand in warning. "We're not certain she died under questionable circumstances, but we're taking extra precautions just in case."

Kristen wondered what they had discovered to lead them down this road. "I'll be happy to tell you everything I know, which isn't all that much."

The sheriff rolled his eyes at her remark. "I'm confident you can help us out a great deal. From past experience, I've found you to be very perceptive."

Kristen relaxed a little at his backdoor compliment and vowed to cooperate with Sheriff Miller, rather than get agitated by him. "I'll try to answer your questions to the best of my ability." She folded her hands in her lap to keep herself from fidgeting. "What's causing you to be so suspicious?"

"You don't give up, do you?" Then the sheriff seemed to relent. "There's a possibility Nancy may have ingested something that caused her to have a reaction, resulting in death."

"Surely you don't mean she was poisoned!"

"We're not sure of anything at this point." He scratched his head. "Besides, we have to wait until we get some test results back from the lab, as well as the autopsy results, before we can draw any logical conclusions."

Kristen took a deep breath. "Oh." She was at a loss for words and felt herself getting worked up again.

"You're upset. That's one reason I didn't want to tell you about the complications stemming from Nancy's death."

Some special date this is turning out to be, thought Kristen ruefully. She forced herself to remain composed. "It's okay. Please ask me anything you want." She didn't add that she had nothing to hide, but the look she gave him implied that fact.

"Let's start from the beginning. You obviously needed to use the ladies room."

Kristen cleared her throat, trying not to blush at hearing Miller's blunt statement. "Yes, that's true. We had just finished dinner and were waiting for dessert to arrive."

"So you left the table and entered the restroom by yourself?" he prodded her.

"Yes. I'd had some wine and water to drink, so I needed to use the facilities," she said delicately.

"And?"

Good grief, did he want details? "And I noticed one stall had the door closed, but I didn't hear any sounds coming from it."

"So what did you do next?"

"After I finished"—she felt the color rise in her cheeks but chose to ignore the annoyance—"I came out to wash my hands and touch up my lipstick. I checked my hair and makeup in the mirror."

The sheriff merely nodded as he scribbled notes in his notebook.

"Even though I didn't spend much time in there, I thought it was peculiar I hadn't heard any noise coming from the other stall." She paused, twirling a strand of hair around her finger. "Even if the other lady had wanted privacy, I'm sure I would have heard *something*, but there was only dead silence." Kristen instantly regretted her unfortunate choice of words.

The sheriff didn't seem to notice her crude terminology. "So what did you do next?"

"I called out to see if the lady needed help." Kristen felt her nerves tense under his scrutiny.

"What then?"

Kristen squeezed her eyes shut, trying to remember the sequence of events. "I looked under the stall and noticed the occupant was wearing black slacks and dress shoes. Upon closer inspection, I saw a turquoise earring."

"Did you recognize it as Nancy's?"

"Not immediately. I remembered Nancy had been wearing turquoise jewelry, but I wasn't sure the dropped earring was hers." Kristen stared at the wall, thinking. "But I thought it could have been Nancy's and then I started to worry."

"Was it at that point that you decided to find help?" Sheriff Miller peered closely at her face, watching her expression.

"I waited a minute then called out again." She inhaled sharply. "When I didn't receive a response, I rapped on the door."

"Of the individual stall?"

She nodded. "By then I was starting to feel frightened, so I looked through the crack between the door and doorframe."

"And did you recognize the woman as Nancy?"

"Yes, right away. I'd complimented her on her blouse when I spoke to her on the way to our table. It was the first thing I noticed when I peeked in the stall."

"So let me get this straight. You interacted with the deceased earlier in the evening?"

The deceased? Kristen felt her hackles rise. "Of course I did. I imagine most of the diners talked to her too. And, for the record, I also spoke to others and even waved at a few."

"I didn't mean to ruffle your feathers. I'm only trying to pinpoint exactly what happened."

"I guess I'm on edge." She sighed loudly. "Nancy was a very social person, so she probably interacted with several people tonight."

"Did you notice anything out of place when you walked by her table or when you were in the restroom?"

"No, not really. I suppose when I walked by her the first time, I was just excited about our night out, which hasn't turned out all that well, by the way."

"Probably not." The sheriff didn't seem to have much sympathy for her. "So, she was behaving normally when you visited with her?"

"She seemed her usual bubbly self. She looked very attractive, and I would have never guessed she was ill." *Or would meet her death shortly afterwards.*

"What about her husband?"

"She didn't introduce us. He may have been chatting with someone else, I don't remember. Nancy and I only exchanged a few pleasantries. Since we were following the hostess to our table, we didn't want to detain her too long."

"Sure, that makes sense."

Kristen was glad Miller was behaving more reasonably. It took some of the pressure off this incredibly difficult conservation. "I noticed Nancy drinking red wine, but I'm not sure they were eating anything yet."

"We can review the customer orders to determine what Nancy had selected and most likely ate."

"Do you think she may have had an allergic reaction or food poisoning?"

"It's too early to tell, but we'll run some tests to determine that."

"But no one else seems to have exhibited any of the same symptoms." Kristen glanced anxiously behind her through the small window in Barney's office that overlooked the dining room. "Unless someone else has taken ill?"

"Not that we're aware of, thank goodness." Miller flipped to a fresh page. "Now let's get back on track. After you realized Nancy had serious problems, what did you do next?"

"I ran out of the bathroom to find help. I stopped by our table first to let Brett know I was okay. I'd told him I'd only be gone a minute, and I was gone longer than I intended." Kristen considered what to say next. She still felt it was odd that Mr. Meyers hadn't tried to track down his wife. She voiced her concern to Sheriff Miller, who nodded soberly. She had a feeling if it ended up that Nancy had indeed been poisoned, Mr. Meyers would receive an interrogation that would make this one seem mild in comparison.

"What did you do after you told Mr. Stevenson about the situation?"

Kristen was probably imagining the sarcastic tone the sheriff used when saying Brett's name. She knew Brett had behaved with the utmost courtesy during Johnny's murder investigation. She didn't take time to ponder the implications further.

"We went to the hostess stand, where we talked to Patricia. She left us alone for a moment to locate Barney, and the four of us walked to the bathroom. Not to be disgusting, but the smell of vomit was overpowering, whereas when I had been in the restroom a short while earlier, I only noticed the smell when I checked inside Nancy's stall."

"It's likely she threw up shortly before you entered the restroom the first time." He jotted her observation down before continuing. "And probably died soon afterwards."

"I guess so." Kristen could feel tears well up, but she was determined not to break down in front of the sheriff. She sniffed. "She didn't appear to be breathing when I saw her. That's why I ran for help."

"Were people starting to stare when the four of you traipsed to the bathroom together?"

"She nodded. "Some of the diners were watching us."

"And when you reached the bathroom, did you take the lead?"

"You mean checking on Nancy? No, I'd already seen her. I let the others go ahead of me. While they were trying to get a pulse and determine her status, I decided to call 911. I went outside the bathroom door to make sure no one else entered."

"That reminds me, are you sure no one else was in the restroom at any point?"

"I don't see how anyone else could have been present when I was there the first time, and it was even more crowded when the four of us were there together."

"I don't suppose anyone knows if someone snuck in between your visits?"

"Maybe one of the other diners noticed someone enter."

"We'll make sure we ask." The sheriff was interrupted by a sharp knock on the door. A deputy entered, and Kristen was shocked to see him carrying a vase—one filled with wildflowers purchased from the Nature Station.

Oh no, she groaned inwardly. She had a bad feeling that unlike the dainty flowers, whatever happened next wasn't going to be pretty!

CHAPTER 4

Sheriff Miller looked at the plants in astonishment. He noticed Kristen's flushed and worried face. "Is everything all right?"

"I'm just wondering why Deputy"—she stammered, not knowing his name—"brought my flowers into the office."

Miller glanced questionably back and forth between Kristen and the deputy. The deputy, a husky middle aged man, seemed to dwarf the dainty wildflowers and vase he held gingerly between his large hands. His latex gloves only made his hands appear larger. Miller shrugged and said, "I'm not sure, but if you'll excuse me for a moment, I'll see if I can find out."

Leaving Kristen to ponder her own thoughts, Miller and the deputy left the room. She began to chew her already stubby nails, a bad habit she often gave into when nervous or upset. In an effort to take her already uneasy mind off the fact that her flowers may have contributed to this awful situation, she wracked her brain for anything she could think of that seemed abnormal at the restaurant.

She sat alone for what felt like years—though Miller couldn't have been gone for more than a couple of minutes—

before she heard the door rattle open and the sheriff entered. This time, his gloved hands were gripping the vase full of flowers.

Eying them uneasily, she waited patiently for the sheriff to speak, wondering what he'd ask. She didn't have to wait long.

"What can you tell me about these flowers?" His tone had reverted to the terseness she'd experienced before when dealing with him.

"There are three species of flowers in that vase, spiderwort, butterfly milkweed, and foxglove beardtongue."

The sheriff looked alarmed. "Foxglove?"

"Relax, this plant isn't poisonous." She had a sudden revelation. Were they trying to blame Nancy's illness on innocent wildflowers? The ones she'd sold Barney? *Oh no, I could be in a heap of trouble.*

"What about the other ones? Are they safe to eat?"

Kristen considered his question. "I don't know. I've never contemplated eating them."

Evidently Miller thought she was trying to be flippant. "Can you use your plant expertise," he spit out the words, "to help us narrow down whether these plants could have made Nancy ill and caused her death?"

"I'm afraid I'm not an expert on poisonous plants. I always tell people never eat a plant unless you know it's safe. I can't picture Nancy taking one out of the centerpiece vase to munch on it." Kristen looked at him incredulously. "Is that what you think happened? That's plain crazy."

"I'd prefer you to keep your opinions to yourself." Miller paused. "If you'd care to tell me anything you know about these particular plants, I'd really appreciate it."

Kristen wondered what she could tell the sheriff about these plants that might prove to be helpful. She bolted upright in chair, suddenly recalling milkweed's poisonous properties. In fact, monarch butterflies, insects that used milkweeds as a primary host plant, were poison to its predators if ingested. "The orange plant, butterfly milkweed, is related to other milkweeds."

The sheriff didn't look impressed. "So?"

"Some species of milkweeds can be poisonous if ingested." Kristen touched the dainty hourglass shaped flowers, reveling in their beauty. "However, I'm guessing that an adult human would need to eat quite a bit of milkweed to become severely ill, let alone die from its toxins."

"You can rest assured we'll be researching the possibilities."

Kristen nodded, knowing she'd be doing the same thing. "And the spiderwort," she said, pointing to the periwinkle flower, "may cause skin irritation in some people if they encounter the fluid from the stem."

"Good grief, why wouldn't Barney have the common sense not to use them as centerpieces?"

Kristen wanted to crawl under Barney's messy desk and hide. But she knew she needed to come clean and face the music, or in this case, Sheriff Miller. "If you must know, Barney has an arrangement with the Nature Station to purchase an assortment of wildflowers to use for the busier weekend evenings."

"You're telling me he bought these deathtraps from you?"

"I'm not going to tolerate that kind of behavior from you! We had a business arrangement. It's quite common for wildflowers to be used in floral arrangements." Kristen could feel herself losing her cool. She felt the sheriff's insult directed toward her, the Nature Station, and her beloved plants. Still, she urged herself to bring her emotions under control. "Like any plant, prairie plants have their medicinal and other practical uses." She took a deep breath. "But in some cases, native plants, or even domestic plants, may be detrimental to one's health."

"Okay, I get that. But why would you sell poisonous plants to a restaurant, where people are *eating*?"

"First of all, the diners aren't supposed to be eating the centerpieces. Secondly, the butterfly milkweed is not even poisonous unless a large amount is consumed." Kristen had gotten fired up, despite her intentions to remain calm. "Thirdly, I work with these plants on a regular basis, and I have never experienced any side effects from them."

"I see your point." The sheriff seemed sorry he'd mentioned the subject. "Is there anything else you can tell me?"

"I'd like to know why these wildflowers were brought into the conversation. If you feel Nancy may have eaten something that caused her to have a severe reaction, I can understand that. But why are you questioning me about flowers that were not on tonight's list of culinary specials? They aren't meant to be eaten; they're supposed to create ambiance."

Sheriff Miller shifted uncomfortably in his chair, and Kristen couldn't help but gloat. At least she wasn't in the hot seat—at the moment.

"We're trying to cover all the bases," he said vaguely.

But Kristen knew there was more to the story than that. He had to have some reason to be questioning her about the flowers, but she relented. "If I ever get out of here," she said meaningfully, "I'll verify the facts about these plants."

"We'd really appreciate your assistance."

"I'd be happy to help." She hesitated before continuing. "But I'd like you to level with me first. We were dining at the finest restaurant in the county. Why would you jump to the conclusion that it was the wildflowers and not the entree items that may have killed Nancy?"

Miller looked her straight in the eye. "Because it was obvious that the vase at Nancy's table had been tampered with. And before you pounce all over that tidbit, that's all I'm saying."

Kristen interpreted his look as 'subject closed.' She decided to heed his unspoken warning. "I'll do some digging and see what more I can unearth about these plants. I'll be in touch as soon as possible. Am I free to leave?"

"Yes, you can leave...for now."

Kristen wasn't sure what to think as she stood to exit Barney's cramped and cluttered office. She'd only been trying to assist someone in need, and by doing so, she felt like she'd gotten in over her head. She couldn't believe she'd been thrown into yet another investigation. She straightened her back and held her head high, though as she glanced woefully at her bare feet, she wished she were fully dressed. She headed directly to her table, ignoring curious looks from the other diners as she sought the comfort of Brett's strong arms and his common sense approach to life. She knew she'd need his help to get through this mess. So much for their night out to celebrate the closing of a murder investigation. In doing so, she'd gotten them involved in yet another mysterious death.

CHAPTER 5

Unsure whether her date was being questioned by one of the deputies, Kristen was relieved when she saw Brett seated at the table. He took one look at her desolate expression and opened his arms to hug her. Nestled up to him, she enjoyed the relative peace and tranquility, a relief after the sheriff had put her through her paces. She sat motionless for a moment, soaking up Brett's scent, a mixture of soap and subtle aftershave. She could almost forget the horror of the evening—well almost.

"Dare I ask how everything went?" he asked.

"About as well as can be expected." She pulled away and turned her head to look at him. "Did they question you, too?"

"Yep. Too bad I wasn't able to tell them much."

"So, if we're both done talking with the authorities, are we free to leave now?"

Brett shrugged. "They told me to wait until they announced they were finished."

Kristen was exhausted. She wanted to go home. She took a swig out of her half empty water glass and eyed the untouched cheesecake. "As long as we're stuck here, do you want to polish this off?"

"Sure," said Brett with a grin. "I can't believe you're hungry after dealing with the sheriff."

"I'm not really," she said as she picked up a fork. "But it's chocolate covered cheesecake, the epitome of comfort food."

"I see what you mean!" He took a bite and moaned in pleasure.

"I'm not sure how anyone can eat at a time like this," said the sheriff as he came to their table and glowered at them. "But when you two lovebirds are finished eating, you're free to leave."

Kristen was irritated with herself for feeling a stab of guilt. Her perfect evening had been ruined. Why couldn't she savor the rich dessert without the sheriff's disapproval? "That's good to know." She lapped up some chocolate sauce that was trapped in the corner of her lip. "If you have further questions, you know where to reach me."

"Yes, and I'm sure you're planning to stick around town."

"Excuse me?" Kristen bristled at the sheriff's attitude. "No, I'm not planning to leave town, but why is that your business?"

Miller sighed impatiently. "Since you're the one who found yet another body, we're bound to need more information from you. Next to Mr. Meyers, you're our most important witness. Besides, you promised to do some fact checking on the plants we discussed."

"Oh, sure," she said, feeling ridiculous. She wished the sheriff didn't annoy her so much, though she suspected he enjoyed doing so.

Brett prodded her gently by taking hold of her elbow to nudge her out of the booth. "We hope you conclude the investigation as soon as possible," he said in his most polite and respectful tone.

"Thanks," Miller said gruffly before turning away to consult with a deputy who had just finished talking with another witness.

Before the sheriff could detain them any longer, the couple walked rapidly across the dining room. Kristen noticed only a few of the original diners and staff members remained. She supposed they were fortunate to be leaving now since they had been the first on the scene. Brett held the door for Kristen, and she felt a whoosh of humidity as they stepped out of the air conditioning and into the warm and sultry summer night.

When they reached Brett's truck, he put his arms around her and pulled her toward him tightly before leaning in for a tender kiss.

"Mmm. That was the best thing about tonight."

Brett looked crestfallen. "I'm sorry things didn't work out the way I'd hoped."

"Oh no, I didn't mean it like that," Kristen rushed to reassure him. "I only meant your kisses never fail to leave me breathless." She stood on her tiptoes, reaching even higher than usual in her still stocking feet to kiss him.

"Yeah, I see what you mean." He pulled away with regret. "Now let's get you home. You've been through an ordeal tonight."

"Don't worry about me." she said woefully. "Unfortunately I've been through something similar before when I stumbled over Johnny's body. I just feel badly for the Meyers family. When I was talking to Sheriff Miller, I was concentrating on the facts, not my emotions."

"It's got to be tough for them, but give yourself a break. You have to admit it's probably tough on you, too." He opened the door for Kristen, and she climbed into the truck. Both of them were relieved to be headed home.

"It's tough to face the fact that Nancy's gone," said Kristen. "I thought the world of her. I've known her for ages, with her being a nurse all those years before retiring. When she started working at the Nature Station, I got to know her in an entirely different way."

Brett merely patted her knee, and they drove the short distance to her house in silence. Peaches was waiting for them at the backdoor. Kristen rushed over to the dog, burying her face in her pet's orangey fur. Even though she'd found comfort, and more, in Brett's embrace, there was nothing quite like some dog affection to make her feel better.

"Why don't I fix some tea?" She reflected on how ludicrous her offer to make tea sounded on what was supposed to have been a special evening. What had started off so well had gone downhill quickly.

"That sounds perfect. Maybe we can wind down for a few minutes, and then I'll let you get some rest." Brett paused. "Unless you'd like me to stay with you tonight." He looked at her longingly.

Kristen caught the look in his eyes and wasn't sure if he was strictly concerned for her wellbeing or if it was more than that. He wasn't the type of man to take advantage of a woman whose defenses were down after an encounter with death, but he was also a man strongly attracted to her. She felt it wise to postpone anything more serious until yet another mysterious death was resolved.

"No, I'll be all right." She started water boiling on the stove in her cozy kitchen while Brett pulled two mugs from the cabinet.

"If you're sure…"

"Don't worry about me. I'm perfectly safe here, even if Nancy's death was *not* from natural causes." She hastened to add, "Which I'm sure it was." She said it emphatically in an effort to reassure herself.

"I'm just worried you're too upset. I thought you'd be more comfortable having someone with you tonight." His warm smile told Kristen he'd be the perfect gentlemen if he did stay.

"I'll be fine. Believe it or not, I'm so tired I think I'll sleep really well, despite the unfortunate turn of events." *What an absurd euphemism for the death of a friend*, Kristen thought sourly. Thankfully the kettle started singing, interrupting her dark thoughts. She busied herself dousing boiling water over the teabags. She inhaled the fumes from her herbal blend in an attempt to relax a bit. Brett took his own regular tea, and they walked into the living room, where Kristen collapsed gratefully on the old, but comfortable couch. She eyed her feet, somewhat dirty from going shoeless. She couldn't wait to get into her comfy clothes, but for now, she was content to sip the calming tea and snuggle next to Brett. She sighed in pleasure, and for the first time in the past few hours, felt happy.

She was jolted back to reality by Brett asking, "So what do you think happened to Nancy?"

So much for relaxation, she thought, but didn't blame Brett for being inquisitive. After all, she had plenty of her own questions. "I have no idea, but the sheriff seems to think Nancy could have died from unnatural causes."

"I got that feeling too."

She took a sip of tea. "In fact," she said, hesitant to share this morsel of information even with Brett on the off chance it was actually possible. "Sheriff Miller was questioning me about the wildflower centerpieces."

Brett's look of puzzlement indicated he didn't receive that line of questioning. "Why on earth would he do that?"

"They're speculating that Nancy could have been poisoned."

"What's that have to do with wildflowers? It's hard enough to believe someone would poison Nancy, but do you mean to tell me they're trying to pin her death on prairie plants?"

"I'm sure they won't know anything for certain until they perform an autopsy and run some tests." Kristen couldn't believe how far her knowledge on murder investigations had come in the past couple of months, and it wasn't due to the murder mysteries she gobbled up by the dozens. To be cautious, she shouldn't assume Nancy was murdered until she heard it from the sheriff. Besides, she reasoned, even if Nancy did die from poisoning, it could have been accidental. How could it be proven otherwise?

"Hey, you're a thousand miles away." Brett playfully punched her in the arm, but he was concerned. "Are you sure you're going to be okay staying alone?"

"Yes, I'm sure." She yawned, indicating she was bushed and probably would sleep well and for the entire night.

Brett took her unspoken hint, even though Kristen had no intention of driving him off. He drained his cup and set it on the coffee table. He put his arm around her and kissed her deeply, then pulled away. "I'd better let you get some rest."

"Yeah," said Kristen weakly. "The Nature Station opens at noon tomorrow. I may skip church if I'm not feeling up to attending. I have a few things I need to finish before work."

"I'll call to check in on you." He tweaked her nose. "Just try to stay out of trouble and leave the investigating to the sheriff's department."

"No worries on that. I have no intention of getting myself further involved," she said, though she remembered her promise to research poisonous plants and was itching to get started…maybe tomorrow. She really did need some sleep.

They walked through the kitchen to the back door.

"I had a wonderful time tonight. At least until the sheriff's department arrived on the scene," Brett said ruefully.

"You had a lovely evening arranged, and we were having a great time." Kristen's voice trailed off as she thought of what had happened to end their perfect date.

"Hey, I'd better get going. Just don't let it get to you." He lingered for a final kiss before opening the door to leave.

"I know, but it's hard not to." She hugged him one last time.

"Bye." He walked slowly to his truck; knowing she'd be watching until he left, he waved.

She stood at the door afterwards, staring into the pitch black night. She knew one thing for certain: regardless of the consequences, she was going to get to the bottom of Nancy's mysterious death.

CHAPTER 6

Kristen locked the doors and rinsed out their mugs before shutting off the lights and heading upstairs. She washed her grimy feet and donned loose-fitting, cotton sleep shorts and a ratty, old t-shirt. Feeling somewhat better wearing her most comfy clothes, she settled into bed with a book, trying to unwind after the eventful evening. She read a couple of chapters before she had problems keeping her eyes open.

Shutting off her light, she fell asleep mere minutes later. She slept deeply for a few hours then was jolted awake for some unknown reason. She wondered what she'd been dreaming about to jar herself out of such a deep sleep.

Then the events of the previous evening came back to her. She groaned, realizing it was probably disturbing thoughts of poisonous plant possibilities that had destroyed her slumber.

Feeling restless and unable to will herself back to sleep, she decided to spend the wee hours of Sunday morning on her laptop; she didn't want to delay researching noxious plants any longer. Luckily, she'd last used her computer in her bedroom, so she powered it on, willing it to hurry through its introductory functions as she settled back against her bed pillows.

Finally it came to life, and she logged onto the internet, curious to search for the plants she'd sold to Barney in an effort to enhance diners' experiences, not disrupt their digestive systems or ultimately cause their death. She shuddered at that thought and forced herself to continue. For better or worse, she had to know if her plants might have contributed to Nancy's untimely demise.

She wished she had some direction to guide her search. Miller said the vase at Nancy's table had been tampered with, but what did that have to do with the arrangement of native plants? The only thing she knew for sure was that the sheriff's department had confiscated the wildflowers.

She began her search for Spiderwort. Despite its icky name, it was a lovely plant. She couldn't imagine it causing someone's death, much less being used as a murder weapon. She told herself to stop jumping to conclusions. The last she'd heard, Nancy's death hadn't been classified as a murder. Still, any death caused by unnatural means was baffling.

She knew for a fact Nancy wouldn't have voluntarily ingested something with the potential to make her ill, much less be lethal. With her nursing background, Nancy was an expert on the medicinal uses of local native plants; she knew which ones were irritants or possibly poisonous. She had even experimented with home remedies, using some of the plants grown at the Nature Station.

A shocking thought hit her. Could Nancy's death have been the result of a do-it-yourself cure gone bad? *No way!* Kristen had just worked with Nancy earlier in the week, and she hadn't complained of any ailments then. Many of the workers who volunteered their time and efforts at the Nature Station were retired and openly discussed their minor health issues. Kristen figured Nancy was no different than the others; she would have mentioned it if she'd been doctoring herself. In fact, she would have been proud of being able to concoct her own treatment.

Kristen shook her head to clear the cobwebs from her still sleepy brain. None of it made sense. She focused her thoughts on the computer screen. A dozen entries had popped up under spiderwort, giving her plenty to read. She knew the basics about the plants growing on her property, but in order to help determine whether a native plant had contributed to Nancy's death, she needed more detailed information. Once she compiled the data, she'd pass it along to Sheriff Miller, and he could have the proper tests run.

Kristen gulped back a sudden lump in her throat; she still had a problem accepting the fact that her friend was gone. She'd been so vibrant when they'd visited at the table at Barney's. At least Kristen had a plan now. She'd do her best to help determine what had caused Nancy's death.

She skimmed through several entries. Sure enough, spiderwort could cause minor skin irritations. Good to know, but it was doubtful Nancy had died from itchy blisters. Though from personal experience, Kristen had encountered several plants that made her skin crawl with oozy, painful blisters that could itch like the devil. While producing extreme discomfort to sensitive humans, they weren't life threatening. Still, she sent the most relevant material to the printer.

Next was foxglove beardtongue. She knew most people were leery when they heard the term "foxglove" and even more so if they knew the scientific name for this plant: *Penstemon digitalis*. Still, Kristen was sure this variety was harmless, unless for some strange reason the plant caused an allergic reaction specific to some individuals. She scanned through the websites confirming her knowledge, and then printed a fact sheet for the sheriff.

She fluffed her pillows before searching for the next plant on the list, butterfly milkweed. The search engine generated multiple listings for this beautiful plant. Kristen sifted through them, looking for details relating to its toxicity. After finding several sites describing the attributes of several other members of the milkweed genus *Asclepias*, she knew she needed to narrow her search to verify if *Asclepias tuberosa*, the scientific name for the milkweed in question, could have caused such a violent reaction. She was having a hard time retrieving the definitive information she needed and was beginning to feel frustrated and a little drowsy.

She checked her bedside clock and was amazed to see it was already four-thirty in the morning. Deciding to call it quits for now, she shut down her laptop, vowing to refine her research on butterfly milkweed when she was feeling fresh. She wasn't sure if she could fall back to sleep, but she decided to try, even though she could already see the beginnings of the sunrise creep into the room. Her lightweight curtains did little to prevent the early light from shining through her bedroom's old fashioned, double-hung paned windows.

She hunkered down, willing herself to try to fall asleep. She could rest more easily knowing she'd started the data collection she'd agreed to perform for Sheriff Miller. After she slept, it would be easier to focus her efforts on the remaining plant, which was the most important. After all, milkweeds were known to be toxic under the right circumstances.

The question was, could butterfly milkweed have been toxic to Nancy? Kristen thought it was unlikely. Nancy handled native plants on a regular basis. Surely if she had a reaction to this particular plant, they would have discovered it earlier. Even more disturbing, how could Nancy have come into contact with a lethal dose of a particular plant? The more she considered it, she realized something was fishy, and it wasn't the weekend seafood specials at Barney's. If Nancy had in fact died from a poisonous plant, Kristen figured it was no accident. Her mind whirled with possibilities and questions.

Stop thinking! she chided herself. Squeezing her eyes shut against the early morning sun, she stretched out underneath the light sheet and finally dozed. When she awoke later, the sun was streaming full force through her windows. Though a light breeze stirred the curtains, the room was beginning to feel warm. She squinted at the clock, astonished to see it read almost ten o'clock. She never slept that late, but then, she'd been through a lot during the previous evening, and her nocturnal research hadn't helped matters.

She stumbled out of bed, anxious to start her morning ritual of coffee brewing. Peaches was curled in her favorite corner of the kitchen. She looked expectantly at Kristen, probably wondering why she'd been neglected for so long. Kristen patted her on the head, filled her food and water bowls, and turned her loose outdoors. Though it was too late to get ready to attend church, she didn't need to be at the Station until shortly before noon, their opening time on Sundays. Even with today's Family Nature Hike starting at twelve, she didn't need to worry about arriving very early to set up. They had organized what little needed to be done before they closed Saturday afternoon. She savored being able to take her time getting ready. Besides, she wanted to plan her next move, which included more research. Setting the coffee to brew, she raced back upstairs to shower while it perked.

Her hair still damp, Kristen fortified herself with a cup of strong java and finished dressing, opting for a sage green t-shirt bearing the Station's logo and khaki shorts. She'd already fired up her laptop, anxious to finalize her research on butterfly milkweed and whatever else she might run across in the process. During her pre-dawn quest for plant knowledge, she'd bookmarked some helpful sites. Her plan now was to pillage them for additional information.

She took a swig of coffee and felt her senses gradually perk up with the infusion of caffeine into her groggy system. She returned to one of the sites she'd visited earlier that morning, diving deeper into the terminology. Sorting through information on milkweeds that weren't native to the area, she finally found the plant in question. She confirmed what she'd already known and discovered earlier. It appeared that the species with narrower leaves were more toxic than the wide-leaved species. Though she considered butterfly milkweed leaves to be narrow, she still wasn't convinced Nancy could have died from sampling the plant no matter how wide its leaves were. Not wanting to ponder the mysteries of plant classification further, she continued scrolling through pages and links until she pulled up a fact sheet produced by the USDA Natural Resources Conservation Service that featured butterfly milkweed.

Butterfly Milkweed may be toxic when taken internally, without sufficient preparation. Milkweed species, as a group, are known to contain cardiac glycosides that are poisonous both to humans and to livestock, as well as other substances that may account for their medicinal effect. Resinoids, glycosides, and a small amount of alkaloids are present in all parts of the plant. Symptoms of poisoning by the cardiac glycosides include dullness, weakness, bloating, inability to stand or walk, high body temperature, rapid and weak pulse, difficulty breathing, dilated pupils, spasms, and coma.

So it confirmed butterfly milkweed could be toxic to humans if ingested in large quantities. The big question was, how much was too much? Since this plant was used to effectively treat a number of common ailments, it must be safe in small quantities.

She printed a few pages to show the sheriff. It wasn't for her to decide whether butterfly milkweed had killed Nancy Meyers. They'd need to perform tests to determine whether cardiac glycosides were in her system. Kristen knew Nancy had vomited, but that was a common symptom of several other poisons. She had no idea whether the woman had exhibited any of the other symptoms caused by cardiac glycosides.

Kristen shook her head. Nancy was well versed on harmful plants as well as their medicinal uses. In fact, she wouldn't have even needed to conduct the search Kristen had just completed; she'd already know enough to steer clear of the plant and wouldn't have used it to spice up her salad greens.

She glanced at the clock, shocked time had flown by so quickly. Her stomach rumbled with hunger. She never forgot to eat, but she'd skipped breakfast in her haste to track down useful data online. Now she closed up her laptop, gathered the papers from the printer, and headed downstairs to fix herself some lunch before opening the Nature Station for the afternoon. She prepared a sandwich to take with her, grabbed an apple from the fridge, and filled her water bottle before pouring more coffee into her aluminum travel mug. Her cell phone rang just as she was heading out the backdoor. "Brett? Hi there," she said, feeling her heart speed up a tad at the thought of talking to him.

"How are you feeling today after such an eventful first date?"

She laughed at that. On their actual first date, they'd searched the scene of Johnny Thomas' murder, looking for possible clues. And now, during what was supposed to have been their first real "out on the town" date, they'd gotten themselves embroiled in another mysterious death. What were the odds?

"I'm a little tired, but I'm doing okay."

"I can imagine. Did you get any sleep at all?"

"I read for a while to unwind and fell asleep shortly afterwards." She paused briefly, unsure how Brett would react to her helping the sheriff with research. Brett knew her well enough to know she may start off doing only research, using her biology and native plant background for fact finding, but would she stop at that? Probably not. "I woke up a few hours later and couldn't get back to sleep, so I searched online for information related to native poisonous plants."

Brett exhaled loudly but didn't utter a word. He was probably counting to ten. Kristen knew he was worried she'd get in too deep if she started investigating in full force.

Kristen felt she needed to fill in the gap in conversation with something unrelated to Nancy's death. "We close at five tonight. Would you like to come over afterwards? The weather should be perfect for grilling." Especially if she wheeled the grill to the shade, and they sat nearby, with Brett drinking an ice cold beer and Kristen sipping a cool, crisp, dry white wine while the meat cooked.

"You know I can't resist your home cooking, but you'll be working all afternoon. I'll tell you what. Why don't I grab some stuff at Swede's Groceries before I come over, and all we'll have to do is relax and let the grill do the rest."

"Sounds good to me. If you're coming over this evening we can talk then. Right now I'd better get to work."

"Okay, I'll see you later."

By the time the call ended, Kristen had reached the Red Barn, the restored one hundred-year-old structure where they would be checking in afternoon hikers. She unlocked the door and let herself in, flipping on the light switches to the massive main area. Her phone rang again. She wasn't surprised to see it was her parents' number. At the rate she was going, she'd never get a chance to munch on her simple lunch.

"Hi, Mom!"

Her mother, Joannie, was always taken aback when her children—Kristen, her older brother Mark, and younger sister Morgan—greeted her by name when she called. Having standard landline phone service with no caller ID, she was amazed at modern technology. Still, it didn't take her long to start asking questions.

"I heard the awful news about Nancy's death in church today. No one seemed to know any details other than she had eaten at Barney's. Didn't you and Brett eat there last night? Were you there when it happened?"

Her mother sounded worried, and Kristen winced. Not only would she have to break it to her mother that yes, she had been present when Nancy died, but also tell her she was actually the one who discovered the poor woman. She straightened her shoulders, though her mother couldn't see her.

"Unfortunately, we were. We even spoke to her on the way to our table."

Should she tell her mom about finding Nancy? She wasn't sure if Sheriff Miller would appreciate it, but she wasn't as scared of him as she would be of Joanie if her mother found out she'd been withholding information from her.

"Later in the evening, I went to use the ladies room, and I found Nancy…dead."

She heard only silence on the line and knew her mother was stunned, though Joannie recovered herself enough to ask, "You found another dead body?"

"It's a long story, Mom."

"And I want to hear all of it."

Of course she did. Kristen refrained from groaning aloud. "Why don't you come over tonight after we close. I've already invited Brett. We're planning to grill out for supper."

"I wouldn't want to intrude on your evening…"

"Oh, don't worry about it. We're probably going to be discussing Nancy's death anyway. You may as well stop by, and we'll talk about it together."

It seemed like a good solution. Kristen loved her parents and enjoyed spending time together; she was fortunate they lived close-by. But she had been looking forward to a quiet evening with Brett, especially after their date had ended up with questioning from the sheriff and his deputies, plus all the excitement beforehand. She knew from past experience that time spent with her family was rarely quiet.

"Well, if you're sure."

"Of course I am. We close at five, so how about you stop by around five-thirty."

"All right, and I'll bring something for dessert."

Kristen perked up a little. Her mom's cooking was delicious. "That sounds great. Brett's picking up a few items from Swede's," she said, though she made a mental note to alert him about the extra people joining them for dinner.

"We'll see you then." Joannie paused. "And Kristen, be careful. I don't know what happened, but I have a funny feeling about the entire situation."

Kristen shuddered. Unfortunately, she was picking up a few bad vibes herself about Nancy's untimely death. She was glad Brett and her family were coming over that evening. She had no doubt that, together, they would get to the bottom of things.

CHAPTER 7

After ending her phone conversation, Kristen finally had a chance to eat, which helped settle her nervous stomach. She couldn't quite shake the feeling that Nancy's death would be just as big of a mystery as Johnny's murder. She went about her duties, eating her light lunch as she prepped for the afternoon. Though the weather was predicted to climb to eighty-five degrees, with the humidity percentage even higher, she knew they'd have a crowd of hikers arriving shortly to take advantage of the entrance discounts offered during the Family Nature Hike. She was glad Hope was scheduled to arrive shortly. Not only would Kristen appreciate her help handling the crowd, but today she needed a dose of Hope's feisty personality.

Speak of the devil! Just then Hope arrived, poking her head through the main entrance of the Red Barn.

"Hey, what's up?" she called to Kristen. "I heard you had quite an exciting evening."

"Yeah, that's putting it mildly."

"I know what you mean. But my evening ended up being not so exciting."

"I figured that when I saw Todd at Barney's." Kristen paused thoughtfully. "Have you had a chance to talk with him?"

"Not too much, and I'm dying to know what happened to Nancy." Hope quickly sobered. "That was a poor choice of words."

"It's okay. I know what you meant."

The two were silent for a moment, both of them remembering the once lively Nancy who had helped at the Nature Station only a few days earlier.

"I'll check in with Todd later today. He worked overtime last night, went home for a few hours of sleep, and he was due back early this morning." Hope's usually cheerful face looked worried. "I don't understand why Nancy's death has the entire force working around the clock."

The entire force didn't consist of very many in a rural and normally sedate county like theirs, and each small town only employed a few officers for patrols; it seemed everyone was on the job. Kristen had seen the Eklund's night officer on the scene last night, assisting with questioning, she supposed. Still, a lot of manpower was being used to check into what, or whom, had killed Nancy.

"I only know enough to be dangerous," she said, thinking of her earlier plant research. She decided to let her friend in on what she knew. If Hope learned something important from Todd, Kristen could tap into her as a source.

Hope gave her an odd look. "I think you know more than you're telling. Spill the beans, and I'll make it worth your while."

"Don't worry. I'm not deliberately withholding anything from you. It's all so fresh, and I'm trying to decide what to tell you that isn't just a figment of my imagination."

Or apparently the sheriff's, since he's the one who put suspicions into my head.

"We don't have long before we open. Tell me what happened." Hope squeezed Kristen's shoulder. "If I know you, you were probably involved in some way."

"Unfortunately, you're right about that. I was the one who found Nancy."

"Oh my goodness, not again!" Hope's eyes widened in wonder.

"Brett and I were having a fantastic dinner. We'd just ordered dessert, and I went to the ladies room to freshen up. It's a long story, but I found Nancy slumped over in the bathroom stall."

Hope's eyes nearly bulged out at that information, so Kristen hurried to fill her in the details, finishing with the intensive questioning afterwards and her promise to aid in gathering information on poisonous native plants.

Hope was stunned into a rare loss of words after Kristen's account of the tragic evening. It was a few seconds before she spoke. "I'm going to get in touch with Todd right now to see if there's anything he can tell me. Nancy was our friend, and you're involved up to your neck in this, so I have absolutely no qualms about fishing whatever information I can out of Todd."

Kristen grinned at her loyal friend, though she also knew she wouldn't do anything to betray Todd's trust. "If you could get an update on the investigation, I'd appreciate it. I'd like to know how to direct our efforts."

Hope didn't even blink at the thought of uncovering what they could. "At least you don't seem to be under suspicion, which is great news. After all, not only are you the one to discover the... body," she said, breaking off with a slight gulp. "But the plants we supplied Barney's are under scrutiny. The sheriff wouldn't have asked you to do research if he didn't think you were innocent."

It was Kristen's turn to gulp. She hadn't considered that she could be implicated. Even on the slim chance her plants had caused Nancy's illness and death, it wasn't like she had been the one to actually feed them to Nancy. But the sheriff didn't know that for sure, she reasoned. In fact, he didn't seem to know much about plants at all, remembering with amusement how he'd reacted to some of her woodland wildflowers observations at the scene of Johnny Thomas' murder. That's why he was relying on her to assist with digging up information on poisonous plants, which wouldn't be a smart move on his part if she really had tried to bump off Nancy. She breathed a sigh of relief, knowing that once again, she'd been in the wrong place at the wrong time. But no matter what had gone wrong with Nancy, she was determined to discover the facts.

"Can you please try to contact Todd now? I have everything ready for hiker registration." She glanced up at the sound of a car door slamming and noticed a family gathering their things to start a hike. "I'll handle things here while you talk to him. After registration ends at one o'clock, and depending on what you learn from Todd, we can decide what to do next."

"Sounds good to me," said Hope, already punching numbers into her phone.

Feeling energized and proactive after her chat with her best friend, Kristen walked briskly to the registration table, ready to greet the afternoon's first hikers. She'd be busy for the next hour, and that would take her mind off the night before. After the registration rush, they could begin tracking down the truth.

A steady flow of hikers filtered in between noon and one o'clock. Finally there was a lull in the action. Kristen looked at her watch, amazed to see how quickly the hour had gone. Sure enough, Hope was walking in her direction.

"What'd you find out?"

Hope looked perplexed. "I'm not sure, but maybe you can shed some light on it."

More curious than ever, Kristen asked, "What do you mean?"

"I was able to catch Todd during lunch, and he gave me a rundown on the investigation." She paused. "And I *do* mean investigation."

Kristen didn't like the sound of that. "Are you trying to tell me they actually think Nancy was murdered?"

"Yep. At least the sheriff's department is treating Barney's as a crime scene. They've come to an initial conclusion that Nancy was murdered."

"Oh my…goodness!" Kristen stuttered in astonishment. Though of course she knew something was up with the way things were being handled, right from the start, it was a shock to hear murder spelled out in black and white. "Why do they think Nancy was murdered? Couldn't her death have been accidental?" Her mind flashed back to seeing the deputy holding the vase of wildflowers. She needed to contact Sheriff Miller as soon as possible to pass on what she'd learned about potential plant toxins.

"You already knew her death was being treated as suspicious since the circumstances were rather unusual. Maybe it was an accident, but the department isn't buying that."

"Nancy was the picture of health, ate right, and exercised regularly. Since she was a retired nurse, I'm sure she was faithful about yearly physicals and tests. I guess I can

64

understand why they jumped to conclusions right away. She wasn't the type to just drop dead from a medical issue."

"And that's not all," said Hope, pausing dramatically. "The paramedics noticed a few things when they initially examined her."

"Like what?' Kristen was eager to learn more.

"You told me she had vomited, which can be a side effect of many poisons."

"Or even food poisoning," Kristen added, wondering if that were the case. She hadn't heard of other diners becoming ill, but she supposed Nancy could have eaten something earlier in the day that could have been the cause.

"Since no one else became ill, they started checking out other options as well."

"At least they're exploring all possibilities." Kristen waited for Hope to continue, sensing there was more to the story. There was.

"Nancy's body was bloated and her pupils were dilated, which narrows the possibilities."

Kristen's thoughts shot back to what she'd discovered about butterfly milkweed. While many of the symptoms would only be noticed on a living person, she remembered bloating on the list of cardiac glycosides poisoning symptoms, but she couldn't recall the rest of the symptoms. She wondered if anyone had noticed Nancy exhibiting other symptoms before she died. She couldn't believe the sheriff hadn't already contacted her to see what she had learned about plant poisons. She knew he was busy, but he should be following up on this potential lead. Of course, he could be doing his own research. Even without a plant background, he could search online, just like she had. Still, she'd call him as soon as she was done talking to Hope, and she could fish for information, as well as passing on what she knew.

"That fits with what I learned about the toxins in butterfly milkweed." Kristen twirled a lock of hair around her finger absently. "I wonder if other plants or substances contain the same toxin," she said, still refusing to believe that Nancy had ingested enough butterfly weed to do her harm.

"That's easy to check on our end. Meanwhile, I'm sure they're analyzing the stomach contents." Hope said with a grimace.

Kristen could understand how she felt, since she'd seen firsthand the contents of Nancy's stomach. How appalling!

"What about her dishes and glassware?"

If the death was being investigated as suspicious from the start, she hoped they'd taken steps to preserve everything on the table. Of course, service at Barney's was exceptional. Perhaps her dishes had been cleared, and it would be hard to determine what, if anything, could have caused her violent reaction.

"Luckily, her wine and water glasses were still on the table, as well as her half-eaten dessert on its plate."

"Well, that's good news at least. She may have had more than one glass of wine, even one while waiting for her table at the bar. I would imagine she must have ingested the poison early on for it to take effect while she was still at Barney's."

"That's a good point, but there's more," said Hope, savoring her role as informant. "Her bread and butter plate was also on the table, and that's what made the deputies question the wildflowers."

"Oh?" Kristen raised her fair eyebrows. She couldn't believe Hope had been able to finagle all this information from Todd, who had been rather closed-mouthed about the Johnny Thomas murder case.

"Apparently there were bits and pieces of plants on the dish, next to her half-eaten roll."

"If there was still food on the plate, that's probably why it hadn't already been cleared."

"Right. I would think it would be fairly simple for the medical examiner to determine the cause of death based on what they've already found and what you can tell them."

"Which I'll do as soon as we've finished talking. Since they have evidence from the table, and perhaps information from other diners if Nancy's behavior was unusual, it shouldn't be difficult to pinpoint what killed her."

"I agree." Hope was acquiring a flare for drama. "That just leaves figuring out who did it."

"Simple enough," said Kristen sarcastically. "First things first, I'm calling the sheriff right now to pass on what I know."

"If he's in, just head on down to the department. I can handle things here."

Kristen entered the number into the phone and was glad when it was promptly answered. "May I speak with Sheriff Miller, please?"

"He's rather busy at the moment. May I tell him who's calling?

"This is Kristen Matthews. I need to discuss some issues relating to Nancy Meyers."

There was a pause from the lady on the phone line. "Let me check with him."

Kristen pondered the situation while she was on hold. Determining the cause of Nancy's death as soon as possible would allow law enforcement to get a jump on who did this awful act. Her thoughts were interrupted by the switchboard operator. "Ms. Matthews, the sheriff asked me to have you come to his office as soon as you can."

"Sure thing. I'll leave right away." She ended the call and turned to Hope. "I'm going into Eklund to visit with the sheriff."

"No worries. I'll be fine here. Just go." She hugged Kristen.

"I'll pick up the papers I printed off earlier and be on my way." Kristen left the Red Barn and walked rapidly to her house. She grabbed the printouts from her kitchen counter where she'd left them earlier in the day. So much had happened since last night; it was hard to believe it was only shortly after one o'clock in the afternoon. Locating the keys to her trusty red Chevy pick-up, she hurried out of her house, the back door slamming loudly behind her.

Her truck roared to life, and she backed quickly out of her driveway. The sheriff's department building was only minutes away from her house. She couldn't wait to do her part to help them get to the bottom of this nasty situation. One way or another, she was determined to track down the truth about Nancy…and her killer!

CHAPTER 8

The woman manning the front desk looked up from her computer screen when Kristen arrived at the sheriff's department. Kristen introduced herself and was ushered down the corridor, directly to the sheriff's office. At least she wouldn't have to linger in the stuffy, utilitarian waiting room she'd waited in a couple of months ago when she'd accompanied her friend, Ruth Ann Swanson, to this same building. All of a sudden feeling anxious, she took a deep breath as the clerk knocked on the office door.

"Come on in," she heard Miller call from his office. Hesitating only a second, her confidence restored, she entered the room.

The sheriff stood, greeting her politely. At least they were starting off on the right foot today. Kristen shuffled her papers and cleared her throat, anxious to start discussing the issue at hand.

"So what's on your mind?" he asked her.

Kristen placed the papers on Miller's desk, allowing him to leaf through them before speaking. "I did some preliminary research on toxins found in the prairie plants that were in the vases on each table at Barney's."

The sheriff grunted as he scanned the contents. "Can you summarize all this in a nutshell? I don't have time to learn botany. I have a murder investigation to run."

Kristen's eyes flicked to the man, surprised he'd leaked that they were classifying Nancy's death as a murder. She knew she needed to keep her mouth shut about what she'd learned from Hope. She didn't want Todd to get in deep trouble and also wanted to keep the lines of communication open with the handsome deputy.

"Of course. I'll make this short and sweet. You can read the printouts on your own. What I found online verifies what I told you last night. Foxglove beardtongue is harmless. Spiderwort can be toxic to people who are susceptible, but as a minor skin irritation, nothing fatal. However, butterfly milkweed'—she felt her pulse racing at the news she was about to deliver—"may be toxic to humans and livestock if ingested in large quantities."

"I don't care if cows can get sick from the darned plant. I want to know if Nancy died from it."

Kristen flinched. The sheriff's remark wasn't particularly politically correct in the rural town of Eklund where many families' livelihoods were linked to agriculture. Kristen's family raised beef cattle and would have been unhappy if one of their animals had encountered a poisonous plant.

"I can't tell you if she died from it, though I'm sure the medical examiner can determine whether she did. Can you run some tests to see if the toxin, cardiac glycoside, is in her system?

"Of course we can. It's not necessary for you to tell me how to do my job. I only needed to know which direction to go. There are hundreds, thousands even, of ways to poison someone."

My, my, was the sheriff testy today. Kristen really couldn't blame him. "I'm not trying to be negative, only helpful."

"And you have been. I didn't mean to bite your head off, but last night was a long night and the afternoon's half over. We're trying to proceed as quickly as we can with the investigation."

"Sure, I understand." She hesitated, not wanting to shatter their wary truce. "I find it hard to believe Nancy ate enough butterfly milkweed to kill her." There, she'd gone and said it.

The sheriff shrugged his shoulders, and Kristen took that as encouragement to continue.

"She was well versed in medicinal, as well as harmful, plants. Butterfly milkweed is a plant that, if prepared properly, may be used to treat a number of common ailments."

The sheriff interrupted her line of reasoning, "Yeah, but if it's not, it can be dangerously lethal, which is probably what happened in this case."

"But not likely. Who else would have known butterfly milkweed, or any other native plant in the vase, could be used as a murder weapon?"

Miller eyed her coldly. "Who else indeed?"

Kristen shifted uncomfortably, willing herself to remain calm. "My point is, not many people would choose it as a way to kill someone. I knew milkweeds were toxic to many animal species, but I wouldn't have ever thought to use is as a murder weapon...if I were to ever consider murdering someone, which I wouldn't ever do," she finished feebly.

He raised his eyebrows but otherwise ignored her remark. "Well, that's what we have to go on for now."

She hoped they wouldn't focus entirely on the unusual orange plant. A sudden thought popped into her head. Would one of the other Nature Station volunteers know enough to use a plant as a weapon? She knew David Steward, a retired landscaper, was excellent at plant identification. Did he eat at Barney's last night? She hadn't seen him, but he could have arrived before her to take advantage of an early bird special. Her heart skipped a beat. *Oh no!* Robert Wellington was there last night. She remembered waving to him from afar.

She looked up to find the sheriff's curious eyes on her. "Did you remember something important?"

"I was trying to think of anyone else who may have the same plant knowledge Nancy does, or did, rather."

"Did you come up with anyone?" He had picked up his pencil, ready to take notes.

Kristen was cautious. She didn't want to throw out David or Robert's names without being sure they had something to do with Nancy's death. Good grief, she'd been leery of both of them when Johnny had died. She'd checked both of them out, and David had even had a strong motive for killing Johnny. However, what possible motive would he have to kill Nancy? And the same was true with Robert. Yes, she had seen him eating at Barney's, but lots of people were eating there, and they weren't all suspects. She thought back to his possible addiction to alcohol and mysterious retirement from his job at the bank. Even if he had nothing to do with the recent murders, she knew there was more to Robert than met the eye.

She wracked her brain, trying to determine who could have performed this malicious act and why. When she looked up again, the sheriff was watching her closely. "It's interesting to watch your brain in action. Why don't you tell me what you're thinking?"

His tone was polite, but she knew she couldn't get by with trying to evade him. She had to consider Nancy. "I was thinking that Robert Wellington was eating at Barney's last night. He knows his native plants pretty well, and he could have had the opportunity, if not the motive, to kill Nancy."

"Have you been watching police shows again?" Miller smiled in amusement.

"No, I don't watch much television, but I love to read mysteries."

Though he didn't groan out loud, Kristen could tell he wanted to.

"It's up to us to determine whether a suspect has motive. You just never know about people until you dig deeper."

She nodded, knowing he was right. Her eyes had been opened when she'd snooped around town looking for Johnny's killer. Something clicked in her head. When she and Hope had gone to Nancy's house to question her, Nancy had been behaving oddly; she even lied when questioned about a door slamming. Kristen had suspected she lied to cover up the presence of someone in the house. The question was, who was it, and what were they doing there? It had turned out to have nothing to do with Johnny's murder, but did it have anything to do with her own? She wrestled with herself for a moment, not wanting to air dirty laundry about the deceased. Then she decided she needed to tell the sheriff.

As Kristen filled him in on Nancy's actions that day, and the fact that she'd been spotted at Amy's Bakery with none other than Robert Wellington, Sheriff Miller scribbled furiously away on his notepad. When he was finished, he asked, "Why didn't you tell me any of this sooner?"

"I didn't think it had anything to do with Johnny's murder."

"You should have let us decide that."

"I didn't want to spread gossip."

"We keep information like that confidential, so you would be safe telling us."

Kristen thought of what Todd had revealed to Hope and knew that even though he had good intentions, and she was thankful to receive the information, he should have been more discreet.

"I'm telling you now, just in case it has something to do with her death. And by the way, David Steward is another Nature Station volunteer who really knows his plants. Actually, most of them do, but I only saw Robert there last night."

It was possible someone only stopped in long enough to tamper with her food or drink, and she didn't see them. Then of course, there were Barney's employees. Surely everyone had been questioned, but Kristen wasn't privy to that information...unless Hope could persuade Todd to divulge more tidbits. She almost grinned. Hope could be quite convincing.

"If you suddenly remember anything else that could pertain to the case, make sure you tell us—as soon as possible!"

"Oh, I will." She smiled her most charming smile. "By the way, did you learn much from Nancy's husband?"

"I can't comment on that."

Kristen decided to prod him a bit. "If I were running this investigation, I'd be all over him. Nancy must have been away from their table for several minutes. It's a wonder he didn't go looking for her."

"We've checked into that."

"Are you satisfied with his answers?" She was already planning a few questions she'd like to ask him when she had the chance.

"I'm not going to answer your questions, so quit wasting your time."

"Okay, I understand, but you can't blame a girl for trying." She winked, mimicking a move better suited to Hope.

Sheriff Miller only shook his head while rising from his chair to signal he was done talking with her. Apparently, she'd worn out her welcome.

"Thanks for your help, and if you happen to stumble across any other information or run more research, let me know."

"You can be sure of that." She let herself out of his office and returned the way she'd come, down the long, bland hallway. She left the building breathing deeply. Though the afternoon was warm and humid, she was glad to be outdoors. She couldn't wait to get back to work and mull things over with Hope and then later with Brett and her family.

By the time she returned, the afternoon business was starting to wind down. In this weather, it didn't take long for even the most enthusiastic young hikers to grow weary. She parked her truck and walked over to the start of the trail that went to the prairie on the left and into the woods on the right. She greeted families as they ended their afternoon. A few had questions for her; some had snapped photos of interesting plants and wanted her help to identify them. Since she was so familiar with the plants growing on her property, she normally had no problems providing assistance. However, sometimes a question stumped her, but not so much as the mystery surrounding Nancy's death. Her mind wandered as she moseyed back to the Nature Station office where Hope was staffing the small but popular gift shop. Hopefully, they'd had a successful afternoon.

Sure enough, she walked in as Hope was finishing a transaction. From the looks of things, a lot had transpired in the time she'd been away.

Hope pounced on her as soon as the customer walked out the door. "Tell me what happened!"

"Sheriff Miller and I had a fairly decent conversation. He was happy I gave him the plant information and a few other interesting morsels." Kristen felt guilty at implicating some of their workers, but it had to be done.

"More importantly, did you learn anything from him?"

"Not really, though he did let it slip that they were investigating this case as a murder."

"Yeah, but we already knew that."

"I know, but I was surprised he told me."

"I guess you're right. Where do you think we should go from here?"

"Since we're closed tomorrow, what do you think about meeting for breakfast?'

"At Carrie's Coffee Cup? Sure." Hope giggled. "Especially if it's your treat!"

"Hey, no fair, I paid the last time."

"That's true, but I have a feeling we're going to be going door to door and asking questions–" Hope cleared her throat for effect "–as a result of you being involved in another murder."

"I suppose you're right." Besides, if she couldn't offer Hope a huge salary or paid fringe benefits like health insurance or a retirement plan, the least she could do was buy her a meal every now and then. She knew from past experience that Hope would more than earn what one of Carrie's breakfast specials would cost her.

"Why don't we get started closing down." Hope eyed her watch. "Todd and I are meeting for a quick dinner date before he needs to get back to work. These murder investigations take a toll on a relationship."

Kristen certainly didn't envy her for that, though she knew their relationship was rock solid. "I know I don't need to say this, but see if you can squeeze out some information from your main squeeze."

"That goes without saying, if he even feels like discussing the case. And maybe you can get some background information during your dinner with Brett and your family."

"Sure. We'll probably spend half the evening discussing the latest murder."

"And when we meet for breakfast tomorrow, we'll fill each other in, and go from there."

"Sounds fine to me. How about if we meet around eight-thirty? That will allow us to sleep in a little, but we'll still have ample time to get some snooping done."

Arrangements made, Hope left a few minutes early. Kristen was glad for a little alone time to think before everyone arrived at her house. She wanted to make the most out of their time together to glean whatever information she could.

She longed for a peaceful evening with Brett, where they could converse on things other than murder. Their Saturday dinner date had been turned upside down by Nancy's death, and tonight they'd be rehashing what they knew about Nancy and the people acquainted with her. During the short amount of time they'd been dating, she and Brett had experienced some rocky times together. It looked like they would encounter more ups and downs until Nancy's mysterious death was put to rest.

One thing Kristen knew for sure: bad times could either strengthen a relationship or tear one apart. Needless to say, she wanted theirs to prosper. They needed to move beyond murder for that to happen.

CHAPTER 9

After the last hiker left for the evening, Kristen raced home, hoping for a few minutes to shower and sponge off the grime of the day—not just dirt, but the tremendous tension she'd been feeling ever since discovering yet another body.

She emerged from the bathroom feeling recharged. Dressing quickly in a pair of cutoffs and a red tank top, she slid into comfortable flip flops, glad to free her feet of her heavy work boots.

As she came down the stairs, she saw Brett's truck pulling into the driveway. His timing always seemed to be perfect. She was opening a bottle of chilled sauvignon blanc when he rapped on the backdoor.

"Hey there," she said, wrapping her arms around him and surprising him with a slow, sweet kiss; she had to sneak in what she could before her family arrived. "Would you like a beer?"

"That sounds great." He set his grocery bags down and stashed a few things in the refrigerator.

She had some iced tea brewing on the countertop, but that could wait. They took their drinks out to the front porch to wait for her mom and dad to arrive. Come to think of it, her sister Morgan would probably join them too. Fortunately, this wasn't the first time they had all met, but they were still in the "being polite and getting to know each other" stage, thank goodness. She had the distinct feeling, though, that discussing Nancy's murder would tear down whatever barriers might exist between Brett and her family. She knew she could count on a lively evening.

"What have you been up to today?" she asked as they relaxed with their drinks in comfortable wicker rockers. Shaded by the large white oak gracing Kristen's front yard, it felt good to unwind after the events of the past twenty-four hours.

"You know how it is on your day off. There's always something to do." Brett stretched out his long legs. "I did some yard work and laundry, nothing too exciting."

"It's nice to have time to catch up on those things." She'd probably need to mow her own yard in the next day or two. "Besides, we had enough excitement last night, didn't we?"

"Yeah, but not the good kind. Things started off well enough." He sighed. "I just wish they'd ended up better."

"Me too. But I'm confident everything will get back to normal soon." Kristen took another sip of wine, feeling it work its way through her body, helping her to relax.

Brett smiled. "We don't even have a 'normal,' do we?"

"It doesn't seem like it." She looked at him, feeling the attraction stronger than ever. "But we will."

He started to answer her, but whatever he was about to say was interrupted by the arrival of her family. They waved from the porch, beckoning her mom, dad, and Morgan to join them. Sure enough, Kristen spotted Joanie carrying a nine by thirteen pan of something that was bound to be scrumptious. She felt her stomach grumble in response.

"I'll take that," she said to her mom. "The grill is around back, and we'll be firing it up shortly. Why don't you head back there. We'll be out in a few minutes." Brett jumped up, taking drink orders, then met Kristen in the kitchen, where she was lifting the aluminum foil off the pan, sneaking a look at the dessert inside. She noted its gooey chocolate contents and sighed in pleasure.

Brett poured drinks while Kristen shifted around the contents of the refrigerator, including the salads Brett had picked up at Swede's, to locate the pork chops and hamburgers she'd thawed earlier. She found some dip for carrots and grabbed some chips from the cabinet. Dividing up the food and drinks among them, they exchanged a smile before venturing out the backdoor to the small patio that held the grill and a scattering of chairs.

"Help yourselves to some munchies while we start grilling," said Kristen. Once everyone was settled down with something to eat and drink, she placed the meat on the grill, turning the knob to low to ensure they'd have plenty of time to chat while their meal cooked. Before taking a seat near Brett, she paused to pet Peaches, who was enjoying the extra company. She'd sniffed everyone thoroughly, then she lay down in the corner, this time contentedly sniffing the grill's fragrant aromas.

It didn't take long for conversation to begin. "Have you found out anything more about what happened to Nancy?" her mother asked.

"As a matter of fact, I visited the sheriff's department earlier today, and Hope found out a few things from Todd."

"Well, don't keep us waiting," Morgan said with a grin. "You know we didn't barge in on your evening just to eat."

She sniffed the already savory aromas radiating from the grill. "Everything does smell wonderful, and I'm starved."

"Me too!" Kristen lunged for a handful of chips to tide her over until dinner was ready.

"If you're traipsing off to discuss things with the sheriff, you must be in the thick of things, which doesn't surprise me," said her dad wryly.

Kristen shrugged. It's not like she tried to get herself involved in murders. It just seemed to happen these days. "The sheriff asked for my help doing research on poisonous native plants."

"Oh, I didn't realize you specialized in poisonous plants. We'd better be careful what we eat tonight." Morgan snickered.

"No worries on that," Kristen said with a laugh. It felt good to let her hair down around her family. If they could help her figure out who had killed Nancy, they would. "You know the Nature Station supplies Barney's with fresh wildflowers to use on their tables most weekends during the summer."

"Don't tell me," said her dad. "Your flowers were used to poison Nancy."

Kristen didn't need to hear it spelled out quite like that. "Nothing can be determined until they run some tests, but the sheriff seems to think Nancy was murdered. From what I could find out online, she would have had to eat a huge amount of butterfly weed to die from it. And that doesn't make sense. She was an expert on medicinal uses of local native plants."

Her mother set her glass of iced tea on the small table. "That fits with her nursing background. But what doesn't fit is that she would knowingly eat a poisonous plant."

"Exactly," said Kristen. "Nonetheless, the sheriff asked me to research the plants. I know the basics on some of the common poison native plants and ones used for medicinal purposes, so it didn't take long for me to get the details."

"Besides," chimed in Morgan, "you wanted to clear yourself of any wrongdoing, not that you did anything wrong!"

"Of course not! Even if the plants I sold to Barney were harmful, people aren't supposed to eat them! And if they were curious and took a bite, it wouldn't be enough to make them sick, let alone die!" Kristen stood up and walked over to the grill to flip and season the meat.

"Even if one of your plants did kill Nancy, that means someone most likely fed her the plants unbeknownst to her." Her dad looked puzzled. "And I'm not sure how they would have done that in a crowded restaurant without anyone noticing."

"You would have thought Nancy would have noticed, if no one else," said her mother thoughtfully.

"And why would anyone even want to kill Nancy in the first place?" asked Morgan. "As far as I know, everyone loved her. She was an awesome nurse with a good bedside manner."

"Even if she was giving you a shot, it didn't seem so bad." Kristen smiled at long buried memories of childhood doctor visits. "She talked the entire time, taking your mind off everything, and before you knew it, it was over."

"Nancy was a real people person," her dad agreed. "She enjoyed chatting with everyone and was sincere and caring to others."

Kristen's mind raced, trying to determine who would have a motive to kill her friend.

"What's the matter, Kristen?" asked Brett, finally getting into the act. "I don't like the look in your eyes. You need to stay out of trouble and leave the investigating to Sheriff Miller."

Kristen noticed her dad nodding in approval at Brett's remark. While she was happy they seemed to be hitting it off, she didn't appreciate them both ganging up on her. After all, she was an independent woman who did as she pleased. Of course, it was only recently that she'd found herself engaged in some tricky situations. She supposed they had a good point, but she wasn't going to let common sense deter her from delving into Nancy's suspicious death.

She decided to change the subject and checked the grill one last time. "I think the meat's about finished. Shall we eat inside or out here?"

"It's not too bad in the shade with the breeze blowing." Joannie stood and headed to the kitchen to help make preparations for their impromptu dinner.

Luckily, there wasn't much to be done. Brett transferred the meat from the grill to the platter while Kristen and her mother went indoors to get the other food ready. Soon they were seated back on the patio, chowing down on dinner. They chatted about local news, friends, and family while they ate, not wanting to mar their digestion with thoughts of murder.

Once dishes were cleared away, they got down to business. "So what can we do to help?" asked her dad.

Kristen's lips twitched in amusement.. If she hadn't been so stressed during the previous murder investigation she was involved in, she would have gotten more of a kick out of watching her dad gather information. He didn't seem to worry about his own safety, though he was deeply concerned for Kristen's. "For starters, you can find out what you can about Nancy's husband."

Her dad nodded, knowing as well as she did that the spouse would be a natural selection when it came to targeting someone for initial questioning. *Or an unnatural selection*, Kristen thought to herself, *if he was the one who had actually killed Nancy.*

"I'll be glad to, though I don't know him well. Still, I'll ask around."

Kristen wondered if she could get away with paying a visit to Nancy's house to offer her sympathies to her husband. After all, Nancy had been a regular volunteer at the Nature Station, so it would be appropriate. She added the stop to her list of things for her and Hope to tackle after breakfast. She crossed her fingers that her friend would be able to come through with some news from Todd.

She remembered her previous thought about how strangely Nancy had acted when they'd dropped by her house unannounced while searching for clues to Johnny's killer. Later that same day she'd been spotted with Robert Wellington at Amy's Bakery. Were the events related? Robert was dining at Barney's last night. Surely he couldn't have killed Nancy. Still, Kristen added him to her list of people to check.

"I think it's a good idea to snoop around about Robert Wellington too." Kristen sighed. What more could she find out about the man after interrogating him just a few months ago? Maybe she and Hope could track him down together for an informal conversation. They probably should also delve deeper into Nancy's past.

Perhaps a trip to Amy's Bakery was in order. Since the bakery had started serving gourmet coffee blends to accompany their sweet treats, Amy's business was attracting the coffee crowd. Kristen doubted they'd taken much business away from the gas station, though. A faithful gathering of male coffee drinkers met there regularly to enjoy the strong brew, she recalled with a chuckle.

"What's so funny?" Morgan looked at her sister oddly.

"Nothing much. I was just remembering the experiences Hope and I had asking questions about Johnny's murder at the gas station and other places around town."

"It's no laughing matter," her dad said sternly, probably recalling the close call Kristen had when confronted by the killer.

She quickly sobered. "I realize that, Dad. Don't worry. I'll be very careful."

Brett spoke up. "Just to make sure no harm comes your way, you could leave the investigating to the sheriff's department.

"You're right, I could," said Kristen, though she had no intention of doing so, and Brett probably already knew that.

"Why don't we have some dessert," said Joannie, attempting to switch topics.

"I'll help you!" Kristen rose from her chair and followed her mother indoors, glad to escape Brett's and her family's good intentions for a few moments.

After scooping generous portions of the chocolate concoction into individual bowls, they carried a tray outdoors. Luckily, the others had taken to discussing the weather, always an interesting topic in this rural community. Though she appreciated the input from everyone tonight, Kristen couldn't wait to mull over the new ideas in her head and then get herself organized for her morning sleuthing escapade with Hope.

After they'd finished their dessert, Kristen couldn't contain her yawn. "Sorry about that. I was awake really early this morning."

Her family took the hint, helped her carry everything indoors, and made their way to the door, promising to contact her if they learned anything relevant to the case.

Soon Brett and Kristen were alone in the kitchen. The sun was sinking lower in the sky, casting an orangey glow through the windows. Brett leaned in to brush her lips lightly with a kiss. "I know you're bone tired, and I have a busy day at work tomorrow."

"I'm glad I'm off tomorrow. I don't envy you!"

"You worked all weekend, so I hope you enjoy your day off." He leaned closer to kiss her again, this time lingering much longer before reluctantly pulling away. "I'd better get going. Cassie and I will be in the field the entire day."

Kristen felt an unexpected jolt near her heart. In all the excitement, she'd forgotten about Brett's intern, Cassie. "You'd better take a lot of water with you. It's supposed to be a hot one tomorrow." She kicked herself for making such a lame remark and for feeling even the slightest bit of jealousy.

"I'll be fine, but you need to watch yourself. I can only imagine what sort of trouble you and Hope will get yourselves into with your sleuthing."

Kristen wouldn't normally bristle at Brett's teasing, but she was still thinking about Brett and Cassie working so closely together. "You don't need to worry about us."

"But I do worry about you," he said, putting his arm around her affectionately. "Be sure to call me if you run into any trouble, though my cell phone reception is not always reliable when I'm doing field work in remote areas."

That fact didn't make Kristen feel any better, for reasons other than her own safety. The thought of Brett and Cassie working together in the middle of nowhere did not help matters.

"I will."

He kissed her once more before he left, telling her he'd call her after work.

She watched him pull out of the driveway, knowing she was crazy to think he'd be interested in another woman after the affection he'd shown her the past couple of months. She trusted Brett completely, but she'd never met Cassie and had no idea whether she could trust *her*.

She rubbed her tired eyes while yawning once more, then switched off the lights and headed upstairs. She figured a lack of sleep was probably making her overly suspicious of an innocent work relationship. She hoped she'd feel better after a good night's rest.

Dressed in a cool nightshirt, she climbed into bed with her book, planning to read a couple of chapters to wind down. She'd barely made it through the first chapter when her eyes grew heavy. She turned off her lamp and snuggled down in her bed, falling fast asleep within minutes, all thoughts of murder brushed aside for now.

CHAPTER 10

When Kristen awoke, the sky was only just beginning to glow with soft summer morning light, though birds were already chirping. She glanced at her clock, grimacing when she noted the time; it was only four-forty. Boy, did it start to get light early these days! She attempted to squeeze her eyes shut and get back into sleep mode, which was next to impossible. The sun was rising higher with each minute, and her bedroom was growing warmer.

Since sleeping in on her only day off from work was out of the question, she decided to go for a run. It would be cooler than waiting until evening, and she could use some uninterrupted thinking time, not to mention exercise after indulging in a heaping helping of last night's dessert.

She stretched and yawned one last time before casting off her covers. She dressed in her running clothes, then pulled her bed head hair into a tight pony-tail and went downstairs. Peaches must have heard her stirring—she was already waiting at the back door ready to go outside with her mistress.

Kristen was still tired, so she took it slowly for the first half mile, then picked up her pace as her body grew more limber and her breathing came in sync. She let her mind wander, reviewing the events of the past two days and the few facts she knew about them. She tried to organize her thoughts and drafted a morning "to do" list. However, the direction they took this morning might depend on whether Hope had anything important to report. Still, she made a mental note to visit with Robert Wellington, Nancy's husband, and possibly drop by Amy's Bakery to see what she could find out from her. From conversations with Nancy, she knew she had become a coffee regular there and sometimes picked up baked goods orders for Nature Station events.

She thought back to Saturday evening, trying to remember anything unusual. She hadn't noticed anyone other than Nancy's husband sitting at their table. Nancy had been drinking red wine when she stopped to visit, but there was no food on the table at the time. She'd only glanced casually at the flowers, but it didn't appear they'd been tampered with at that point, although she could have missed it.

A thought suddenly occurred to her. She'd been concentrating on who'd been eating at the restaurant that night, but she supposed one of Barney's wait staff could have been responsible for Nancy's demise. In fact, such a drastic event would have been more easily accomplished by someone who worked there. . They all had an opportunity to monkey with the food, whether they were preparing or serving it. The question was why? Who on earth had reason to kill Nancy? She added a visit to Barney's to her list, then remembered they weren't open on Mondays. It really didn't matter; they could track Barney down at home, if needed.

That's enough for now, she told herself. *We'll play the rest by ear.* She had taken her favorite trails through the timber and prairie, and she saw the Red Barn come into view as she rounded the corner. She slowed her pace to a walk, thankful for the light breeze blowing to help cool her damp skin. The day was already starting to warm up, and the air was thick with humidity. Her breathing labored, she walked toward the house. She couldn't wait to jump in the shower and have a cup of coffee before setting off to meet Hope.

After starting a small pot of coffee perking, she went upstairs to shower. She savored the steamy spray pelting down on her, but cut her time in the bathroom short to avoid adding to the humidity already invading her house. Wrapped in a soft towel, she pulled a pink tank top and black shorts out of her drawer, thinking she should start a load of laundry. She threw her damp towel into the basket with her running clothes and carried it downstairs to the washer. That chore completed, she poured herself a steaming cup of coffee and wandered out to the front porch, on the way grabbing the unread Sunday newspaper to read.

Between the run, shower, and now a dose of caffeine, Kristen was starting to feel awake, despite her early start to the day. She leafed through the paper, enjoying some rare spare time. An article in the outdoor section caught her eye, written about local medicinal plants. One of the plants featured was pokeweed. She grimaced. It was tough to eradicate this weed that grew around some of the more disturbed areas of the Nature Station property. What a coincidence that the newspaper would run an article on a plant that had medicinal properties but could also be toxic if prepared improperly. She was immediately reminded of the possible poison that killed Nancy. She couldn't wait to join Hope for breakfast to discuss the case.

Finished with the paper, she took her cup indoors for a refill and grabbed her laptop. She was curious to learn more about pokeweed. Her interest in poisonous and medicinal plants was growing. She scrolled the numerous entries, clicking on one that sounded promising. Though she knew pokeweed could be poisonous, she wasn't aware of the details. She was surprised to learn the roots were among the most poisonous parts of the tall plant. She would have thought the purple berries it produced later in the summer would have been the most toxic. She scrolled through the list of symptoms, which seemed similar to many types of poisons.

She glanced at her watch, astonished she'd spent so much time engrossed in research. She shut down her computer and went to throw a few items into the dryer before hanging the rest outdoors to dry. She took a notebook from her desk drawer and hastily scribbled down the list she intended to take care of with Hope this morning.

Making sure Peaches had an adequate supply of food and water, she left the house, hurrying to be on time to meet Hope. Soon she was pulling into the crowded parking lot at Carrie's Coffee Cup, a cafe that did a booming business during breakfast hours. She feared that securing a table would be a challenge, but then she spied Hope's car at the back of the lot. Thank goodness her friend had arrived first. Kristen parked near her and entered the bustling coffee shop. She spotted Hope in a corner booth, nursing a cup of coffee.

"Hey, how are you doing?" asked Hope.

"I'm doing okay," she said, sliding into the weathered vinyl seat of the booth across from her friend. "How was your evening with Todd?"

Hope smiled mischievously. "It was nice. I bribed Todd with a home cooked meal before plying him for information."

Kirsten thanked the waitress who had just poured her coffee, and both women placed their orders. "Were you successful?"

"You won't believe it."

"Probably not, so just tell me!"

Hope leaned in closer, enjoying her role as informant. "They're still trying to pinpoint the poison that caused Nancy's death."

"Oh?" Kristen pondered that information and decided to feel relieved. Surely if they couldn't trace the poison specifically, that meant she and her wildflowers were off the hook. Unfortunately, that most likely meant they were scrambling to find the cause. "But they're still confident Nancy died from poisoning."

"Yes, all her symptoms point to it, and her health was otherwise good, so they're pursuing the poison route."

"What exactly were her symptoms again?"

Hope recited the list. "Nausea, vomiting, and burning sensation around the mouth,"

"Had Nancy complained about her mouth burning to her husband?" She didn't think they could determine that post mortem.

"According to Todd, her husband mentioned it."

"Interesting." So why hadn't her husband checked on her? Suddenly Kristen's mind leapt to the article she'd read in the newspaper only an hour or so earlier. Pokeweed! If her memory served her correctly the symptoms were similar. Pokeweed's poisonous properties were fairly well known by gardeners and farmers who raised livestock. It was common in the area, so it could be easily obtained and not likely to be suspected or traced by law enforcement.

"What's the matter? You look like you've seen a ghost."

"Did you read the Sunday paper?"

Hope looked at her quizzically. "I skimmed through it yesterday. Why?"

"There was an article featuring local medicinal and poisonous plants, such as pokeweed. I was curious to find out more, so I searched online for more specific information."

Hope took a sip of coffee. "What are you trying to tell me?"

"I need to check into it more, but I have a hunch pokeweed might be to blame for Nancy's death."

"Nancy would have known better than to mess with that!"

"Exactly, but you have to admit, it would make an excellent murder method. It's virtually untraceable."

Or was it? Kristen wrinkled her brow. It wasn't unusual for her to field inquiries about pokeweed from visitors to the Nature Station. She wracked her brain, trying to remember if anyone had recently asked what it was called. Definitely not one of Kristen's favorite plants, she could still understand why people were drawn to it; the tall leafy stalks produced dark purple berries. After identifying it, Kristen always explained why people should avoid contact with pokeweed, since parts of it were poisonous.

"I guess so," said Hope. "What are the odds pokeweed was used? There are thousands of things that could be used to poison someone. In fact, Todd told me sometimes it was like looking for a needle in a haystack trying to rule out particular poisons. If they have something to go on, it's much easier."

"Well, let's give them some direction," Kristen replied while searching in her purse for her phone. She plugged pokeweed into her browser and searched. She squinted at the tiny entries that popped up then enlarged one that sounded promising. "Here we go. Toxic components of the plant include saponins and pokeberrygenin."

Hope looked at her dubiously, convinced Kristen had gone off the deep end. "Pokeberrygenin? Did you make that up?"

"No way. Look, it's right here." She pushed the phone in Hope's direction.

"Okay, you're right. I agree, the symptoms do match. I guess it's worth a shot." She grabbed her own phone and punched in a few words. "In my text to Todd, I said you'd forward him the website link. They should be able to run some tests on the toxic compounds it listed for pokeweed."

"Sure." Kristen shot the web link off to Todd just as their breakfast arrived. She was starved—she'd been awake for hours and gone for a run to boot—and dove into her biscuits and gravy enthusiastically.

They munched their food in silence for a few minutes, pausing only briefly to swig coffee. "So where do you think we should go first?" asked Hope.

"While we wait to hear from Todd about the possible pokeweed poison, I think we should have a chat with Barney."

"Barney? You don't think he had anything to do with Nancy's death, do you?"

"No, not Barney, but one of his employees could have. He has several longtime employees, but he hires a few temporary people for the summer and around the holidays."

"Okay, so we visit Barney. Then what?" Hope was jotting items in a small notebook.

"At some point I think we should talk with Mr. Meyers."

"I agree, but that could be an awkward conversation."

"That's why we need to stop at Amy's first to pick up something to take with us. We'll pay our respects and see if we can find out anything."

"That sounds awfully cold."

"Yeah, but so is murdering Nancy."

"I guess you have a point."

"And who knows what we'll discover when we visit Amy's Bakery. I bet she overhears some interesting conversations while customers are chugging down her gourmet coffee."

"That's very likely." Hope looked thoughtful. "If we strike out there, we can always check out the coffee crowd at the gas station."

"You'd like that, wouldn't you?" Kristen enjoyed teasing her friend about her conversational skills. Back in April, Hope had chatted up the men at the gas station's coffee counter in an effort to pick up useful information about Johnny Thomas.

Their list made, they discussed other topics while they finished their breakfast. Kristen reached for the check while their waitress refilled their cups one last time. Soon they'd finished their coffee, paid the check, and walked out into the warm, muggy air. The parking lot at Carrie's Coffee Shop had cleared considerably, so they left their vehicles parked there and walked the short distance to Barney's.

They tried the door, although they knew the restaurant was closed. Still, Kristen hoped Barney would be there, maybe doing book work. No answer. They walked around to the back of the building where Barney's office was located. While Kristen pounded on the back door, Hope scouted out the small window in Barney's office. They were pleasantly surprised when Barney opened the door.

He eyed Kristen knowingly. "I figured I'd be seeing you again."

"We did have quite an experience the other night." She patted his arm. "I wanted to make sure you were getting back on track."

"The sheriff allowed me in here this morning. I've been trying to put things back together after the investigators finished their work."

Hope smiled sympathetically. "I'm sure it was a mess." She looked around. "Isn't anyone helping you?"

"I wanted to see how things looked first before I called in help." Barney shrugged. "They were careful in their search, but it's a restaurant, and someone died here. Things need to be put in order, not to mention thoroughly sanitized."

Kristen winced, remembering the stench from the vomit. "I suppose you need to hire a professional service to take care of that."

"Yeah. A crew is coming in this afternoon to get started—that's all arranged. I just need to pick up the pieces."

Kristen imagined he meant trying to salvage his business's reputation after a murder had taken place there. She could understand his feelings; she'd gone through the same thing herself. At least the Nature Station had rebounded, and she was confident Barney's would be successfully back up and running in no time. "Is there anything we can help you with?"

"No, I'll be fine." He sighed heavily, definitely not behaving in his normal cheerful host demeanor. "I just can't figure out why anyone would do this to Nancy. She was a wonderful woman."

"We feel the same way," said Hope. "It's an awful shock."

"The sheriff's department spent hours questioning my staff and searching the place. Even though a cold-blooded murderer is responsible for Nancy's death, it happened here, so I feel a certain responsibility to set things right."

Kristen nodded in agreement. "That's how I felt a couple of months ago when Johnny was killed out at the Nature Station."

A glimpse of a smile crossed Barney's face. "And you probably feel the same way this time."

"I *am* the one who discovered her."

"And I know that couldn't have been easy. Here I've been moping about feeling sorry for myself, but there are many others affected."

"Don't worry, you've got a right to feel down," said Hope. "Maybe the best thing for everyone is to band together and try to figure out what in the world happened here."

Barney's spirits lifted. "You've got a point. Without a doubt, I cooperated fully with the sheriff's department. But since we," he glanced at Kristen, "were actually here that Friday night, we probably have a different take than the investigators."

Kristen nodded. "Exactly. Not only do we have a vested interest in finding Nancy's killer, we may have noticed something they didn't. Not that they don't do a great job!' She glanced meaningfully at Hope.

"They have their hands full," said Hope. "I'm sure they'd welcome any help they can get. It's possible another diner or employee remembers something later that may prove to be important."

"I think a staff meeting is in order." A look of relief crossed Barney's features, probably because he felt like he was taking control of the situation rather than merely reacting to it.

"That's a great idea!" Kristen looked a little sheepish. "I'm sure you realize one of your staff members could be responsible for Nancy's death. After all, it would be hard for another diner to tamper with her food or drink."

"But not impossible," piped up Hope. "Nancy was a popular and well-liked woman. I'm sure several other diners stopped by her table to visit."

"Which gets us back to motive. Who wanted Nancy dead?" Kristen shook her head. "It just doesn't add up."

"There must be more to the situation than meets the eye." Barney gazed out the window, lost in thought.

"Do you know something about Nancy we don't?" asked Kristen. "Since she dined here often you saw who she came with, what she ordered, and other interesting facts."

"You're right. I get to know my clientele in ways you wouldn't imagine." Barney once again looked thoughtful.

"Come on, Barney. Just spill it." Hope was impatient to learn more.

"Yeah, obviously something's on your mind." Kristen was starting to feel annoyed. She didn't have time to mess around. Besides, even though Barney was an icon in the town of Eklund and surrounding communities, who's to say he didn't kill Nancy? She couldn't come up with anyone who would want to harm the poor woman, and she knew the person who killed her would be just as unlikely. Which meant they were back to trying to unearth information about Nancy and the people who were closest to her.

Barney was done hemming and hawing. "I guess it doesn't matter now. I was trying to protect Nancy's reputation, but it's too late for that."

Kristen glanced at Hope, then back at Barney. "We may be snoops, but we're not gossips. Whatever you have to say will stay between us, unless it relates directly to the case. We don't want to hurt Nancy's reputation either, but I think the time has come to dig deeper into her personal life."

Barney sighed deeply. "You're right. I don't really *know* anything, but sometimes I picked up some negative vibes about her relationship with her husband."

Kristen raised her eyebrows, waiting for him to continue. Hope shifted impatiently from one foot to the other.

"She came in here quite a bit with him, but they didn't seem to talk much."

Kristen had noticed many older couples dining together at restaurants, some of them going the entire meal without speaking. It always amazed her when it seemed like she and Brett had so much to say to each other. Still, it wasn't unusual to eat without talking much. That didn't mean they didn't love each other.

"Isn't that normal for some couples?"

"Sure, but there's more to the story." The restaurant owner paused, looking uncomfortable. "Sometimes they dined with others."

"That's quite common." Hope wore a puzzled look on her face.

"You're not getting it. When they were eating with friends, they always seemed to have lively conversations, like they were happy and well matched."

"But when they were alone, they didn't?" Kristen still didn't understand where this conversation was going.

"No, they didn't. And when they talked with certain friends, they seemed very friendly."

"Who was being friendly?" asked Hope, her annoyance apparent.

"Nancy acted friendly with some of the other men, not to mention her husband's well known dalliances with other women."

"Oh," was all Kristen could say. She hadn't realized Meyers had been sighted with other women; her already low opinion of him sunk even lower. Her mind flashed back to the time she and Hope had visited Nancy's home. She had seemed flustered that day and had blown off a door slamming in the back of the house. Could she really have been having an affair? Kristen had tried not to focus on it, but Barney's words were making it sound more likely. "Was it any particular man Nancy flirted with, or was it more than one?"

Barney face flushed bright red, and it wasn't from schlepping Saturday night specials to hungry diners. "Robert Wellington. I'm sure you remember that he was eating here when Nancy died."

CHAPTER 11

"Robert?" Kristen sputtered in astonishment. She couldn't think of a man less likely to flirt with a married woman…or any woman. Still, she knew there was more to Robert than met the eye. Thinking back to April when she'd run into him at Swede's with a cart full of booze, she wondered again if he had a drinking problem. Alcoholism would certainly impair his judgment, although it definitely was not in keeping with his conservative banking background. When her dad mentioned Robert's sudden retirement a few months ago, though, she'd thought it odd.

"Back up a minute. Nancy was friendly to everyone. What exactly is your definition of the word?" asked Hope.

"I have no proof of anything," said Barney. "It's just a feeling I got around them. You know, looks and smiles between them, sitting close together, that kind of thing."

"Did you tell the sheriff?" asked Kristen. Nancy's husband was already near the top of Kristen's list of suspects; the man had ample motive if his wife had been cheating on him, or perhaps if he'd been cheating on her.

"Of course, though my observations were fairly vague. I'm not sure he took me seriously enough to look into it any further."

"If Nancy really was fooling around, they can probably dig up evidence of it to back up your statement." In fact, thought Kristen, she would look into it herself. She already had her own suspicions concerning Nancy's faithfulness to her marriage vows.

"Is there anything else you can think of?" asked Hope. "What about Nancy's husband? Is he the jealous type?"

"He didn't seem to mind Nancy flirting with other men. Maybe he didn't pick up on it, since he was busy doing his own flirting."

Or maybe she was doing it to make her husband jealous. Kristen had experienced jealousy firsthand, even of a woman she'd never met, like Brett's intern, Cassie. She was sure it would be a powerful emotion in a marriage. She couldn't imagine Nancy's husband not noticing her flirtations, even if he wasn't the most observant or jealous man. If Barney had picked up on it, others would have too, which might make Kristen's job easier. "Do you know much about her husband?"

"He wasn't as personable as Nancy, though he's always polite." Barney paused briefly. "He usually talked to the other diners who stopped by to visit with them, but he wasn't as outgoing as Nancy."

They weren't getting much tangible information out of Barney on the Meyers couple. Kristen switched gears. "I know you're having a staff meeting to discuss the situation, but you never mentioned whether you have any new employees. Unfortunately I don't come in here enough to be familiar with all your people, especially the ones who work behind the scenes."

"I hired a few folks to fill vacancies, plus a couple of others just for the summer." He scratched his head before continuing. "You met Patricia the other night. She's the new full-time hostess and also performs other duties besides seating diners. She started a few months ago." Barney's face became animated as he talked about the hostess. "She's been a great asset to the business."

"Yeah, she seemed friendly and efficient, and even remained calm during our emergency situation," murmured Kristen.

"Anyone else?" asked Hope, jotting a few lines on her notepad.

"I hired two college students for table bussing and dishwashing, Steven Nelson and Tara Koehler. I had one waitress start just last week, Lauren McCauley."

Kristen had only met Patricia. "Were they all working on Saturday?"

"Sure, we're fully staffed on Saturdays."

"I believe Brett spoke with Patricia when he made our dinner reservation. Did you start taking reservations recently?" It occurred to Kristen that if one of Barney's staff members knew Nancy had reserved a table for Saturday, they would have planned ahead of time to bring the poison that night. After all, no one would risk carrying it around with them unnecessarily, especially if it were a poisonous plant requiring advance preparation.

"We began taking reservations shortly after Patricia started. It was one of her new ideas that allows us to plan ahead better."

Kristen nodded, wondering why Barney hadn't instilled the common practice years earlier. "I don't suppose you noticed anyone acting suspiciously or anything out of the ordinary."

"I told the sheriff everything I could remember, and the deputies questioned all my staff. Saturday nights are usually organized chaos. Unfortunately, it would have been easy for someone to get away with something unnoticed."

"That's probably true whether the killer was an employee or another diner," said Hope.

"You've got a point." Barney shuffled his feet. "Listen, ladies, I know you're trying to get to the bottom of the situation, and I can appreciate that. But I've told both you and Sheriff Miller everything I can remember. I need to get back to work if we're going to open tomorrow for business."

"Sure, we understand," said Kristen reluctantly. She knew they were being dismissed, but she couldn't quite believe Barney had told them *everything*.

They said their goodbyes and left via the back door. Once they were headed down the block, Hope eyed Kristen. "What are you thinking?"

"I'm just speculating whether Barney was being straight with us about everything. As observant as he was about Nancy's behavior, he didn't seem to notice much else."

"I'm sure Saturdays are his busiest night. That's probably why they started taking reservations."

"Maybe," said Kristen thoughtfully. "Do you think one of Barney's employees could have seen Nancy's name on the list and decided to make a move?"

"It seems logical. Maybe Nancy or her husband told someone they were eating dinner at Barney's on Saturday night. I think it was a regular hangout for them." Hope pulled a face. "Not everyone lives on the same strict budgets we do."

"You're right about that. But it might be worth it to check if Nancy actually had a reservation the night she died.

And who in the restaurant had access to the list or took reservations over the phone."

"We can call Barney later to ask. We may have some other questions for him after we're done with our other stops."

"Good idea. I think we should pay a visit to Robert Wellington."

"Are you sure *that's* a good idea?"

"You mean because he may have been extremely close to Nancy, close enough to want her dead?" Kristen looked perplexed. "No, it's probably not a good idea to visit him, but that doesn't mean we aren't stopping by his house anyway."

Hope whipped out her phone. "If that's the case, I'm letting Todd know where we're going and why we're going there."

"Now *that's* a good idea." Kristen frowned. "Then again, maybe we should just let the sheriff's department handle Robert. He was on my original 'to do' list, but we've got enough going on today."

"But you heard Barney say they didn't seem to take him seriously."

"Can't you convince Todd to look into it a little further?"

"I can try, but that doesn't mean we can't still have a casual chat with him ourselves."

"Maybe I can ask Dad to talk to him, since he knows Robert from his banking days. That way we can tackle the other people on our list. If we need to follow up with him later, we can."

"Sure. Let's see what we can do."

Kristen rang up her dad while Hope tried to get in touch with Todd. Neither of them was successful, so they left messages.

"I hate to say this, but our next stop should be to visit with Nancy's husband," said Kristen.

"I'm not looking forward to it, but since Nancy worked so much at the Nature Station, we have every right to pay our condolences."

"Besides, he knows I'm the one who found Nancy."

"Okay, let's get this over with. But don't you think we should take something to his house?"

"You mean food?" Kristen thought for a moment, deciding to kill two birds with one stone. "Let's drop by Amy's Bakery to pick up something for our visit with Mr. Meyers."

"And she'll be able to fill us in on anything she may have heard in her shop."

"You've got it." Feeling better to have their plan set, Kristen and Hope ambled down the sidewalk toward their friend's shop. Since Eklund's downtown was only a few blocks long, they reached their destination in a matter of minutes.

Inside the bakery, the aroma of newly ground coffee beans competed with the savory aromas of fresh-from-the-oven goods. The place was bustling with late morning business.

"It's too bad we ate a big breakfast," said Hope, eying a tray of éclairs.

"Breakfast was excellent," Kristen said as she patted her full stomach. "But we can always take something for later."

Amy finished ringing up a customer's order and smiled in their direction. "What can I do for you two?" She waggled her eyebrows. "Are you here for something to eat or to sniff out information?"

Kristen chuckled. "A little of both."

"Can I interest you in some blueberry muffins?" Amy asked, then lowered her voice. "I've been wanting to talk to you. Hold on and I'll have my assistant take over for a few minutes."

"We'll have some coffee while we wait," said Hope.

"Help yourself. We have Monday Morning Joe brewed in one carafe and Vanilla Nut Cream for our flavored blend." Amy slid two mugs across the counter. "I'll join you in a minute."

Anxious to hear what Amy had to tell them, Kristen filled her cup with coffee, then walked to a table in the corner where they were less likely to be overheard. It wasn't long before Amy carried her own mug of steaming coffee to their table.

"I take it you're trying to help solve Eklund's latest murder."

Kristen smiled wryly, thinking of how what should have been top secret information traveled quickly in the small town. "We're doing our best. Even though I was the one who stumbled across Nancy on Saturday night, I have no clue what happened to her or why someone would want her dead."

"We've been doing a little digging around town, trying to do what we can to assist the sheriff's department," added Hope.

"Oh, so Todd has sanctioned this investigation?" joked Amy.

"Not exactly." Hope shifted uncomfortably. "But he knows us well enough to guess we'd be asking a few questions."

"It's hard not to get involved since Nancy was our friend. Besides, I think the sheriff's department needs all the help they can get." She glanced at Hope. "Not that they can't handle this investigation, but things are a bit complicated, and it's difficult to know where to start."

"At least that's how we feel." Hope smiled. "Maybe you can point us down the right path."

Amy took Hope's opening. "It's not like murder is a common occurrence in the peaceful town of Eklund, and now we've had two in just a couple of months. Ever since I started serving coffee, I have people hanging out here at all hours of the day. It used to be they would come in, make their selection, and then they'd leave. Now they spend more time here, and I have a chance to talk with them and also witness interactions between my customers."

Amy had done wonders with the bakery, taking advantage of her previously large waiting area's wasted space and converting it into an intimate seating area. The serving counter had been scooted farther into the commercial kitchen, making more room available for the coffee crowd. An artistic blend of mismatched antique chairs and tables, most likely purchased at sales, made the bakery cozy and eclectic. A sofa, a couple of armchairs, and a low coffee table were nestled in one corner. The walls had been painted a warm gold to hide the utilitarian white previously adorning them. All in all, the bakery now exuded a friendly, welcoming feeling that drew folks inside.

"I'm sure it's also a nice boost to your business," Kristen said, wondering where Amy was headed with her comments. "Coffee houses are becoming increasingly popular again."

Amy beamed with pride. "I wish I'd done it sooner. Even calorie conscious customers can drink as much coffee as they wish and not worry about their waistlines. Though I do serve real cream." She winked.

Hope swirled her coffee around in her cup. "I bet you've started attracting even more customers than before."

"Yes, it's been wonderful for business. I still cater to my faithful bakery customers, who also love a cup of something warm when they're here, plus new customers who come in just for the coffee."

After rising so early, another serving of caffeine was just what Kristen needed. She took a swig of the rich brew. "So tell us about these coffee-holics."

Amy smiled but seemed nervous all of a sudden. Hope tried to reassure her. "It's okay to talk to us. You can trust us to be careful with any information we learn."

"Oh, I trust you both. It's just hard to discuss something that may affect the deceased's character or possibly point fingers at an innocent person."

Here was someone else concerned about Nancy's reputation. Apparently Kristen didn't know Nancy as well as she thought. "It's likely we've already heard something similar from our other contacts. Just tell us what you know, and we'll figure it out."

"I just feel so badly." Amy paused and cleared her throat. "Nancy stopped by the day she died to pick up a few items for breakfast on Sunday, along with some coffee beans."

"Was that out of character for her?" Kristen already knew Nancy was a frequent customer of the bakery.

Amy shifted in her chair. "No, not at all, but she was acting a bit oddly. I didn't think much of it at the time, but when I heard the next day..." Her voice trailed off.

Hope patted Amy's hand encouragingly. "We understand. Who would have thought that was the last time you'd see her. You'll feel better if you get this off your chest."

Kristen nodded. "What exactly do you mean by odd?"

"We all know Nancy had a bubbly and dynamic personality. That's one reason I can't understand why someone would want to harm her. But on Saturday she seemed absent minded. I asked her what she had planned for the weekend, and she told me they had reservations at Barneys."

Kristen raised her eyebrows at Hope. "Just as we suspected, she could have told anyone about her dinner plans."

"Yeah, so now we know more than just restaurant staff knew where she was eating Saturday night." Hope looked thoughtful. "I don't suppose you remember if anyone else was here at the time."

Amy grinned. "I was getting to that. I'd better just spit it out. Nancy was with Robert Wellington. She met him here quite often."

Kristen exhaled slowly. She couldn't avoid talking to Robert after hearing this news. "And I saw Robert at Barney's on Saturday. That's quite a coincidence, isn't it?"

Hope piped up. "I wonder why Nancy was acting absent minded. It wasn't like her to be spacey."

"It wasn't anything major, but not typical Nancy behavior. For example, when she placed her order, she changed her mind three times. Then she gave me a ten dollar bill to pay for almost twenty dollars' worth of items."

"And Robert was with her the whole time? Did they come in together or meet here?" Kristen was curious to know if they were merely friends or something more.

"Sometimes they met here, but on Saturday they came in together. I'm not sure if they rode together or met outside first."

"I need you to put aside your feelings about Nancy and be honest. Would you say they were more than friends?" Kristen hated digging up dirt on a woman she had liked and respected for years.

Amy looked glum. "It sure looked like it to me."

"So, Nancy was acting a little ditzy and Robert was with her. Were they behaving any differently than usual?" Kristen hated to picture Nancy and Robert together, as both of them were married to other people.

"I don't know. I tried not to pay much attention to them when they were together. It didn't seem right. I did wonder, if they were having an affair, why would they flaunt it in a small town like Eklund?"

"That's asking for trouble," agreed Hope. "Is there anything else you can tell us? We know you're busy here, and we have other stops to make."

"I'll give you a call if I do. By the way, I assume you don't have any changes to this week's orders?"

"No, we're good." Kristen drained her coffee and pushed back her chair. "Thanks for the coffee."

"Yeah, it hit the spot," said Hope.

They selected an assortment of muffins to take along when they called on Nancy's husband and left the bakery, pausing outside the brick faced shop to regroup. "Do you think we should drop in on Robert?" asked Kristen.

"Let me check in with Todd first." They sat down on a bench under a shady maple along the town's main stretch and Hope pulled out her phone to call Todd. Fortunately, she was able to catch him this time.

While Hope was chatting with Todd, Kristen pulled out her own phone and rang up her parents. Her mom answered, and Kristen brought her up to speed on what she and Hope had learned from Barney and Amy.

"I was wondering if you could check on something for me."

"Sure, I can try. What do you need?"

"First of all, what's Nancy's husband's name? I meant to ask you last night. We're headed over there pretty soon to pass along our condolences."

Her mother chided her gently. "And do some snooping, I'm sure."

"We're just trying to gather some background information."

"Well, his name is Ted. Now what else did you need?"

"Ted." It was nice to put a name with the face, though that wouldn't make an uninvited call on the widower any easier. "Say, had you ever seen Nancy and Robert out together?"

"I saw them in the same place sometimes, but that's not necessarily being together."

"I know what you mean. They both worked at the Nature Station, though I never noticed them acting like they were more than friends."

"And they might have actually been just friends. Even if they were romantically involved, it may have nothing to do with her murder."

"That's true, but something caused a killer to strike, and this is the most likely lead we have at the moment. What else is there?"

"I'm not sure, but if I know you, you'll keep rooting around until you find out what happened to Nancy."

Kristen ended the call then turned to Hope, who had just finished her conversation with Todd. "Did you find out anything interesting?"

Hope shrugged her shoulders. "Not too much. Todd said they questioned Robert, but they didn't learn much from him."

"Go figure. So I take it he didn't admit to having an affair with Nancy?"

"Nope. He just said they were close friends."

"Which could be true, but I still think there's something odd about their relationship."

"Something odd about whose relationship?"

Kristen and Hope had been so engrossed in their conservation they hadn't noticed their friend Ruth Ann Swanson walk up behind them. It probably wasn't a good idea to discuss murder investigations while sitting along a public sidewalk, thought Kristen ruefully. Still, she was glad to see Ruth Ann. "We were talking about Nancy."

"Of course." Ruth Ann sighed heavily. "Another murder in our fair town of Eklund. And you're involved in this one too." She hugged Kristen tightly.

"Unfortunately, I'm getting a track record for discovering dead bodies. It's not a good feeling." Kristen grimaced.

"How are you holding up?" Ruth Ann had been a friend of Kristen's family for decades, having gone to school with her parents and taught high school biology to Kristen and her siblings. Most recently, she served as one of the Nature Station's most reliable volunteers. Despite the sultry day, she looked cool and crisp in khaki capris and a mint green shirt. Her strawberry blond hair, touched up a bit from the salon, and bright blue eyes gave Ruth Ann a youthful appeal.

"I'm doing okay, but as you can imagine, we're trying to figure out who would want to kill Nancy."

"It puzzles me, too." Ruth Ann joined them on the bench as the two younger women scooted closer together. "Nancy was a lovely lady, and I can't believe she's gone. I'll miss her terribly. How can I help?"

"We're spending our day off asking a few questions, but we aren't getting many concrete answers." Hope pushed a strand of brown hair behind her ear to keep it from blowing in the light breeze.

Kristen looked at Ruth Ann thoughtfully, Maybe the older woman could help pave their way into Ted Meyers' home. It would also be nice to have her along if they decided to talk to Robert.

"What do you think about tagging along with us to pay our respects to Ted Meyers?"

"I was planning to drop by anyway, so we may as well go together. In fact, I have some fresh baked cookies in my car. You're welcome to ride with me."

"That's a good idea. Nancy's house is a few blocks away, so we would probably have taken my truck if we hadn't run into you," said Kristen with a grin, though it faded quickly when she thought they could possibly need a get away car handy when talking to either Ted or Robert. Kristen pondered whether the men who appeared to be closest to Nancy would have harmed her. If so, they needed to stay on their toes when they talked to the men.

"Are you merely expressing sympathy to Ted, or do you have an ulterior motive for visiting with him?"

Kristen had never been able to pull anything funny with Ruth Ann when she'd had her as a teacher, and it was obvious she couldn't fool her now. "Of course we want to visit him as friends of Nancy's. We bought some muffins at Amy's to help pave the way since we also want an opportunity to chat with Ted."

Ruth Ann raised her eyebrows. "Any particular reason why?"

"He was her husband, so it makes logical sense he would know Nancy the best," said Hope.

"To be honest, I thought it was strange he didn't seem worried when she didn't return from the ladies room after a few minutes." As they walked to Ruth Ann's car, Kristen filled her in on what all had transpired that fateful Saturday evening and what they'd uncovered since then."

Ruth Ann shook her head. "I can't believe Nancy would have an affair, but that's not to say I hadn't seen her around town with Robert."

"It doesn't make sense to me that she'd be seen in public with her lover in a town this size," said Hope practically. "Everyone knows each other's business, and if they don't, they aren't afraid to speculate."

"I agree, but we've heard from more than one person that Nancy and Robert were close...maybe *very* close," said Kristen.

By then they'd reached Ruth Ann's car, and she unlocked the doors of the well maintained Buick, moving a few things around to make room for her riders.

"So you're probably planning to visit Robert too?" she said as she started the car and pulled away from the curb.

"Depending on what we learn from Ted, that's the plan," said Kristen. They rode in silence during the short drive to the Meyers' house. Fortunately, no cars lined the driveway, but the garage door was open, revealing a vehicle parked there. "We'll follow your lead, Ruth Ann, while you offer your sympathy, since you know Ted."

"We'll sit back and observe and maybe ask a few subtle questions," added Hope.

"Well, try not to be too pushy," said Ruth Ann. "Even though I want to figure out who killed Nancy as much as anyone, I don't want to upset her husband. He's been through so much the past few days, and I'm sure he's been questioned extensively by the sheriff's department."

Kristen looked curiously at Hope, who shrugged her shoulders. She felt sure Hope would have passed along anything she knew about what transpired when the sheriff questioned Ted. "Ruth Ann, have you ever known us to be pushy?"

"Of course! You wouldn't have opened and managed The Nature Station so successfully the past few years if you weren't!"

The women chuckled as they got out of the car and walked toward the front door, though they knew there was some truth in Ruth Ann's statement. They quickly sobered as the door opened. Ted Meyers stood there, looking extremely rough around the edges. It appeared he hadn't showered or shaved since Saturday evening. He wore a rumpled t-shirt and khaki shorts, and his eyes were bloodshot. He attempted a weak smile as he greeted them.

"Hello there, Ruth Ann. It's nice of you to call." He looked questioningly at Kristen and Hope. His eyes paused on Kristen as if trying to picture where he'd seen her.

She stuck out her hand. "Hello, I'm Kristen Matthews. I saw you the other night when I stopped by your table to chat with Nancy." She paused. "I'm also the person who discovered her in the restroom."

"Ah yes, I remember you." He cast his eyes downward, as if trying to gather his composure. "You're the owner of The Nature Station."

"Yes, that's right," she said, stumbling for the right words. "We loved working with Nancy, and we'll truly miss her."

"She enjoyed helping at your events. It kept her busy while I..." He stopped talking.

There was an awkward silence as the women stood there waiting for him to continue. Finally Hope handed him the muffins, introduced herself, and expressed her sympathies.

"Thank you so much," he said, then remembered his manners. "Please, why don't you come inside?"

"We'd love to, but just for a minute." Ruth Ann offered Ted the plate of cookies she'd brought.

"Thank you for thinking of me. I'd appreciate some company. It might help me forget some of the dreadfulness of the past couple of days. Let's have a seat."

They followed him into the living room, the women seating themselves on the couch, and Ted in an armchair. When Kristen had visited Nancy previously, she was charmed by the coziness of the couple's home. Today the curtains were drawn, blocking the day's bright sunlight, and the house seemed drab and depressing.

"I can't believe you haven't had a swarm of visitors stopping by."

"Oh, there have been several." He gestured toward the kitchen, where the table was laden with food. "But most of them only stay for a minute to drop off a dish and then leave."

"They're probably not sure what to say to you," said Hope.

"I know. I suppose it's only natural." He sighed, looking glum.

Since Ted appeared to have plenty of food on hand, and he didn't seem interested in eating any of it, Kristen wondered fleetingly if he would notice if she took the muffins from Amy's home with her. Probably not one of her better ideas. What was wrong with her? Why was she thinking about muffins at a time like this, when a friend of hers was dead? She had work to do. Glancing around the room, she looked for something that would help them get to the bottom of things. Nothing jumped out at her.

"None of us are used to people being murdered in our quaint town." Kristen thought she'd gone too far when she saw the man flinch. "I'm sorry. I didn't mean to state it quite like that."

"It's okay. Besides, it's the truth. And it's not like you're here to interrogate me, like Sheriff Miller," he joked half-heartedly.

Kristen felt guilty at that comment, since she had every intention of asking Ted a couple of things. But she'd also been on the receiving end of the sheriff's questions, so she could understand how difficult it would be, especially when the man had just lost his spouse. Whether there was any love lost between the two was an entirely different matter, though.

"Oh, so he had some questions for you?" Kristen eyed him sharply, thinking the man seemed sad but not exactly heartbroken.

He shifted in his chair uneasily. "Well, yes, as Nancy's husband I'm the person closest to her…or I was."

Ruth Ann reached over to pat Ted's hand. "Oh dear, it must have been dreadful answering the sheriff's questions while you were bereaved, to boot. I know what that's like." She cleared her throat before continuing. "I suppose you probably know by now that Johnny Thomas and I had been seeing each other when he was killed. Not only was I suffering from losing him, but the sheriff acted like I had something to do with it!"

In showing her support for Ted, Ruth Ann had set the stage for Kristen to continue. "I remember, I'm the one who took you down to the sheriff's department. What a day that was, not one I care to repeat. I hope you held up okay under his scrutiny, Ted."

"I know what you mean, question after question, he really fired them at me."

"Were you able to tell him much?" Hope spoke up with a deceptively demure smile.

"I outlined our schedule for the day and evening, of course. He wanted to know if Nancy had been feeling well, had any enemies, and that type of thing. They were hard questions to answer, given the circumstances, but when I thought about it later, they made sense. After all, we were married for almost forty years."

"Well, I don't think *any* of it makes sense." Kristen's voice started to rise. "Nancy was a good woman. Who could have possibly wanted to kill her?" Her eyes met Ted's. "Do you have any ideas?"

He looked uncomfortable, but that could be attributed to three women throwing questions that were difficult for him to answer. He shrugged. "Nope."

Interesting, thought Kristen. She found it hard to believe the man had no suspicions of his own. "Did Nancy act any differently the day she died?"

"Not that I noticed, but we had both been on the go all day, so I didn't see much of her until it was time to get ready for dinner."

That's right; she had been spotted at Amy's Bakery with Robert earlier in the day. What else had she been up to? And for that matter, what had Ted been doing all day? Figuring out how to poison his wife?

"Did you meet anyone before dinner?"

He looked at Kristen oddly. "Why would you ask that? It's none of your business."

Hope straightened her posture and came to her friend's defense. "We're just trying to help. Nancy was our friend, and Kristen is the one who found her. I'm sure you can imagine how difficult that would be."

"I apologize if I asked one too many questions," said Kristen, smiling charmingly at the man. "I can't help but wonder, 'what if I had I had found her sooner?' Could she have been saved?" She speculated again why Ted had not come searching for Nancy, especially when he had known she wasn't feeling the greatest.

Ted rushed to reassure her. "I understand how you feel because I feel the same way. I could kick myself for not coming after her. To be honest with you, we had had a few drinks, and I was sitting at the table relaxing and watching the other diners. If I had known I'd never see Nancy alive again, I would have done things differently."

"How could you know?" asked Ruth Ann, before posing a question of her own. "When you were enjoying your drink and people watching, did you notice anything, or *anyone*, out of the ordinary?"

"I've thought long and hard about that. Nancy and I dined regularly at Barney's, and we knew most of the employees and many of the patrons. In fact, we talked to several of them that night. Sure, there were some people I didn't recognize, but for the most part, I knew just about everyone."

"So you realize you probably *know* the murderer." Kristen blurted this out, and then immediately regretted it. Ted was sure to kick them out of his house after her tactless remark. "I apologize again for my comment."

"No, you're right. I'm sure we know the person who did it, and it's not a comforting thought." He leaned back in his chair. "I'm not offended by your directness. In fact, I know how you helped to catch Johnny Thomas' killer. You must have a knack for this type of thing. You have my blessing to do what it takes to find the killer. Nancy would have wanted you to help. She had a lot of respect for you and even mentioned her admiration Saturday night after she talked to you." He suddenly grew silent.

"Did she say anything else?" prodded Hope gently.

"Lots of stuff, but is any of it relevant? I have no idea."

Kristen was having a hard time reading Ted. Though he seemed sad and wanted her to help find Nancy's killer, he didn't provide them with much useful information. Was he hiding something? She assumed there was much he wasn't telling them. She could understand him wanting to keep certain things private, but a murder investigation could uncover all kinds of secrets. He may as well be as up front as possible to save time for the investigators and bring the killer to justice faster…unless *he* was the killer, which was entirely possible. He would have had ample opportunity and a possible motive if Nancy had been unfaithful, or if *he* was unfaithful. Perhaps he was trying to keep marital issues quiet, but whether he was the killer or not, their personal issues could have led to Nancy's demise. Kristen snapped out of her thoughts when she heard Ruth Ann's gentle voice.

"We've bothered you enough for the day." She patted Ted on the shoulder. "I'm sure you need some rest after this ordeal."

"I can rest after I have some answers. They haven't released…" He paused and sucked in a deep breath. "…her body yet. I can't even make funeral arrangements. It's just not right."

"I'm sure the sheriff's department is working diligently to narrow down the cause of death. They're conducting a variety of tests at the crime lab. Hopefully those results will lead to the killer," said Hope.

Kristen jumped in. "Once you've had a chance to reflect more on the days leading up to the murder, you may remember something that could be important to the case."

Ted nodded. "I've been doing a lot of thinking the past couple of days. Perhaps something significant will click into place soon."

Kristen fished in her purse for a business card and handed it to him. "Just give me a call if you want to chat. Or better yet, contact the sheriff's department. I'm positive they'd welcome input from you."

Ted rolled his eyes. "I'm not so sure about that, the way they've been grilling me. Thank you, ladies, for coming. I can't tell you how much I appreciate your support."

The women parted with Ted on the front porch. They remained silent until they were seated in Ruth Ann's car and she'd started the engine. Kristen knew one thing was certain. With three women observing and listening to Nancy's husband, a lively discussion was bound to ensue. But whether or not they had learned anything useful from the visit was up for debate.

CHAPTER 12

"I don't get it!" said Hope.

"What's there to get?" asked Ruth Ann as she rounded the corner and headed back toward Eklund's downtown area.

"He's moping around about Nancy, but he doesn't seem to know anything about what happened. He was probably sitting right next to her when she was poisoned. How could he *not* know something?"

"Who's to say he doesn't know anything? I think it's a matter of not telling us," said Kristen thoughtfully.

Ruth Ann nodded in agreement. "I've known the Meyers for years. I don't think Ted was being dishonest, but I got the feeling he wasn't being totally upfront with us."

"Maybe he didn't want to open up too much with Kristen and me there."

"That would be understandable if he didn't ask for help with tracking down Nancy's murderer in the next breath," said Kristen. "He can't have it both ways."

"And as much as I hate to say it," said Ruth Ann with a sigh, "he could have been the one to poison Nancy."

"It sounds like the sheriff's department is checking into that possibility. And until they have more leads to follow, they'll continue to hound Ted," Hope said.

"That's why I don't understand why he's not more forthcoming. He gave no indication Nancy may have been having an affair." Kristen was growing frustrated. "What's he trying to hide?"

"Maybe the fact that he murdered his wife," Hope said jokingly, though it was no joking matter.

"And there we were at his house, sniffing around for information," said Ruth Ann. "But he wanted you to help. None of it makes sense."

"I'd like to find a way to speak with him again, but first we need to talk to some other folks to learn more about Nancy, and Ted too, of course."

"Ruth Ann, are you planning to join us when we visit Robert?" asked Hope.

The older woman glanced at her watch. "Sure. I can do that. We're not far from his house. Why don't we stop by to see if he's home."

"Do you think we should come up with some sort of game plan first?" asked Kristen. "After all, we can't march into his house and accuse him of cheating on his own wife with Nancy."

Hope cracked up. "We'll definitely need to be more subtle than that. Maybe we can ask him if he wants to contribute money toward flowers or a memorial in honor of Nancy on behalf of the Nature Station."

"That's a great idea! We should have already thought of that." Kristen sighed. "Though from what Ted said, he hasn't even made any arrangements yet."

"We can mention some sort of business concerning the Station. We can see if he'd like to help at an event to cover the time Nancy had been scheduled to work," said Ruth Ann, as she pulled into Robert's driveway.

Kristen glanced out the car window, wondering if Robert was home and what sort of mood he'd be in. "Okay, let's lead off with asking for a memorial donation and then see if he's willing to work at this Friday's Tree Identification Workshop. If I remember correctly, Nancy had volunteered to assist with that event."

"Perfect," said Hope as they hopped out of the car and walked up the steps of Robert's sedate ranch style house. The garage doors were closed, making it difficult to tell if anyone was home.

Kristen rang the doorbell, and they waited, a little anxiously, for someone to answer. It wasn't long before a petite woman with gray hair and warm brown eyes opened the door. She greeted them then paused, waiting for them to state their business.

Ruth Ann took the lead. "Hello, Mrs. Wellington. We're here to speak with Robert. Does he happen to be home?"

Mrs. Wellington glanced at them, looking puzzled when her eyes landed on Kristen and Hope.

Kristen stuck out her hand. "I'm Kristen Matthews, and this is Hope Johnson. We're from the Nature Station, where Robert volunteers. We want to ask him a couple of questions, if that's okay."

"Sure, that's fine, but I'm afraid Robert's not here at the moment," his wife said in a gentle and soft spoken voice.

"I don't suppose you know when he'll be back, do you?" Ruth Ann smiled her most charming smile. "We've come to discuss a couple of things relating to Nancy's death—Nancy Meyers, that is."

Mrs. Wellington's eyes widened in surprise. "Oh. Well...I'm not sure exactly when he'll return," she muttered with a look of disdain. "You may be able to catch him down-town. He told me he was going to stop by the library."

"All right, we'll try to catch him there. But just in case we miss him, would you mind asking him to call me when he gets a chance?" Kristen handed her a business card. "It's important."

"Of course." By now, the other woman had gathered her composure.

"So sorry to bother you," said Ruth Ann.

"It's no problem at all." Mrs. Wellington shut the door, leaving the women looking at each other in bewilderment.

No one said a word until they were again safely inside Ruth Ann's car. "Did you notice how Robert's wife reacted to the mention of Nancy's name?" asked Kristen.

"It was hard not to notice," agreed Ruth Ann. "She's normally the epitome of decorum. She must have really been irritated with Nancy to react the way she did."

"Or irritated with Robert's behavior around Nancy," suggested Hope.

"If Nancy and Robert were truly having an affair, or even if they were just good friends, but Robert's wife assumed they were having a fling, she could have had a strong motive to kill Nancy," reasoned Kristen.

"She's probably dealt with a lot during their marriage, if Robert has or had an alcohol problem." Ruth Ann turned the car toward the library. "If she thought Robert and Nancy were too friendly, it may have been the last straw. It would feel like a slap in the face to stand by him through thick and thin, only to be jilted for another woman."

"I agree, but we only talked to Mrs. Wellington for a couple of minutes. We're reading a lot into her facial expression and one remark," said Hope.

Kristen rummaged in her purse for a pony-tail holder to pull back her hair. She eyed the digital thermometer on Ruth Ann's dashboard. It read eighty-seven degrees, and it wasn't even noon yet. The high humidity only made it feel hotter. The thunderstorm predicted for later that day would be a welcome relief.

"We'll try to nail down Robert," said Kristen. "If his wife thinks he's been cheating on her, he doesn't have anything to lose by opening up to us."

Ruth Ann found a parking place near the library's main entrance. Although the building had been constructed decades ago, it was recently upgraded to make it handicap accessible. The original part of the building retained its architectural integrity, and the library had increased its square footage by adding on in the back for additional stack space, computer terminals, study areas, and meeting rooms. The facility was popular with Eklund residents. Kristen could understand why Robert spent time there. She used the library to supplement her book habit, since she loved to read but couldn't afford to buy all the latest best sellers hot off the press.

They walked through the front door, enjoying the blast of cool air from the air conditioner. The librarian at the main desk, Marian Sanders, glanced up as they entered, then did a double take when she noticed the three women. They weren't normally sighted together at the library. Marian maintained order in her domain and probably wondered what they were up to.

Kristen sauntered toward the desk. "Have you seen Mr. Wellington here this morning?"

"Oh, so you didn't stop by to check out our new releases?" Marian laughed.

"Actually, I'd love to, but I'll wait until after we've located Robert."

"He's in the seating area near the periodical section." She winked at Kristen. "Don't worry, I'll save you a couple of cozy mysteries we just received."

Just one more thing to love about small town life, though there were a few others she could do without. "Sure, that would be terrific. Thanks."

By then, Hope and Ruth Ann had scouted out Robert, and they made their way to where he was sitting, scanning through the pages of a popular financial magazine.

"I guess old habits die hard, Robert," said Kristen, referring to the magazine he was reading.

Robert visibly jumped, then put down the magazine and smiled while taking in all three of them. "Hello, ladies. This is a nice surprise."

As the women sat down on the comfortable armchairs in the reading nook, Kristen realized she probably shouldn't have used the 'die hard' expression. Poor Robert looked like he'd seen a ghost, making her all the more curious about his relationship with Nancy and his possible involvement in her death.

"Your lovely wife told us we might find you here."

He flinched at the mention of his wife. It was possible she wasn't as gentle at home as her earlier docile demeanor implied.

"Oh, she did? Well, yes, now that I'm retired, I spend quite a bit of time here. And the Nature Station too, as you well know."

"Oh yes, and you know we appreciate the hours you spend working there," said Hope, smiling charmingly at the man.

"And that's why we've hunted you down, so to speak," said Kristen, immediately regretting yet another poor choice of words. *Oh well, if he has anything to hide, it will do him good to squirm a little.*

Ruth Ann spoke up. "We're contacting everyone who volunteers at the Station to see if they'd like to contribute something toward a memorial for Nancy."

In the silence that ensued, Kristen watched Robert's reaction. He looked uneasy. "We talked with Nancy's husband earlier today," she said. "He hasn't made any arrangements yet for her funeral. Still, we want to do something to show our support for her family and how much we appreciated her volunteer service."

Robert's face seemed to go from ghostly white to bright red in about ten seconds. "Of course I'll contribute." He dug in his wallet and pulled out some bills, his hands shaking slightly.

Ruth Ann patted him on the shoulder gently. "Are you all right?"

"Yes, I'm okay. I'm still in shock. Nancy was a wonderful lady, and we grew to be friends in our time working at the Nature Station." He put his face in his hands. "I just can't believe she's gone!"

"Neither can we," said Hope soothingly. "We appreciate you donating toward her memorial. It's helping us to band together and try to do something positive after the shocking news of her death."

Kristen watched Robert scrunch down farther in his chair, trying to avoid making eye contact with any of them. "We know how you must be feeling. We feel the same way!"

"You *can't* feel the same way." Robert's eyes were dangerously close to tearing, and his face had returned to its earlier pallor. "I've lost one of my best friends."

"Just friends, or something more?" The words were out before Kristen could stop them.

"Where on earth did you get an idea like that?" Anger, or perhaps embarrassment, made him flush again. The man changed colors as often as a chameleon.

Ruth Ann tried to calm him. "Now, Robert. It's common knowledge that you and Nancy were seen around town together. It's only natural for people in a place the size of Eklund to speculate about the nature of your friendship."

"I suppose you're right," he admitted, still appearing shaken. "We made no effort to hide our friendship, because that's all we were, friends!"

"We believe you," said Kristen, though she wasn't sure she did. "I didn't mean to upset you by insinuating that you were anything other than friends. It's just that Nancy died at the hands of a deranged murderer, and chances are good it was someone who was close to her."

He stared at them, speechless after their comments.

"You don't happen to have any ideas about who could have done such a thing, do you, Robert?" asked Hope. "Kristen said you were at Barney's on Saturday night. Did you notice anything unusual?"

"Not really. She was with her *husband*." He spat out the word. "They seemed to be enjoying each other's company."

"Did Nancy and Ted have issues…more so than any other married couple?" asked Kristen. She felt sure that during forty years of marriage they'd been through several ups and downs.

Robert paused, as if considering what he should tell them. "Her husband was a louse."

"Oh, how so?" asked Ruth Ann. This was news to her, despite the rumors she'd heard about other women.

"He cheated on her more than once in the past. Nancy recently confided in me that he was having yet another affair. She thought it was more serious than his other flings and suspected it was with a younger woman."

"How did she know?" Kristen could understand Nancy accusing Ted of being unfaithful, but with a younger woman? Then again, if Robert was to be believed, Nancy'd had much practice over the years putting up with Ted's infidelity.

"She wouldn't say how she knew or who she thought the woman was, but I think she'd been checking up on him. Maybe Ted figured out Nancy was on to him, and he decided to poison her."

"In a busy restaurant? Why would he do that?" asked Ruth Ann.

"Why not? There were people all over the place and several distractions. It's a possibility," said Robert, his voice rising.

Marian threw them a glare and put a finger to her lips. Fortunately, there weren't many patrons in the area, or they would have needed to choose another location to finish their interrogation.

"But the same could be said for you, Robert," said Kristen in a particularly unwise moment. "You were there that night and could have killed her just as easily."

"Trust me, I wouldn't go anywhere near that table with *him* sitting there." The normally mild-mannered Robert's feathers were definitely ruffled.

"Calm down everyone, or we'll get ourselves kicked out of here." Hope glanced over her shoulder toward the circulation desk. "Robert, we really did come in to ask you about making a memorial contribution, as well as ask you to fill the slot Nancy had volunteered for, Friday's Tree ID workshop."

Kristen tried to rein herself in. "I'm so sorry, Robert. I had no intentions of accusing you of murdering Nancy."

"She's right. Besides, what possible motive could you have for killing her?" asked Ruth Ann with a practical note to her voice.

"We're all on edge, I guess. Still, I had no excuse to get so carried away." Kristen smiled engagingly at Robert. "Will you forgive me?"

"Sure. We're all upset about Nancy's death. You're the one who discovered her, so I'm sure you want some answers." He sighed. "Just like the rest of us. I still think her snake of a husband had something to do with it."

"He certainly would have opportunity and probably a motive, if he's been unfaithful to her," said Hope.

"He may have wanted her out of the way to move on to greener pastures," agreed Ruth Ann.

"And maybe money was involved that could make a divorce tricky." Kristen scowled. "Killing a woman to avoid a messy divorce is a bit extreme." She looked questioningly at Robert, wondering if he knew about the Meyers' finances, or if he would tell them anything. "From your experience at the bank, was there anything unusual about how they saved or spent their money?"

Robert shifted uncomfortably in his chair. "I'm sure you understand it wouldn't be prudent for me to discuss their banking. All I can tell you is they were well off and didn't need to worry. In fact, Nancy received a small inheritance that she kept in a separate fund. And no, I'm not breaking a bank confidentiality code by telling you that. Nancy told me that herself."

Robert may have been prudent with information he'd garnered from working at the bank, but nonetheless, he'd spilled the beans on Nancy's personal finances. Still, did it matter if Nancy had a pot of money all of her own? Possibly, if someone else wanted it.

"Really? Did Ted know about it?"

"I assume he did, Kristen. But it was hers to use, and it gave her a sense of freedom in case things went bad with Ted."

"Do you mean in case she wanted to leave him?" asked Hope.

Robert looked forlorn. "Possibly, though Nancy never confided if she had concrete plans to divorce him. I just know Nancy's cheating husband made her miserable. That's all I had better say. Anything else would only be my biased opinion."

Kristen needed to mull over this tidbit. It was apparent Robert and Nancy were close, but after witnessing his actions, she was convinced he hadn't done it. His bitterness over Nancy's death was directed at Ted Meyers, whether he had anything to do with it or not. Kristen's mind churned through the possibilities. "Since you and Nancy were close friends, do you know of anyone else who may have wanted to harm her? I can't imagine her having any enemies, but she must have had at least one."

Robert hesitated a moment before answering. "Not really."

Kristen looked him directly in the eye, sensing he was being evasive. "You need to level with us, Robert."

"Nancy was well liked, not at all like Johnny Thomas." Hope looked apologetically at Ruth Ann. "If someone had a grudge against her, that person would stand out among everyone else. Knowing who hated her enough to want her dead will make or break this case."

"She's right," Ruth Ann agreed. "Just think about it. If you don't want to tell us, that's fine. But you need to tell the sheriff. Trust me, I know about these things." She winked at Kristen.

"Yeah, I get it, but I don't *know* anything. It's only conjecture." Robert stared out the window. "I knew Nancy was upset about her *husband*." His lips twisted in a grimace as he spat out the word. "But she didn't seem quite herself the past few times we were together. I can't pinpoint what exactly was different."

"That's the type of information that could prove to be vital," said Kristen encouragingly. "You need to talk to Sheriff Miller as soon as possible. He's a professional and will try to keep sensitive information confidential."

"If you don't mind, I'd like to be left alone for the moment. I need to do some thinking about the last days of Nancy's life." He shook his head. "You don't need to worry. Once I get my thoughts together, I'll pay a visit to the sheriff."

Kristen realized none of this was easy for the man. He'd been through a lot after losing his friend. She suspected Robert had pined for Nancy in a more romantic manner, though their relationship seemed platonic on the surface. Plus, he was not the type of man to divulge personal information about his friends or family. "Let us know if there's anything we can do to help."

The women said their goodbyes and walked toward the front desk, where they paused to speak with Marian.

"Are you finished already?" she asked, looking at the clock behind her. "We're still open a few more hours in case you'd like to continue harassing our patrons."

Ruth Ann wasn't about to take any guff from the edgy librarian. "Oh, cool it, Marian. We didn't mean any harm. We only want to get to the bottom of this nasty situation."

"I know that. I was only giving you a hard time." The librarian smiled then quickly sobered. "Robert and Nancy met here quite often, you know."

"No, we didn't," said Kristen, curious to learn more about the two friends. "I'm sure you observe all kinds of interesting behavior and friendships."

Marian took the opening to continue, keeping her voice low. "You don't know the half of it. The library is a calm and peaceful place, almost like a sanctuary for some. Those two met here at least once a week. I can assure you they were just friends, though I'm positive Robert had a mild crush on Nancy. But she was like that. Everyone loved her."

"Well, not *everyone*," said Hope. "Did Nancy meet anyone else here?"

"Not that I noticed." Marian paused for a moment "I saw her husband in here a time or two."

"Are you saying *he* met someone?" asked Ruth Ann. "Who?"

"I can't say they had an arranged meeting, but I saw him talking to other women, and they appeared to be pretty cozy with each other."

Kristen assumed Marian wasn't referring so much to the library's homey seating areas as to those who may have rendezvoused there. She pondered whether Ted purposely met other women there, or if they just happened to run into each other among the stacks. In all her years of being single, Kristen had never considered hanging out at the library an ideal method to meet men. She had better success at the grocery store. She chuckled at that thought, since most of the men she met there had known her since she was a child. The other women looked at her strangely. "Never mind."

"Listen, Marian. We understand if you don't want to confide in us about the people Ted or Nancy may have associated with here at the library. But be sure to talk to the sheriff if you remember anything significant," said Ruth Ann.

"Oh, I will," the librarian replied. "I'll mull things over and decide what's relevant and what isn't."

Kristen handed her a card. She'd have to restock soon if she kept passing them out at this rate. "If you'd prefer to talk to us, give me a call."

Marian studied the card, possibly weighing her options. "Sure thing. Oh, and don't forget the books I saved for you."

Kristen checked out her books, thinking she'd better start reading the short stack of mysteries for inspiration on how to proceed with this murder investigation. After a couple of days of snooping around, they'd hit a dead end—not the same dead end Nancy had come up against, thank goodness.

CHAPTER 13

Ruth Ann and Hope were waiting for Kristen outside the library. Hope eyed the books she carried. "What are those? Reference materials to help us refine our strategy?"

"Very funny. My vote is we should grab a bite to eat at Monty's and regroup," suggested Kristen.

"It doesn't seem possible to think about food after everything we've already eaten today," said Hope. "What do you think, Ruth Ann?"

"That's fine with me. I'm starting to get hungry, and maybe we can stir up some trouble at the café."

Ruth Ann had a point. Like Carrie's Coffee Cup where they'd breakfasted that morning, Monty's sandwich shop boasted its share of regulars who might have observed something interesting about Nancy or Ted. Besides, they needed to review what they'd learned so far and develop a game plan. "That's a great idea. Something to consider, everyone seemed to see Nancy and Robert around town, but what about Ted?"

The women walked down the block toward Monty's. "We haven't really posed that question, but we can start now," said Hope.

"Marian mentioned him frequenting the library, so it's possible he met women elsewhere around town," said Ruth Ann.

Before long they were standing outside the entrance to Monty's, studying the daily specials written on the chalkboard sign. They went indoors and found a corner picnic-style table. Monty himself came to take their order. *Good*, thought Kristen. They could quiz him for information before he went back to the grill.

"What can I get for you lovely ladies today?" Monty had his pen poised over his notepad, ready to jot down their requests, although Kristen suspected he would have no problem remembering them. He probably knew the "usual" orders for all of his regulars. He was the perfect person to help them uncover more information.

They placed their orders, all opting for one of the Monday specials. Kristen leaned in closer to Monty. "If you have a moment, we'd like to talk to you."

"Don't worry, our sandwiches can wait a few minutes," said Hope. Luckily, they had arrived before the noon rush, and the shop wasn't busy yet. She patted the bench next to her. "Have a seat."

Monty wiped his hands on his apron and sat down. "What can I do for you?"

"We were wondering if Nancy Meyers stopped to eat here often." Kristen tried to sound casual, though she felt sure Monty knew what she was up to.

"Sure, she came by once a week or so."

"So you knew her fairly well?" asked Ruth Ann.

"That's hard to say. She was always very friendly when she ordered, but other than that, I didn't know her any better than I knew my other customers." He was thoughtful.

"Sometimes she came alone, but oftentimes she had some-one with her."

Someone? Bingo. "Did she have lunch with the girls or maybe her husband?" Kristen couldn't remember where Nancy's children lived, and if they were close enough to lunch together on occasion.

Monty wrinkled his brow in an effort to remember de-tails. "I know why you ladies are here." He looked point-edly at Kristen, though all three of them had contributed their fair share to their sleuthing effort today. "There were days when she ate with other ladies, like you, Ruth Ann."

"Of course! I wouldn't turn down an invitation to eat here!"

"And some days she ate with Ted, her husband." He paused. "A few times she came here with another man. Rob-ert Wellington, I believe."

This was nothing new. They had pretty much elimi-nated Robert as a suspect. "Anyone else? Or did you notice anything out of character for Nancy in recent days?"

He scratched his balding head. "I'm not sure."

The women watched Monty expectantly, allowing him to gather his thoughts.

Monty cleared his throat. "I don't know if this means anything or not, but she had lunch on Thursday, I think…" His voice trailed off. "I think she met someone here."

Hope glanced at him curiously. "You think? Was there some doubt that she met someone? Didn't you see them?"

Monty seemed flustered. "Let me explain myself better. I'm just kind of remembering it now—I didn't think much of it at the time. Nancy arrived just before the lunch rush.

When I asked for her order, she only wanted coffee. She told me she'd order food later."

"And did she?" prompted Kristen.

"Yeah, she came to the counter and placed an order for a couple of sandwiches. When I took them out to her, she was sitting with another lady."

"So that's why you think she may have met someone for lunch." Kristen was thoughtful. Maybe they had finally stumbled upon some useful information.

"I can't say for sure they actually met by design or if Nancy just saw someone she knew, and they decided to have lunch together."

"Of course, that makes perfect sense," said Kristen, though her mind was still trying to process what Monty had told them so far.

Hope was one step ahead of her friend. "Did you recognize the lady she ate lunch with?"

"Yes, this could be really important," added Ruth Ann. "Did their conversation appear to be serious?"

Monty grinned at them good naturedly but held up his hand in mock defense. "Hold on, ladies! Let me finish. The woman looked familiar, but I don't know her name or how I recognized her. I do know I've never seen her in here before."

"What did she look like?" asked Kristen, growing impatient. She felt they were close to learning something significant.

Monty looked perplexed. "She was a little younger than Nancy, in her fifties if I had to guess. I know you're probably wondering about her appearance, but I'm not into details. She had reddish hair, I remember that."

"Auburn or lighter?" asked Hope. "Was she plump or in decent shape?"

"Her hair was a darker red color, I guess auburn, and I'd say she was medium build, not in bad shape for someone her age."

Ruth Ann cleared her throat in response to his remark, though she had no reason to be sensitive. She took care of herself, and it showed. "I don't suppose you noticed whether she had straight or curly hair. And what color were her eyes?"

"Her hair was a little poufy, but not really curly. Maybe wavy is the best way to describe it. Her eyes? I didn't get that close of a look, and probably wouldn't have remembered anyway."

"What do you think they were discussing?" asked Kristen, not confident Monty would be able to divulge much.

"I have no idea what they were talking about, although they did seem to be in deep conversation. I suppose it could have been about something fairly serious. They didn't even notice me at first when I brought the food to their table. Nancy was gracious as usual when she thanked me. Maybe I'm only imagining it, but it seemed like she needed to pull herself together, as if she had been upset earlier and didn't want me to notice."

That was interesting. Kristen pondered whether the women's conversation was connected to Nancy's death. Was the woman Ted's mistress? Kristen frowned. They needed to figure out who the mysterious woman was.

Evidently Hope agreed. "Monty, you've been very helpful. If you remember anything else about the woman Nancy lunched with, please let us know."

"In fact, it wouldn't hurt to tell Sheriff Miller," suggested Ruth Ann.

"Even if you can't remember where you've seen her, maybe they'll be able to figure it out." Kristen knew she'd be keeping her eyes peeled for red-haired women. It wasn't much, but it was all they had right now.

Monty left them, promising to bring their orders soon. The women were silent for a few minutes, each contemplating the information they had gathered so far. Kristen wondered if any of it was useful. She absently checked the messages on her phone. She'd missed calls from her Dad and Brett. She excused herself from the table and went outside to first return Brett's call.

Though the day was shaping up to be hot and muggy, and she knew she'd soon be a sweaty mess, it felt good to inhale the fresh air. She had so much on her mind after their busy morning and the past two days; she needed to compose herself.

She glanced at the buildings lining Eklund's bustling downtown street. Constructed in the early nineteen hundreds, they featured well maintained shops housing a variety of small businesses. Terra cotta planters boasting vast arrays of blooms decorated the sidewalks fronting each shop. She focused on the flowers for a minute, willing herself to relax before making her first call to Brett.

He answered right away, apparently within cell phone range. "Hi! How are you holding up? Any news on Nancy?"

As Kristen began to fill him in, she heard a woman's voice in the background. "Are you busy? I can call later."

"No, that's just Cassie. She didn't realize I was on the phone and thought I was talking to her. Go ahead."

Kristen tried to ignore the strange sensation in the pit of her stomach. "Oh, well, Hope and I started the day off with breakfast. Later on, we met up with Ruth Ann." She told him about the progress they'd made during the morning.

Brett whistled. "You ladies have been busy. I just hope you haven't ruffled anyone's feathers."

"No worries on that. Besides, with the three of us, it's like birds of a feather flocking together."

Brett laughed, probably not so much at her lame joke but at the thought of the women pestering the people of Eklund for answers to the town's most recent murder. He quickly sobered. "I'd like to get together with you myself tonight, if you're free. I'm worried about you. Whether you realize it or not, you're bound to set off alarms if you ask the right person the wrong questions."

Kristen sighed, knowing he was right, although she wasn't about to stop investigating now. Still, some quality Brett time would keep her out of trouble, wouldn't it? "If you come over for dinner after work, we can talk about the investigation. I'm hoping by the time we're done for the day, we'll have something substantial to report."

"I'm sure you will, since the sheriff's department must not be conducting their own investigation," he said dryly.

She laughed, though she wasn't sure if he was joking or getting irritated with her disregard for her own safely. "Of course they are, silly. I'm actually authorized by the sheriff to assist this time, remember?"

"I think they wanted your technical advice on poisonous plants. Knowing what I know about the staid sheriff, I doubt he pictured you traipsing around town hunting down the murderer all by yourself." He paused. "Then again, maybe he did."

Kristen couldn't help but feel amused. "We've already gone over this. I'm *not* by myself."

"Okay, you've convinced me. Speaking of plant poisons, have they narrowed down what poison was used to kill her?"

"We're still waiting to hear the official verdict. They were running tests on pokeweed today."

"Wow, I've heard of that plant's poisonous potential, but I never realized it could be used as a murder weapon."

"I agree it's a pretty creative method. But it's just a hunch of mine that might not be right."

"My bet's on you."

Kristen smiled, glad their conversation had gotten back on a more positive track. "Why don't you come over around six."

"That'll work. Do you want me to bring anything?"

"Nope. I've got it covered with leftovers from last night. Besides, I'm going to stop by Swede's Groceries to…" She hesitated. "Never mind."

"Ask a few questions? I've gotten to know you pretty well during the past few months, so don't think you can fool me, especially when your safety's at stake."

"Oh, come on! I'm just going to feel out Marty for some information." The lead checker had proven to have eye-opening observations related to Johnny's death. Maybe she could help Kristen out again.

"Is she the ultra-chatty redhead?"

Redhead. Kristen swallowed the disturbing thought. Everyone knew Marty, including Monty. She'd worked at Swede's for years. Kristen had gathered from Monty that the woman who dined with Nancy was not from Eklund. Or maybe she was new to the area if Monty had seen her somewhere before. "Yeah, she's the one."

"Listen, I need to get back to work. I'd tell you to enjoy your day off, but I know that's pointless."

Kristen bristled. "I *am* enjoying my day off."

Brett chuckled. "Calm down. You know what I mean. I'll see you tonight!"

Kristen stared at her phone for a moment, contemplating whether she had time to return her dad's call. She glanced in the window and saw Hope and Ruth Ann talking, but their food hadn't arrived yet. Kristen punched in her dad's number.

When Ken answered, she could hear loud machinery noise in the background. He was probably cutting, raking, or preparing to bale hay, never-ending summertime activities on a cattle farm. She was surprised he'd even heard his phone.

"Hi, there. What have you been up to today?"

Her dad rarely called unless he had a good reason, such as checking up on her. "Hope, Ruth Ann, and I are about to have lunch at Monty's."

"So the three of you have been working together?"

"We're trying. Say, Dad, do you know of any redheaded women who are new to the area?"

He laughed. "That's a strange question, but I suppose you have a lead you're trying to pursue."

"That's right." She relayed what Monty had told them.

"I can't think of anyone, but I'll ask your mom and Morgan. They'd probably know more than I do about red-heads. Besides, with women messing with their hair color all the time, it's hard to keep track."

He had a good point. If the woman Nancy met was in her fifties, odds were slim her red hair color was all natural.

Monty hadn't mentioned any gray streaks. "Have you had a chance to do any sleuthing today?"

"Not yet, but I hope to later this afternoon once we've finished this field. Anything particular you want me to check out?"

"Maybe you could drop by two of your favorite haunts, the grain elevator and gas station, to see what you can find out about Ted Meyers and Robert Wellington. Can you also ask around about redheads?" Kristen knew how weird that job sounded, but she could count on her dad to be subtle in his questions.

"Sure. I need to market some grain anyway, and I'll pick up something cool to drink at the gas station. I'll see what I can find out about Ted, Nancy, Robert, and even mysterious redheads, while I'm there."

"Are you sure you don't want some coffee instead?" It didn't matter how hot it was or the time of day, coffee was usually the preferred beverage for her parents.

"Naw, maybe later. Besides, their coffee would taste likes sludge by late afternoon. I'd better get busy, but I'll let you know if I find out anything."

"Thanks, Dad, and be careful, okay?" Kristen decided to use that comment on him before he could tell her the same thing.

"You too!"

She smiled to herself as she entered the cool sandwich shop. Her friends and family were working together to help gather clues for the investigation. She felt certain they'd make a discovery soon that would lead them to solve Nancy's murder. Right now, though, she had other things on her mind, such as the tantalizing food Monty had just delivered to their table.

CHAPTER 14

Kristen made a beeline for their table and noticed Hope punching words into her phone. "What's up? Anything new?"

"I just got a text from Todd. The preliminary tests are pointing toward pokeweed poisoning as the cause of Nancy's death. The lab is going to run more detailed tests to confirm the possibility, but they want to thank you for pointing them in the right direction."

"No problem. I'm glad my hunch paid off. I can't believe the initial results came back so quickly." She dove into her sandwich, surprised how hungry she was after the treats she'd indulged in that day. Maybe investigating murders burned more calories than other activities.

"I'm sure the lab expedited the analysis, given the situation. What were you up to on the phone?" asked Hope, wiping a blob of mustard from her face.

"Who says I was up to anything?"

"We do." Ruth Ann exchanged smiles with Hope. "Your serious expression gave away that you were probably badgering the poor person on the phone."

"Very funny. I talked to Brett and Dad, so I wasn't badgering them, at least any worse than usual." Kristen took a bite of her gooey sub before continuing. "Dad has been busy and hasn't had a chance to do any snooping, but he hopes to later. Brett's coming over for dinner, and it gave me the idea to talk to Marty at Swede's about Ted and Nancy. I'll ask Marty a few questions when I'm doing my grocery shopping."

"That's certainly one stop shopping. Thank goodness, Marty's usually willing to share her thoughts on things," said Hope, politely referring to the checker's gossipy personality.

"And that can work in our favor," agreed Kristen. "Besides, they have some great specials going on this week."

"And with our salaries, we need to be frugal," laughed Hope.

Kristen wrinkled her brow. "Which means we can't afford to visit Barney's very often."

"One of these days you will." Ruth Ann smiled encouragingly.

"I hope so, but for now it makes me appreciate the times I go there all the more. But Nancy and Ted dined there often. They knew the staff, and the staff knew them. Are we missing the obvious?"

"What do you mean? Should we focus our efforts on the people who work there?" asked Hope.

"I think maybe we should quit worrying so much about a red-haired woman who probably has nothing to do with the murder and take a closer look at who was working or dining at Barney's on Friday night."

"I agree. That makes sense," said Ruth Ann. "Maybe Barney will be willing to give us a list of his employees and the reservations for the evening."

"Since they started taking reservations recently, that should simplify things." Hope took one last bite of her sandwich. "On a busy Saturday night, most diners probably reserved their tables in advance."

"That's the key, right there," said Kristen. "Whoever killed Nancy had to know she was going to eat dinner there."

"You're right. I can't imagine being able to whip up a pokeweed poison on the spur of the moment,' said Ruth Ann emphatically.

"No, I wouldn't think so," agreed Kristen. "Now all we need to do is talk Barney into releasing that information. I'm not so sure he'll part with it."

"Maybe not, but I bet the sheriff's department has it," said Hope knowingly. "And if Barney won't give it to us, I'm sure I can finagle it out of Todd."

Kristen was amazed at her friend's confidence. During their first murder investigation, Todd hadn't been too willing to share vital information, probably fearing the wrath of Sheriff Miller, which she could well understand after tangling with him herself. Fortunately, they were getting along better this time, which reminded her to check in with the man to see if there were any developments he might share with her. She shouldn't be too optimistic in that regard, but it wouldn't hurt to try.

Satisfied for the moment they were doing what they could to track Nancy's killer, she relaxed and finished the rest of her iced tea while plotting their next move.

Echoing her thoughts, Ruth Ann said, "What next, ladies? We've accomplished a lot today, but we still don't know anything definitive."

"I was thinking the same thing," said Kristen, her brief relaxed state already forgotten. She could rest after the killer was caught.

"We already know we need to contact Barney about his employee and reservation list," Hope reminded them. "Let's tackle that chore first."

Kristen wasn't looking forward to approaching the normal jovial restaurant owner again. She thought they'd learned as much as they were going to from him. She was glad to have Ruth Ann along this time for back-up. Maybe he'd be more willing to help with her there, a chum from school days and a long-time customer. She smiled at Ruth Ann. "Are you sure you're ready for this? You didn't sign on to help us all day."

"Nonsense," she said. "What else do I have to do today? The Nature Station's not open on Mondays, so I can't work there this afternoon."

"That's what we like," joked Hope. "Not only are you a great sleuth, but you're a loyal volunteer too."

"The older you get, the more talents you have. Just remember that." She winked at the younger women. "And by the way, lunch is on me."

Knowing it was pointless to argue, Kristen and Hope merely thanked her, threw a wave in Monty's direction, and went outdoors to wait.

Ruth Ann joined them after she'd settled the bill, and they made the short trek to Barney's Supper Club. As they were walking, Ruth Ann pulled out her lipstick, using her compact mirror to check her appearance. She blotted her face with her powder puff, then fluffed her hair with her fingers. Satisfied, she turned to the girls. "Let me handle this."

Kristen grinned at Hope and shrugged her shoulders. Maybe this was one of the talents Ruth Ann had referred to a few minutes ago. Kristen could use a break, and she prepared herself to pick up a few pointers.

She wasn't disappointed. Ruth Ann knocked loudly on the front door of Barney's then waited patiently for an answer. After what seemed like ages, Barney came to the door, glaring out the window at them. When he caught sight of Ruth Ann, his eyes lit up, and he swung the heavy door open, ushering them into the darkened eatery.

Kristen couldn't help but feel a little creeped out, seeing the normally elegant restaurant in broad daylight. Though they had been there earlier in the day, they had come in the back door and talked in Barney's office. Despite the warmth of the day, she shivered in the low lit, cooler entryway. She told herself she was being ridiculous. There was no reason for the strange feeling that washed over her, even if a murder had taken place here just a few days ago. She heard voices in the main seating area and figured it was Barney's employees. They must have interrupted the staff meeting he had mentioned. She tried to listen to the conversations that were starting in the absence of their boss, but she could only hear muffled talking.

She directed her attention to Barney and Ruth Ann, who were having their own quiet conversation. She glanced at Hope, who raised her eyebrows as she watched Ruth Ann place her hand gently on Barney's arm. "We'd really appreciate it if you could give up copies of your staff listing and reservations for Saturday night." It wasn't long before the man scurried off, probably to copy the information Ruth Ann had requested.

"I guess there won't be any need for me to put the moves on Todd tonight," said Hope ruefully.

"Nonsense," said Ruth Ann with a smile. "We'll probably need other information."

"Well, at least I've picked up a few tips from you."

The women laughed, and Kristen was amazed at how the mild-mannered retired biology teacher had turned into a siren to pave the way for them to acquire sensitive information. She wouldn't have believed it if she hadn't seen Ruth Ann's charismatic maneuvers with her own eyes.

Before long, Barney returned, papers in hand. He passed them to Ruth Ann with a flourish. She thanked him profusely, and Barney's cheeks flamed at her attention. They left the building before he could change his mind about giving in to their request.

"Wow, Ruth Ann," said Kristen. "Where on earth did you learn to flirt like that?"

"Well, Barney had a crush on me way back in high school. Though we eventually grew up and married other people, I could always tell he still had a soft spot for me."

"Why, you little temptress," said Hope, her eyes dancing in delight. "And no harm done."

"Why don't we go to the park to take a peek at the lists," suggested Kristen. The women walked over to the small square near the courthouse and sheriff's department. The trees were well established, the graceful oak and maple trees decades old. Their shade was a welcome relief on the warm day, and the leaves blew gracefully in the breeze. They sat at a picnic table scanning the names on the papers.

First they reviewed the reservations list. Kristen's heart skipped a beat when she saw Brett's name there. It was hard to believe such a lovely evening had turned out so horribly. Together they scanned through the rest of the names, including Nancy and Ted's.

Kristen turned toward Ruth Ann. "Do you recognize most of these people?"

"Well, sure. Half the town of Eklund is on the list, not to mention a few folks I know from surrounding areas."

That didn't help much. "Does anyone particular jump out at you?" Just then, Kristen noticed footsteps coming up behind her, muffled by the thick mat of grass.

"Are you three women out for a picnic today?"

Oh crap. She recognized the man's deep, authoritative voice. She felt like she'd been caught doing something naughty by the school principal. She turned around and was disappointed to see Sheriff Miller towering over them, a glower on his face. "No, but we had a nice lunch together at Monty's."

"So I heard. It appears you've been making the rounds all about town. What's next on your list? A trip to the beauty shop?"

Actually that was probably a good idea. Not only did Kristen's long hair need a trim, but she knew they'd probably learn a wealth of information—or gossip—that could relate to the case. "No, but I really do need to schedule an appointment, now that you mention it."

"Is there something we can do for you?" asked Hope with utmost respect, probably due to the fact he was her boyfriend's boss.

"No, not at all. I just needed some fresh air after being in my office for too long."

"Really? I would have thought you would have been out trying to uncover answers to help solve this case." Kristen tried to keep the contempt from her voice, but she wasn't sure she'd succeeded when Miller gave her a scathing look.

"Why would I need to when you ladies have taken care of that chore for me? Nonetheless, the entire force has been busy working diligently on the case." This time he glared in Hope's direction.

Flinching a bit from the nasty look, Hope gathered her wits and said, "Yes, I know how hard Todd's been working."

"I trust that's all he's told you?"

"I'm not sure I know what you mean. We talk about other stuff, too."

"You know what I mean," said the sheriff. "He'd better not be leaking vital information to you."

"Of course not," she said meekly.

"Did you come out here to chastise us?" Even the normally calm Ruth Ann was getting perturbed by the sheriff's surly behavior.

"No, Mrs. Swanson," he said contritely. He'd been an early student of Ruth Ann's, and old habits die hard.

"I take it you haven't caught Nancy's killer yet?" Kristen did not mean to sound accusatory; she was merely curious.

Still, the sheriff seemed to be feeling defensive. "No, not yet," he snapped. "Though we are pursuing several leads." He reached over and snatched the papers away. "What are you doing with these?"

Ruth Ann cleared her throat before answering. "Our good friend Barney gave them to us," she said, as if it were the most normal thing in the world for a local business owner to provide information to three amateur detectives.

"Oh, so you're good friends with the leading restaurateur of Eklund?" He paused for effect. "How interesting."

Why would he say that, Kristen wondered, eyeing the man closely. Surely the sheriff wasn't suspicious of Barney.

However, a murder occurred at the restaurant, the victim's food or drink apparently poisoned, so why wouldn't Barney be under suspicion. He was a likable man, but that didn't leave him off the hook. Nancy was a well liked woman without any known enemies, but she had ended up dead. Maybe he was fishing for information from them or trying to irritate the women for some other unknown reason. In the heat of the afternoon, she felt her hackles rise higher than the outdoor temperature. She rose to his bait. "Just what exactly do you mean by *that* remark?"

Miller smiled at her, appearing to be cool and confident, despite the heavy material of his uniform. "Not a thing," he said innocently. "Is there something I need to know?"

"As a matter of fact, I was planning to contact you this afternoon to discuss a few things." Kristen spoke in a straightforward manner, though she was seething at the man.

He crossed his arms across his chest, waiting for her to continue. When she didn't, he said, "Oh? What about? Don't think you're going to be getting any inside information from me."

"I wouldn't think of it," she fibbed. "I thought you asked me for assistance in researching possible plant poisons, which I did." She paused, taking a deep breath of the muggy air. "How's that going by the way? Did my hunch about the pokeweed pay off?"

"I can't really say, though we do appreciate your help. Unfortunately"— he cleared his throat before continuing in a more sarcastic tone of voice—"that does not give you the right to, or the need for, sensitive information."

Hope glanced at Kristen, slowing shaking her head. Kristen knew she had to cool off or she'd say something that could implicate Todd. "I don't expect you to reveal state, or county rather, secrets. But you might be surprised at what I could tell you if you'd just trust me."

"Trust you? After you and these other two have been prancing all over town trying to interrogate half the people in Eklund?"

Ruth Ann spoke up. "Now, now. We've just been doing our civic duty, nothing more than that."

Civic duty? Where did she come up with that, Kristen wondered. Maybe the sheriff would buy it. "You can't expect us to sit back and do nothing after our friend was murdered almost right before our eyes."

"As a matter of fact, I *do* expect you to go about your regular business. If I need your help, I know where to find you. And I'm sure the murderer does too, so you might want to keep that in my mind before you get too deeply involved. I've got enough on my plate trying to solve a murder with limited resources without worrying about providing extra protection for nosey women."

Oh no, Kristen thought. Now she'd managed to irritate Miller. His cool exterior was definitely more ruffled than it had been mere minutes earlier. She knew better than to goad him further, though it was tempting.

"We aren't nosey, just worried about the safety of our fellow citizens of Eklund. We've had two murders occur in our small town in a matter of months. We've every right to be concerned."

"Kristen's got a point," chimed in Hope, turning on the charm with a grin thrown at the stoic sheriff. "We won't be able to rest until this murder is solved."

"If that's the case, maybe you can all have a slumber party to keep each other out of harm's way," the sheriff said snidely. "Chances are you'd stay up half the night plotting ways to get yourselves into even more trouble."

Kristen chose to ignore his comment before plunging ahead with a question she'd wanted to ask before their verbal sparring threw the conversation off track. "Tell me, sheriff, is Barney really a suspect?" Though she'd felt some unexplained odd sensation when standing in the entryway of his restaurant, she found it hard to believe he'd kill one of his diners. He didn't seem the murdering type, and besides, it would be bad for business. He'd worked hard to make the grand restaurant a success in the tiny town, where oftentimes small business had to struggle to survive. She couldn't imagine him throwing it away to murder one of his best customers.

"That is none of your concern." He glared directly at Kristen. "But now that you mention it, *everyone* who was at Barney's that night is a suspect."

Kristen couldn't help but feel intimidated by his remark, though she guessed he was only bluffing.

"Don't leave town, Ms. Matthews—just in case I need your help, of course." Miller strode off toward the sheriff's department without another word.

CHAPTER 15

Kristen wheeled her cart around Swede's, flinging a few essentials into it. She was still shaken by her encounter with the sheriff, though she would never admit it to the spiteful man if questioned. She doubted she was a suspect in Nancy's murder, but the sheriff's comments were enough to make her think twice about the investigation. Her desire to hunt for answers may have waned after the tongue lashing she'd received, but she needed to stock up on groceries anyway, so she may as well see what she could find out from the ever chatty Marty. Besides, she reasoned, if she actually were a suspect, she'd better get busy trying to clear herself.

She'd parted ways with Hope and Ruth Ann shortly after Sheriff Miller dropped his bombshell. Ruth Ann decided to stop by Betty's Clip 'N Color to make a hair appointment, possibly trying to glean information about a mysterious red-haired woman. Hope went home to prepare a home cooked supper for the overworked Todd. She promised to see what she could learn from him, though Kristen suspected Todd might be tighter lipped if the sheriff had an opportunity to talk with him before quitting time.

Pondering what she needed for her dinner with Brett, Kristen leaned over to reach some plump green grapes from the produce section and was shocked to see Ted Meyers enter the store. What in the world was he doing there? Not only was he supposedly the bereaved widower, but he had a house full of food he didn't even want. Even if he did need food, he didn't seem to be the domestic type, though with Nancy no longer around to take care of household chores, she supposed he'd have to learn. She hoped he'd get what he needed and leave, just in case Marty felt the urge to fill her in on information relating to Nancy's death. She certainly wouldn't want the man to overhear that conversation, even if he had given her the green light to delve into the situation.

She avoided making eye contact with him and went about her business, tossing some locally grown fresh strawberries into her cart. She grimaced when she thought of her own small garden. She hadn't had a chance to do any weeding for a while, and she might be in for a shock when she visited it next. She made a mental note to take a peek later that afternoon. Meanwhile, Ted had meandered out of her range of vision, probably around the corner into the canned good section. Feeling a bit like Angela Lansbury, she cautiously crept down the aisle, wanting to follow the man without being seen or running directly into him, which was easier said than done in the town's small grocery store.

She spotted him two aisles away putting a couple of boxes of crackers into a shopping basket. With all the food that friends and family had delivered, she couldn't picture him running low of snacks. There were several home-baked goods in his kitchen, including the muffins and cookies they'd delivered when they'd paid their respects earlier that morning. He veered toward the deli area where he selected some imported cheese. She followed him into the liquor section, where she watched him choose a bottle of wine. She gulped, knowing Nancy may have died from drinking poisoned wine. Just a couple of days later her husband was selecting munchies at the local store. She could understand him wanting to drown his sorrows in a glass, or bottle, of wine, but didn't he have any at home? She wouldn't want to venture into the grocery store so soon after a loved one's death.

Pondering this thought, she wasn't paying enough attention to her whereabouts, or Ted's rather, and she was jarred back to reality by nearly crashing her shopping cart into the unsuspecting Mr. Meyers.

"Oh, I'm so sorry," she stammered. The poor man had been through enough without ending up injured.

"Oh, don't worry about me. I'm all right. Besides, it was bound to happen sooner or later, the way you've been stalking me through the store."

Cursing her ineptness, she was at a complete loss of words, or at least words that would explain her actions. She decided telling a white lie was the best course of action. "Oh, I wasn't following you."

He raised his eyebrows. "Really? I find that hard to believe, not after you've been running all over town asking questions."

"I thought you *wanted* me to ask questions. I'm confused. Isn't that how we left it this morning?"

"Certainly, but you've been asking all the wrong questions, sticking your nose into my business." He leaned in close to her. "How is that going to help you find Nancy's killer?"

Kristen tried to back up to create more personal space; she was feeling threatened by the man. In doing so, she nearly knocked a bottle of vodka off the shelf. Luckily, it wasn't an expensive brand, but still, she didn't want to pay for a broken bottle.

"You've got that right. I'm asking all kinds of questions. Some of them have to do with you. I'm afraid that's unavoidable in a murder investigation." Good grief, she was starting to sound like Sheriff Miller.

"Yeah, well, make sure you're not asking anything that will get me"—he paused before continuing—"or *you*, in trouble."

Trying not to let the man intimidate her, she told him, "Sheriff Miller is considering anyone who was at that restaurant Saturday night a suspect." She looked him squarely in the eye. "So maybe you're already in trouble!" Perfect, now she sounded like a third grader.

Despite her childish remark, he seemed to take her seriously, tossing her another glare before flouncing off down the aisle toward the checkout. She hoped Marty was picking up on the interesting vibes that were sure to be radiating from the widower. She tried to calm down and finish her shopping. There was no sense trying to leave the store now or she'd run smack into Ted again, though hopefully not literally this time. Since she was stuck in the liquor section for a few minutes, she might as well make the most of her time. She looked at the wine specials and selected a crisp, dry white wine, thinking the pinot grigio would be just the thing to cool her off on a muggy summer evening, especially after the run-ins she'd experienced this afternoon.

Figuring Ted would have had time to leave the store by now, she rolled her cart cautiously toward the checkout lane. Thankfully, she saw no sign of the irritated man, so she went to the counter and started unloading her cart. The perky Marty greeted her enthusiastically.

"Imagine that. Both Ted Meyers and Eklund's newest super sleuth in my store."

"What are you talking about?" she asked with a smile, trying to play dumb.

"I would think there could be some awkwardness if the two of you met up. After all, I understand you're the one who discovered Nancy's body, and you're getting a reputation for solving mysteries."

Kristen chuckled. "I hardly think I'm qualified to solve a murder mystery."

"You don't have to wear a badge to attempt to figure out what happened." She started to ring up Kristen's purchases. "And the prime suspect just left the building."

She was surprised to hear Marty refer to Ted in that manner. "Since we're on the topic of Ted Meyers, what can you tell me about him?" She wrinkled her brow. "Don't you think it's odd he came to the store? I was just at his house this morning. He had a ton of food in his kitchen, and he didn't seem to be interested in any of it."

Marty leaned closer, keeping her voice low. "To tell you the truth, I wondered the same thing. We've had several people order food from the store to be sent over to the house."

"Really? It makes it even odder that he was shopping here. I suppose you're familiar with his habits?"

"Sure thing. And the same is true with most everyone in town." The grocer spoke with pride. "Though Nancy did most of their food shopping."

"And today Ted was here buying a few snacks and some wine. I guess he'll be the one to do the shopping from now on, so that makes sense."

"That's true. I guess I'll have to learn to get along with the arrogant man. Though if the sheriff has his way, I won't have to deal with Ted Meyers for long."

Kristen was beginning to feel fatigued after a long day of questioning people. If Ted was indeed the prime suspect, she wanted to know why right now, before she wasted any more of her precious free time.

"What makes you think he's the prime suspect?" She couldn't quite decide for herself how she felt about the man, though she wasn't impressed with the bullying techniques he'd attempted a few minutes ago.

"For starters, for as long as I can remember, he's always had another woman on the side."

Something didn't quite ring true. Kristen had known Nancy for years, and she always seemed happy. If her marriage weren't stable, wouldn't she have acted accordingly? And even if Ted were a womanizer, did that mean Nancy had to die? Why?

"How do you know he had flings with other women?"

"I saw him."

Okay, that was credible. "With the same woman or various women? Did you know any of them?" Maybe she was finally getting somewhere.

"A little of both, actually." Marty began putting the groceries in Kristen's cloth bags. "Sometimes he'd be with the same woman for long periods of time, and then I'd see him with someone new, maybe only once or twice."

They'd already established the fact that Ted was attracted to women besides his wife. What Marty told her supported it, but so what? Kristen noticed how the sun from the store's front windows shone on Marty's red hair. The woman's lightly freckled complexion and light green eyes made it evident her hair was its natural color, even if she had help from the salon to cover the gray.

"Had you ever seen him with a red-haired woman?"

Marty paused her grocery packing briefly. "Come to think of it, yes."

Kristen asked the obvious question. "Did you know her?" Marty knew most everyone who passed through Swede's, especially since they did a lot of local business. If she didn't know them, she'd probably be curious enough to find out who they were.

"Actually, no."

Marty was being uncharacteristically close-mouthed. "Did you see them together here at the store?"

Marty narrowed her eyes. "No, and now that you've asked, I'm trying to remember exactly where I saw them together."

Funny, that was pretty much what Monty had said. Whether the red-haired woman had anything to do with Nancy's murder or not, she was still a mystery. "Let me know if you remember where you saw them, okay?" She changed the subject. "Ted was acting pretty fishy earlier."

"When I rang up his groceries he seemed about the same as usual, which I found to be very unusual, now that you mention it."

"I agree. He's just lost his wife, a woman most of us liked and admired."

Marty cleared her throat but didn't say anything right away. Kristen waited patiently until she finally spoke. "Not everyone liked her."

"No, I suppose not," said Kristen, wondering what point Marty was trying to make. "Is there something specific you're trying to tell me?"

"I'm sure it has nothing to do with her murder. It's more of a personal issue." She finished ringing up Kristen's items. "I grew up with Nancy. We were in the same class all through school."

"And you weren't friends?" Even though the Eklund school district consisted of the town and surrounding rural area, its size was limited by the sparse population. If you didn't like someone in school, it could be hard to avoid them.

"Not only were we not friends, but we always seemed to be competing." Marty had a faraway look in her eyes as she continued. "You name it. Whether it was for the best grades, a prized spot on the cheerleading team, or even friends...or boyfriends."

Kristen wondered if they had fought over Ted. Maybe that would explain why she seemed to harbor bitter feeling toward him. She remembered Nancy and Ted had been high school sweethearts, probably marrying shortly after high school. Surely Marty couldn't have hated Nancy enough to wish her harm—or be capable of harming her? What could have possibly triggered the normally good na-tured woman to turn to murder after all these years? Did Marty still harbor feelings for Ted? She snapped out of her thoughts when she noticed Marty had finished and was waiting for her to pay. She pulled her card from her wallet, swiping it through the reader, trying to act naturally. Surely she was mistaken about what Marty had implied. Even if she were the killer, she wouldn't open up to someone she knew was trying to track down Nancy's murderer.

Kristen said a hasty good-bye, grabbed her bags, and walked to where she'd left her truck hours earlier at Carrie's Coffee Cup. What a long day! She wanted nothing more than to go home and take a nap and forget this entire mess.

She cranked her truck's air conditioning on full blast, but the hot air that came through the vents did little to cool her. She was home before the air even started to cool. Hauling her groceries through the back entrance, she felt the clammy air of the kitchen, not much cooler than outdoors. Before she put away the food, she switched on the air conditioning and started closing windows. She tried to avoid using the air until she couldn't stand it anymore, since the large, older house was expensive to cool and heat. The time had come, though. She decided to put away her purchases, curl up on her bed, and try to get some rest. The past few days had caught up with her. She hoped a cat nap would refresh her before Brett stopped by later.

Finally, the windows closed and the groceries stashed, she climbed the stairs, her feet heavy and her mind weary. She fell onto her bed, right on top of her lightweight blanket. She was asleep in a matter of minutes.

CHAPTER 16

When Kristen finally awoke, she squinted at the clock, astonished to see it was almost five o'clock. She couldn't believe she's been asleep for a couple of hours. If she'd dreamt of anything in particular, she couldn't remember it. As the dregs of intense sleep left her, she felt her mind clear and a wave of optimism wash over her. Maybe if she tried to think more about the murder case and perhaps discuss it with Brett when he arrived, something would click in her brain. The nap had done the trick. She felt even better after a shower and dressed in lightweight khaki shorts, an aqua shirt, and comfortable flip-flops. She dried her hair and touched up her make-up then headed downstairs to make sure things were in order for supper. She checked her watch. Brett should be there in a few minutes. She couldn't wait to see him. Not only was she very attracted to him, but he was so easy to talk to. Their romantic relationship continued to grow, but she also enjoyed their friendship.

She pulled a bottle of chilled white wine from the fridge and poured a glass to drink while she puttered around in the kitchen. Taking a sip, she let her mind wander back to what they'd learned that day. She wondered if Hope or Ruth Ann had discovered anything pertinent after they'd gone their separate ways. She'd check in with them in the morning; she'd see Hope first thing when they began their work day at the Nature Station. She made a mental note to check in with her family, too, though she was confident they would contact her if they had any news. Either her dad hadn't gone into town, or he hadn't been able to find out any significant information.

She was jarred out of her thoughts by Peaches barking. Brett must have arrived early. She wasn't surprised. He was usually on time unless work delayed him. Maybe he was just as anxious to see her as she was to see him. Her heart skipped a beat at that thought. Sure enough, she saw the tall, dark-haired, handsome man walking up the back sidewalk. She went outdoors to greet him and threw her arms around him, inhaling his fresh scent. He must have taken time to shower, too.

"Hey, how was your day?" he asked, wrapping his own arms around her. "It sounded like you'd been keeping busy when we talked earlier."

"You've got that right. I was so worn out after such a hectic day that I had to take a nap when I got home."

Brett looked at her with concern. "I can't wait to hear the latest."

"Let's have something to drink while we talk. It's so hot outside. Why don't we go indoors for now." They went inside, and she pulled a frosty bottle of Brett's favorite brew out of the refrigerator and handed it to him.

"Yeah, it probably won't cool off until after the sun goes down."

They carried their glasses into the living room, where they snuggled next to each other on the couch. Kristen propped her feet on the coffee table. She filled Brett in on what all had transpired since they'd chatted at noon.

"No wonder you're exhausted. You've been hard at it all day."

"I just wish we'd learned something worthwhile. It seems like everything we did today was a waste of time. We asked a lot of questions, found some answers, but who's to know whether any of it's relevant or not."

"I'm sure some of it is, though you may need to fit a few more pieces of the puzzle together before everything makes sense." He patted her knee. "Though I'd feel more comfortable if you'd let the sheriff and his deputies handle the details."

"Oh, I forgot to tell you about my chat with the sheriff. Probably because nothing positive came out of that conversation."

"Oh, no. What happened? You normally get along so well with the man." Brett's sarcasm came partly from his own interaction with Miller.

"Not much out of the ordinary. The three of us were resting in the park, and he snuck up on us and basically told us to mind our own business." Come to think of it, that's what Ted had told her too.

And now Brett joined in the act. "Hmmmm, sounds familiar." He kissed her softly on the cheek.

"Believe me, by the time we were done today, I almost took a vow to back off. Luckily, I feel revitalized after my nap and shower, not to mention a tasty glass of wine and some good company."

"So now you're ready to plunge ahead?" he joked.

"I may wait until tomorrow." She snuggled closer to him. "I want to make the most of our time together."

His stomach grumbled, and he blushed. "Sorry about that. So much for a romantic moment."

"That's okay. There's time for that after we eat." She stood up and started toward the kitchen. "Thank goodness for leftovers."

They prepared their supper and sat down at the kitchen table to eat, all the while chatting about their days.

"We've talked mostly about what I've been up to today," said Kristen. "What have you been doing? You were doing field work when I called at lunch. It was a hot one."

"Luckily, I'm usually in the shade," the forester teased. "Even if today's humidity managed to make field work a little sticky."

"I guess I'm not the only one who gets into sticky situations." Kristen loved their easy going conversations.

"Yeah, Cassie and I had to stop for ice cream this afternoon to cool off."

"Oh…how nice!" Kristen fought the urge to say more, knowing the atmosphere would become as thick as the humid night air if she acted like a shrew.

"I wanted to thank her for all her hard work. She's been a big help since she started."

"Oh, that's great for you." *But maybe not so great for me.* All of a sudden the pleasure Kristen had felt earlier began to seep away as Brett talked glowingly about his female summer intern.

"I'll miss her when she goes back to school later this summer."

Brett was apparently not tuned in to the slightly jealous moods of his short-term and still insecure girlfriend. "Oh, that's still a couple of months away. There will be plenty of time for the two of you to work together." *And get to know each other better.*

"That's true. I'd better make a list of everything I need help with, because after she goes back to college, I'll be back to a one-man-show."

"I'm sure you'll manage just as well as before Cassie was hired," she said.

"I'm not so sure." He looked glum. "It's nice to have someone help with all the paperwork."

"I understand. I don't miss that part of my state job."

"You're lucky you get to run things the way you want at the Nature Station."

"That's true, but my tradeoff is an unsteady income and no paid benefits."

"But you have some benefits the rest of us don't have," he said and grimaced. "Like being your own boss."

"I get to boss around Hope and the volunteers, which is not as wonderful as it may seem. They're all stubborn and independent, just like me, so they pretty much do their own thing."

They laughed, and the awkwardness of the earlier moment passed. Kristen told herself to calm down. After all, she reasoned, Brett had to work with Cassie every day, but he *wanted* to spend time with her after work.

Just then, Kristen heard her cell phone beep, the signal that a text was coming through. It was from Hope, and it said simply, **Definitely yes on pokeweed**. At least Hope had been able to glean that important tidbit from Todd, though Kristen doubted they'd learn much else from him if the sheriff had anything to say about it. Even though the message was succinct, Kristen got the point. Nancy was poisoned by a plant that almost anyone could access. Then again, how many people knew the plant could be poisonous, or at the very least dangerous if ingested in large quantities? After the recent newspaper article, more people would know, but normally only people with some plant knowledge would know how to prepare and administer it to the point of lethalness.

She was shaken out of her thoughts by Brett's worried expression. He put his arm around her. "What's the matter?"

"Pokeweed, that's what's the matter." She should be happy the exact cause of Nancy's death had been determined, but something was bothering her. She wasn't sure what it was.

Brett was looking at her quizzically, patiently waiting for her to provide a full explanation. She told him what she'd learned from Hope and her own thoughts on who would know how to use the plant as a murder weapon.

"I agree with you. In our line of work, most professionals know about the poisonous properties of pokeweed, but I'm not sure it's common knowledge to the rest of the world."

"So does that mean someone who volunteers at the Nature Station is a likely suspect?" Kristen sighed. She didn't want to consider that option. Then something else popped into her head. "What about someone who attended one of our events?"

Brett looked doubtful. "Do you make a habit of discussing poisonous plants during a bird walk or tree identification workshop?"

"Not really, other than pointing out common plants that may be harmful."

Brett chuckled. "You mean like pokeweed?"

Kristen smiled half-heartedly then chewed on her fingernail while pondering the situation. She knew at one time or another she'd pointed out the plant to people, probably dozens of times. Like most plants, it grew taller as the season progressed, but by late summer it reached several feet high. It was very showy with its burgundy stems, eventually producing clusters of dark red berries. People were curious to learn about the hefty plant.

"You never know what kinds of questions people will ask. They could have asked specifically about poisonous plants."

"Do you remember fielding a question like that?"

"We get so many questions. It's hard to remember them all. Besides, they could have asked Hope or a volunteer or even someone else who was attending an event."

"That opens up the suspect list."

"But think about it. The murderer had to have been at Barney's on Saturday night. I know it's probably a longshot, but if we could compare Nature Station event registration sheets to Barney's reservation and employee lists, we could determine who was at both places."

"That's a good idea, but didn't you say Sheriff Miller swiped the copy you had just gotten from Barney?"

"That's true, but maybe we can get our hands on another list. Ruth Ann is the one who talked Barney into sharing it."

"Do you think Barney will be willing to cooperate again if he knew the sheriff wasn't keen on you having access to that information in the first place?" He gazed into Kristen's eyes. "I know you get irritated at the sheriff when he behaves highhandedly. But you have to remember, he's not only trying to protect you from getting in over your head, but he's also trying to make sure you don't interfere with the investigation."

Kristen sighed. "I guess you're right, but that doesn't stop me from letting the sheriff know my theory. Not that he'll take it seriously, which is why sometimes I need to act on my own."

"I'm sure he's starting to take you more seriously after everything that's happened in Eklund during the past couple of months."

"Hope and I will go through the files and pull registration sheets from past events. Maybe something will jump out at me, but I'll also let Sheriff Miller review them."

"That's a great idea. I'm sure he'll welcome your input."

"I doubt it, but at least I can try!" *And I'll still continue to do my own thing behind the scenes, but he doesn't need to know that.*

"Promise me you'll let Miller take the lead on whatever you may find. I don't like the idea of you endangering yourself, though you may have already done that with all the questions you were asking around town today."

"Of course I'll provide the sheriff with whatever information I find." She smiled innocently at him. *And keep a copy for myself.*

By the time they'd finished eating and cleared away the dishes, the sun was still shining, though starting to sink lower in the west sky. It always amazed Kristen how light it could remain as late as nine o'clock at this time of the year.

Brett stretched and yawned. "Sorry. I've been getting an early start on these hot days. It's not very late, but I'm growing sleepier by the minute."

"I understand. If I hadn't taken a nap, I would have been yawning long before now."

"I'd better get going. Are you sure you feel safe staying here by yourself?"

"I'll be fine," she assured him. "Besides, I have to be at work early too, so I'll be heading to bed shortly after you leave."

"Just make sure everything is locked up tight."

"Don't worry. I've been living on my own for a long time, even before brutal murders took place in the vicinity." She patted Peaches, who had been hovering nearby. "Besides, I have this big, furry dog to alert and protect me."

"That makes me feel better," he said as the friendly Peaches licked his hand.

They said their good nights, lingering outdoors to gaze at the romantic sunset. "I'll talk to you tomorrow."

"I'll be thinking of you."

She had no doubts he would, just as she'd be thinking of him. She waved as he backed his truck out of the driveway. Walking slowly across the grass, she felt her feet grow damp from the heavy dew. She admired the lightning bugs zipping to and fro. Before she went back inside for the night, she gave one last look at the western sky. Instead of the vivid sunset she'd seen only moments before, clouds were blowing in as the wind picked up. She thought she heard the low rumble of thunder in the distance and could hear the leathery leaves of the massive white oak in her front yard rustling. She wouldn't be surprised if the predicted thunderstorm came to fruition. She locked the backdoor, shivering a little. Was it from the air conditioning, the impending storm, or something else? She didn't know, but she would be glad to have the matter of Nancy's murder settled.

She wanted to get back to her normal life. How ironic. She had a feeling that to return to normal, she'd need to continue doing her own explorations. Her resolve to leave matters in the sheriff's hands slipped a little. While she was looking for information to pass along to Sheriff Miller, she'd be sure to file the data away for her own use.

CHAPTER 17

Sure enough, a thunderstorm rolled in shortly after she'd turned in for the night and lasted into the wee hours. However, it didn't keep her awake but instead lulled her to sleep after a grueling day. Peaches, not a fan of storms, had curled up in bed beside her for the duration. She knew she should scold the dog for hopping onto her bed. Nevertheless, she secretly enjoyed the security of having the big dog keeping an eye on her while she slept. With a murderer on the loose, Peaches offered some peace of mind, even if her bark was worse than her bite.

Kristen awoke early, anxious to start the day. Not only did she have Nature Station business to conduct, but she wanted to start digging through their files in an effort to unearth information of importance to aid the investigation.

After a quick shower, she dressed in khaki shorts and an orange Nature Station t-shirt. Much needed coffee had finished brewing while she showered. She relished the flavor of the rich blend as she grabbed a container of yogurt and some fruit to take to work as her breakfast.

She walked across her yard to the Nature Station office, an old shed that had been revamped for the purpose, and unlocked the office door, clicked on the lights, and waited for her computer to warm up. She went over to the file cabinet near Hope's work station and was starting to pull folders from it when the door opened and Hope entered.

"Good morning!" Kristen called to her friend.

"Same to you." Hope yawned. "I woke up early and couldn't get back to sleep, so I thought I may as well come in to work."

"Maybe you can knock off a little early."

"That would be great. I'm sure a second cup of coffee will help."

"My own cup's about empty. I'll get some started." As she measured out the ground coffee, throwing in an extra scoop to wake them up, Kristen filled Hope in on what she planned to do that day.

"As soon as I get situated, I'll be glad to help."

"Good. Two heads are better than one."

"Even if they're sleepy heads?"

Kristen grinned. "Of course. We kept pretty busy yesterday, on our one day off, so it's understandable we'd be tired today."

"At least we don't have an event scheduled for today, so we can work on getting caught up on things."

"That's true. And we don't normally have huge crowds of hikers on Tuesdays, so we'll take it a little easier today."

"At least we're pretty well organized for tomorrow's Kid's Camp."

"Yeah, just a few last minute details, and Friday's Tree Identification Hike doesn't take too much advanced preparation." Kristen turned away from the coffeemaker. "That reminds me. Has anyone asked you about pokeweed lately?"

"Not that I remember. Of course, I'm not normally the one who leads the hikes and other events, so I don't field as many of those types of questions."

"I know I've pointed it out to people or answered questions about it, but I don't remember to whom I spoke."

"But you don't think someone used one of our plants to kill Nancy, do you?"

"Not necessarily, but they could have gotten the idea from attending one of our events." Kristen sighed. "Not that we would promote using a plant to cause harm, but someone could definitely come up with their own plan from an innocent comment."

"It's ironic that Nancy was well versed in medicinal and poisonous plants. She could have even been the one to trigger the idea to the person who killed her."

Kristen shuddered. "Oh, what a horrible possibility."

"Of course, we're only speculating that someone could have come to one of our events and used knowledge they gained here to poison Nancy."

"That's true, but I still think it's worthwhile to review our sign in sheets to see if any names leap out at us."

"I agree. But what will we do if something clicks? Check them out on our own?"

"I promised Brett I would turn over the information to Sheriff Miller, which I will do"—she paused—"right after we make a list for our own purposes."

"And do what we can to help the process along?" asked Hope knowingly.

"Right after we've had more coffee!" Kristen carried two steaming mugs to the table near the file cabinet where they began to sift through the piles of folders she'd already chosen.

They worked in silence for a while, one person pulling lists and the other running them through the copy machine. Soon they were finished; the stack of paper was almost an inch thick. Kristen bundled the lists into a folder.

"I guess I should get this to Sheriff Miller right away. If there's something important in here. he should know as soon as possible." Kristen really wanted to sort through the papers first, but that task could wait.

"That'll work. In the meantime, I'd be happy to start reviewing the copies."

She was reluctant to pass the job off to Hope without having a look herself, but she knew she could count on her friend to uncover anything unusual. Besides, Hope had a direct line to Todd if she did find something of interest. She shouldn't let her own curiosity hinder the investigation.

"Okay, do you want me to pick up anything from Amy's while I'm out?"

"That would be great. I wasn't hungry for breakfast, but now that I'm a little more awake, I'm starved."

"Any preference?"

"Nope. Surprise me. Amy hasn't baked anything I don't love."

Kristen hopped in her truck and drove the short distance into town, her windows rolled down to let in the already warm and stuffy air. She parked right in front of the department. She would walk to Amy's after she delivered the papers.

She entered the building and stated her business to the woman on duty at the front desk. The clerk gestured for

Kristen to sit down as she picked up the phone and spoke quietly into it. She didn't have to wait long. The sheriff strode down the hallway a minute or two later. He barked out a greeting, making Kristen wonder why she'd bothered to come. She reminded herself it was for Nancy's benefit. It was the least she could do for the poor woman.

She stood and followed Miller down the hall to his office where she handed the folder to him.

"What am I supposed to do with this?" he asked in his brusque manner. "I thought I told you to keep your nose out of the investigation."

"You did, and I'm doing just that, but I thought you might be interested in hearing a theory I have."

"What makes you think that?"

Good grief, was the man in a surly mood this morning. Maybe she should have brought him some coffee to lift his spirits. Though the way he was acting, she'd probably be tempted to spill the boiling liquid on him, but then she'd land in jail. "What I just handed you are registration sheets from Nature Station events."

"So?"

Kristen gritted her teeth in an attempt to keep herself from saying something she'd regret. "I thought perhaps someone who attended one of our events could have learned about poisonous plants from one of us…maybe even from Nancy."

"Do you hold events that pertain to poisonous plants? You already assured me the flowers in the vases weren't what caused Nancy's death. If that's the case, what makes you think the murderer learned about poisons at one of your workshops?"

He had a point. The sheriff didn't know she had knowledge that pokeweed had actually been the culprit, though she was the one who pointed them in that direction. She had to tread lightly, or the sheriff would be even more of a bear than he was now. "If you remember from yesterday, I told you pokeweed could be harmful if the conditions were right—or wrong, rather."

He narrowed his eyes at her. "So you think pokeweed was the culprit?"

"It's a possibility, isn't it? It's certainly easy enough to obtain since it's a common plant in these parts." She eyed him speculatively. "And I'm sure you're testing for various poisons. I'd imagine you'll be receiving those results soon?"

He ignored her comment. "And you think someone who attended one of your events would learn enough, even though I trust you don't teach them how to make these poisonous concoctions, to kill someone?"

"All I'm asking you to do is to consider that someone on these lists"—she gestured wildly toward the unopened folder on his desk—"may have worked at or dined at Barney's on Saturday night. Since you *took* the list we originally acquired from Barney, I can't compare the names to see if there are any matches."

"Don't worry about it. We'll look into it."

That's it? Even though he was not giving up any information, at least Miller was keeping his cool. But did she trust the man to actually review the lists to cross-match names, or would he toss them aside?

"Well, don't you think it's worth a shot?" she said. He only continued to glare at her. "If you need any help, I'd be glad to assist."

"If I need your help, I know where to find you." His scowl deepened. "Now if you'll excuse me, I need to get back to work."

She had little faith she'd gotten through to the pig headed sheriff. She'd have to satisfy herself by reviewing the names on her own and have Hope contact Todd if they found anything of interest.

"Thanks for your time." She rose from her chair and, muttering to herself, left the office without a glance backwards. Once outside the building, she tried to cheer herself up at the thought of indulging in some sweet treats from Amy's. At the very least, it was always nice to talk to the ever practical and jovial woman. She was so intent on her own thoughts, she almost ran smack into customers leaving the bakery. Much to her surprise, it was Ted Meyers with a woman in tow. Not bothering to hide her disgust toward Ted, she ignored him and let her gaze flick over his companion. She looked to be younger than Kristen by a few years. Her dark curly hair and light blue eyes were striking, though her build was short and stocky. As Kristen gave them a curt nod and entered the bakery, she wondered why the girl seemed familiar. And if she wasn't mistaken, Ted's friend had seemed startled to run into her. Was it the light of recognition she noticed in the other woman's eyes?

As her own eyes adjusted to the bakery's lighting, she tried to gather her thoughts. She was already flustered over her run in with Miller, and then to see Ted with another female upset her terribly. Just then Amy popped out from the kitchen to greet her.

"You'll never guess who was just here!"

"Oh, I can guess. I ran into Ted and his honey as I was coming in."

"Disgusting, isn't it?"

"What's the scoop on them? Though the woman, or girl rather, was attractive, she's not the type I'd picture Ted with." Kristen shook her head. "I'm having a hard time picturing him with anyone other than Nancy."

Amy patted her hand. "Go sit down and we'll chat for a minute while there's a lull."

Kristen settled herself on the comfortable couch while Amy grabbed two mugs and filled them with her flavor of the day, Chocolate Chip Cookie. She brought a plate of actual chocolate chip cookies as well and set them down to share on the low coffee table. Not sure what to expect, Kristen took a cautious sip and was rewarded with rich flavor that would probably taste even better if drunk with cookies.

"I don't know how you come up with these interesting coffee flavors." Her stomach grumbled as she took another sip. She'd only managed to munch a few grapes before leaving the Nature Station, and her hunger showed. She picked up a chewy cookie, bit into it, and moaned in pleasure

"For now I have a great supplier," said Amy with a chuckle. "My goal is try my hand at roasting my own beans one of these days."

"That would be cool." Kristen set down her cup. "Now tell me what you know."

"There's not much fact involved, only my observations."

"I think your observations are pretty valuable. I'm starting to think Ted's behavior, not to mention the behavior of one of his women, could have led to Nancy's death."

Amy looked thoughtful. "You're probably right. A jealous lover? Or Ted himself?"

"Either one of those are possibilities. It's not like Ted is even pretending to be much of a grieving widower. He put on a good show when we visited him at home, but I've run into him twice since then, and he seemed to be in a party mode both times." She filled Amy in on Ted asking her to help find Nancy's killer, then their confrontation at Swede's.

Amy shook her head. "I didn't know what to think when he brought that young thing in here. They sat out of the way—here, as a matter of fact—so I couldn't listen to their conversation."

"I was hoping you could shed some light on their relationship. I take it you hadn't seen them together before?"

"No. I did manage to hear them talking while I filled their order. He had regular coffee, and she wanted one of my new iced coffee drinks that have been popular this summer. They both chose cinnamon rolls."

"Yeah, not everyone is diehard enough to drink hot coffee during this weather," noted Kristen. "Did they seem comfortable together, like they had spent time with each other previously?"

"No, they seemed a little awkward, which makes sense if you think about it. We wouldn't be the only ones who'd find it peculiar to see him with another woman in public so soon after Nancy died."

"Good grief, they haven't even had her funeral yet." Kristen sighed. "The girl looked familiar, but I have no idea why. I'm not sure if I've seen her before or if she just reminded me of someone."

"I'd never seen her before."

"I wonder how Ted meets these women."

"I don't have a clue, and I'm not sure I want to know." Amy swirled her remaining coffee in her cup. "I'm amazed at some of the stuff I see when it comes to my coffee house customers."

"And hear? Anything specific?" Amy's keen observation skills could prove to be important.

"Nothing that I haven't already told you." Amy raised both eyebrows. "There's no such thing as baker-customer confidentiality, is there?"

Kristen grinned. "No, I don't think so. I'd appreciate it if you could pass on anything you think of that may be helpful.

"Sure, that goes without saying. I was planning to let you know about Ted and his latest squeeze, and then you walked into the shop right after they left."

"What a coincidence!" Were there other coincidences? Did any of the information they'd gathered so far pertain to Nancy's murder? Kristen drained her cup, feeling depressed about the situation. After her encounter with the sheriff earlier that morning, she wasn't confident they would pursue the same routes. Of course, they had inside information she didn't have access to. Still, she wished the sheriff hadn't discounted her theory so quickly. But since he had, that left her little choice but to see what she could dig up on her own. She knew she could count on Hope, Amy, and Ruth Ann to help. Feeling somewhat better, she glanced up and saw Amy eyeing her curiously.

"What was going on in that blond head of yours?"

"I'm just thinking about what all this means…or doesn't mean."

"You should trust the sheriff's department to handle this," said Amy gently. "I'm sure you remember how things ended when you took matters into your own hands the last time you solved a murder."

"I don't think I'll forget anytime soon." Kristen smiled ruefully and rose from her chair. "I'd better get going or Hope will start to wonder what happened to me. By the way, I'd like to take a treat to her."

"Sure. What would you like?"

"How about one of everything? After all, working to solve a murder burns extra calories," joked Kristen. She selected a few more chocolate chip cookies and threw in some gooey looking brownies for good measure. She had a feeling it would be a long day.

Amy rung up her purchase and bid Kristen farewell. "And I'll be sure to contact you if I notice any monkey business."

"Thanks, I'd appreciate it." Kristen said her goodbyes and left the bakery. As she walked down the street toward her truck, her cell phone rang. She noticed her parents' number on caller ID. Her mother came on the line.

"Did you know about Nancy's memorial service?" Joannie asked, not one to waste time with pleasantries when she had important news to share.

Kristen was stunned. She hadn't heard anything about it. She'd just seen Ted, and he hadn't mentioned a word. Of course, he probably had other things—or people—on his mind. "No. When is it?"

"Tomorrow afternoon." Her mother served on the funeral committee at their church and sometimes learned of deaths and their corresponding arrangements before the general public was told. "We're expecting a large crowd."

"I can imagine. Do you need me to make anything? I'm in town and can grab some ingredients on the way home."

"Sure, we'll need plenty of salads and desserts." Joannie paused. "He sure didn't give us much time to plan the luncheon."

"Unfortunately, it doesn't surprise me about the man, but I know it puts you in a bind."

"Luckily, people feel so awful about the situation that they've been good about donating food. Pastor Mike will be doing the service, of course, and a few close friends and family will be participating too."

"I wonder why they're having the service so quickly. I was just talking to Sheriff Miller, and he didn't mention releasing the body."

"Since it's a memorial service and not a funeral, maybe there won't *be* a body."

Kristen drew in a deep breath. She knew what her mother meant, but it was hard to believe they were talking about Nancy, who had been full of life and helping at the Nature Station this time last week.

Joannie took advantage of Kristen's silence. "Why were you talking to the sheriff?"

"Oh, talking is not really the appropriate word. It was more like I was dropping off what I considered important information, while he alternated between patronizing me and scowling at me." She filled Joannie in on what had transpired earlier that morning.

Her mother tsked in disapproval. Kristen wasn't sure if the disapproval was directed at her or at Miller.

"That man is a complete boor at times, but I suppose he's only trying to do his job and make sure you, and everyone else, remains safe with a murderer gallivanting around town. You know how your Dad and I feel about the circumstances. You've put yourself in the thick of it again."

Her mother had a point. Still, she couldn't help it if she'd been in the wrong place at the wrong time—twice! She was trying to rectify the situation. "I know, Mom. That's why I handed the names over to the sheriff. But he didn't seem impressed." Her voice trailed off, and Joannie jumped in.

"And it's up to you to save the day?" Joannie sighed. "I guess I don't blame you, though I wouldn't have the nerve to stick my nose into such a dangerous situation!"

"I didn't think I would either. I'm just doing what I think needs to be done."

"We raised you to be independent, but that doesn't mean we don't still worry about you when you get yourself involved in a murder investigation."

"You do realize Dad is also trying to dig up information?"

"Of course I do, but he's a grown man." Joannie switched gears. "That reminds me. I meant to tell you that your dad ran into Barney when he was at Farm Supply this morning."

"Really? What would Barney be doing there?" She turned her thoughts back to the restaurateur, ashamed to admit she was suspicious of the jovial man.

"I'm not sure, but I think he raises his own herbs for the restaurant. Maybe he was picking up gardening supplies. You know that store carries a little bit of everything."

"They do, but…" Barney surely wasn't stocking up on bailer twine like her dad was probably doing. He was the owner of a restaurant where a woman had recently died of poisoning. The store sold things like rat bait and pesticides. It would be easy for him to slip something into Nancy's food or drink. But if pokeberrygenin was actually the culprit, then there was no need for him to concoct a poison from something he picked up at Farm Supply. If that were the case, why would the murderer even mess with using a poisonous plant when they could buy a common product over the counter?

"Kristen, are you okay?"

She snapped her thoughts back to the phone conversation. "Yes, I'm fine. I was just thinking about why a murderer would use a plant poison to kill someone."

"Well, that's simple—so it wouldn't be traced as easily."

"I agree, but if something common were used as a poison almost anyone could purchase it, and no one would think anything of it." A light bulb went on in Kristen's head. "Whereas how many people would even know pokeweed is a potentially poisonous plant, let alone how to use it to kill someone?"

"You're right, but this isn't news. However, it surely narrows the list of suspects."

"It just hit me when you mentioned Barney. Not just anyone would have knowledge to use pokeweed to kill someone. And it makes me even more confident that someone who attended a Nature Station event may have been the one to kill Nancy. I just wish Sheriff Miller would see it my way."

"He may be doing just that. By the way, your dad said Barney was feeling pretty stressed about the ongoing investigation."

"I know exactly how he feels!"

"Evidently they've been relentless in their questioning of the staff."

"That's understandable and necessary."

"Well, I'll let you go for now. I wanted to let you know about Nancy's service."

"Thanks. I'll drop some food off at the church first thing in the morning, and I'll definitely plan on attending the service tomorrow afternoon." She signed off and switched directions to head toward Swede's to purchase ingredients for a salad and dessert.

As she walked, she decided she'd whip up a couple of quick and easy stand-by recipes as her contribution to the luncheon following Nancy's memorial service. She was making a mental list as she walked into Swede's where Marty was organizing new stock near the front of the store.

Was it her imagination, or did Marty blush when she saw Kristen. Was she embarrassed about her comments yesterday? It felt peculiar to be suspicious of people she'd known all her life. But she needed to be practical. After all, someone had killed Nancy, and there was a strong possibility she knew the person who did it. She kept her greeting breezy.

"Why hello, Marty! I'm back again!"

"You must be cooking up a storm for that handsome man of yours."

Now it was Kristen's turn to blush. It was true she shopped there more often than she had in the past; now she was cooking more regularly for someone other than herself. Previously, she had only shopped for food once a week.

"Just picking up a few things. I promised Mom I'd make a salad and dessert for the luncheon following Nancy's memorial service. It's going to be held tomorrow afternoon." She watched Marty's face. She looked as shocked as Kristen had been when she'd heard the news about the impromptu gathering.

"My goodness, that was fast," Marty stammered.

"I agree. I just found out a few minutes ago. Mom's been making calls to line up food donations for the luncheon. You'll probably be swamped before long."

"I'm sure we will." Marty said absently.

Kristen had never seen Marty at a loss for words. "You wouldn't know why Ted would plan the service so quickly, would you?"

"No, I have no idea why he'd do such a thing." Again, a blush crept up Marty's neck to her face. "Maybe he just wants closure."

Yeah, so he could get on with his life, though he hadn't seemed to let Nancy get in the way of his activities before she died, so why would he care now? "We all need closure, but a memorial service before the murder investigation has concluded won't be much help."

"It seems you're doing your best to speed things along."

Kristen wasn't sure if Marty seemed upset by the thought or glad she was doing her part. "I'm trying to help."

Digging around for facts relating to the murder had unearthed all kinds of buried secrets in the tiny town of Eklund. Kristen doubted Marty had anything to do with Nancy's death, even if she was acting oddly. After their conversation yesterday, Kristen thought it was possible she still had feelings for Ted after all these years.

She grabbed a shopping basket and scanned the aisles for the salad and dessert fixings. Only a few minutes had elapsed from the time she entered the store until when she unloaded her basket at the checkout counter, but by then, Marty was acting more naturally.

"I do hope they get this mystery solved soon," said Marty in her normal, chatty demeanor.

"Me, too!" Kristen looked Marty directly in the eye. "I know you're in a position to hear things. If you notice anything unusual, you'll give me a call, won't you?"

"Sure thing. Hard telling what I'll hear when the women of the church start coming in to buy ingredients for the luncheon."

"The hard part is knowing whether any of it is significant," said Kristen as she took her bags from Marty. "I'll see you later!"

She left the store, mulling things over once again. So many people were behaving in an odd manner, but how much could be attributed to having a nasty murder occur in town, and how much related directly to Nancy's death? She considered those whose actions seemed out of character: Robert, his wife, Ted, Marty, Barney, just to name a few. She didn't have access to the list of names of those who had been at Barney's that night, but she did know who had been at the Nature Station recently. Feeling inspired, she threw her bags into her truck and drove back to work. She couldn't wait to discuss matters with Hope. Maybe she'd stumbled across something interesting in her time alone at the office. Even if she hadn't, Kristen was confident some of the puzzle pieces were beginning to fit together from the information they had gathered over the past couple of days.

CHAPTER 18

When Kristen arrived at the Nature Station office, Hope was just hanging up the phone. She looked at Kristen questioningly. "Where in the world have you been?" Her face softened at the site of the goody bag from Amy's Bakery.

"Sorry I took so long, but it's been a busy morning."

"Same here." Hope opened the bag, peered inside, and moaned in pleasure at the aroma that escaped.

"Tell me what you found out after I left."

"No, you first. Then we'll decide if my paranoid deductions have anything to do with what you may have discovered."

"We'll need fresh coffee." Kristen brought two cups of coffee over to the work table. "I had another encounter with Sheriff Miller." She filled Hope in on her trip to town.

"I can't believe you saw Ted with a woman so young!" Hope had polished off one cookie before pulling a brownie out of the bag. "And to plan the memorial service at the last minute, especially when things are so unsettled—I don't understand."

"Neither do I. Hopefully we can put our heads together to figure out what happened. Now, tell me what you learned."

Hope shuffled through the pile of papers they had pulled from the files earlier. "I finished reviewing the lists and began to sort through photos of our recent events."

"Good thinking. I must warn you that the good Sheriff Miller practically scoffed at the idea." Kristen rolled her eyes. "He barely acknowledged the papers when I handed them over to him."

"Why doesn't that surprise me? Luckily, we know who comes and goes around here, and though it's not a pleasant thought, one of them could have been the person who poisoned Nancy."

"Or at least gave the idea to someone else. That's something we haven't really considered."

"That puts a whole new spin on things. Let's explore this lead first." She leaned closer to Kristen, showing her names highlighted on the registration sheets. "These are people you told me were at Barney's the night Nancy died. Of course, we don't know everyone who was working there, and as far as diners go, you only listed the people you knew."

Kristen scanned the names. Sure enough, just about everyone they had questioned had attended at least one recent Nature Station event. Hope had highlighted Robert and his wife, Ted, Barney, and Patricia. None of those names surprised her and didn't mean much. This information would be more valuable if they had the list from Barney's. Kristen cursed the fact that Sheriff Miller had grabbed the papers from them before they'd had a chance to review them. As far as the others on the event lists, those living in and around town showed their support by attending events, purchasing items from the gift shop, and volunteering to work there in their spare time. In return, the Nature Station drew people from out of town who patronized other Eklund businesses, so it was a symbiotic relationship.

"It looks like even Ted showed up at one of the prairie walks we held late last summer." From what Kristen knew of him, he didn't seem to be the outdoorsy type. Nancy had probably dragged him along.

"When pokeweed would have probably been in the berry stage, which would cause more people to notice it and comment on it."

"Even if Ted or someone else asked about pokeweed, anyone could have overheard the explanation," said Hope thoughtfully. "I pulled the photo files to see if we recognize anyone by sight who may have been at Barney's on Saturday, but there are still lots more to review."

"No worries. We'll look through the rest together. There were several people I recognized but didn't know, and the same is true with some of the people who attend our events."

"Not to mention the people you didn't even notice."

"That's true. We were supposed to be having a romantic dinner that evening. Naturally I wasn't paying much attention to the other diners."

"Let's take a look to see if something trips our memory."

Kristen scooted her chair closer to Hope's computer screen where they viewed a slideshow of their massive photo collection. They spent almost an hour cruising through the photos one by one. Eventually, everyone in the pictures seemed to jumble together and look the same. Kristen grew bored with the tedious exercise and began to doubt they'd find learn anything of value. Then she noticed someone. "Stop on that frame."

Hope creased her brow. "Who do you see?"

"I'm not sure who she is, but I saw her this morning with Ted."

"Yikes! She really *is* young," said Hope with a wry smile. "Much younger than us."

"I agree, which makes her stand out like a sore thumb being seen around town with Ted, a recent, brokenhearted widower," said Kristen sarcastically.

"I'd guess her to be right around college age, though it's hard to tell these days. Younger women try to look older, and older women try to look younger."

"Can you zoom in on her?"

"Sure." Hope moved the cursor to the curly haired brunette and clicked. Instantly they had a larger view of the woman.

"Even though this photo is almost a year old, the woman looks pretty similar to how she appeared this morning. Black curly hair, fair skin, and pale blue eyes. She's kind of chubby, but really pretty."

"That's right, but she doesn't seem Ted's type."

Kristen thought it was ridiculous that Ted would have a type of woman he preferred, other than his lovely wife. "Maybe they weren't *together*, if you know what I mean."

"You always try to give people the benefit of the doubt, but we need to be realistic. We know she's not one of Ted and Nancy's kids. We've seen them before in other pictures. Who else could this be? Another relative who flew in for the memorial service?"

"That doesn't make sense if Ted only made the arrangements this morning."

"So for now I think we should consider Curly Q one of Ted's women."

Kristen giggled at the nickname then took a deep breath. "Okay. Let's skim through the rest of these pictures. Just because we saw Curly Q doesn't mean she had anything to do with Nancy's murder. It could just be a coincidence." *Coincidence.* There was that word again. Kristen knew much of what they'd seen and heard the past few days was probably irrelevant or coincidental. The question was, how did they decide which information was pertinent and which wasn't, especially when they didn't have the tools available to them that the sheriff department had access to.

"We may run across someone else of interest. Thank goodness we don't have too many more photo folders to scan." Hope stretched and yawned.

"Once we finish these we'll break for lunch and take what we've gathered to Sheriff Miller." Kristen paused. "Or maybe you could just let Todd know. I've had enough of the sheriff for one day. Besides, he doesn't seem to listen to me."

"Oh, I'm sure he does, but he's a powerful man in the county, and he probably doesn't want a naturalist who's stumbled across two bodies to be the one to crack the case."

"Since you put it that way, I guess I don't blame him," said Kristen, her good nature restored.

They went through the rest of the photos. Kristen wished she'd paid more attention to the people working at Barney's that night. She didn't recognize the names Barney had listed as his new hires, other than Patricia. She didn't have a clue who was working in the kitchen and didn't know their waiter either. She hadn't seen him in any of the photos, but they were only snapshots to capture highlights of their events. Not all participants were pictured. Though they were doing the best they could to help track down Nancy's killer, what they could do was limited by not knowing who all had been at Barney's that night.

Before they were all the way finished reviewing the pictures, Kristen heard her cell phone vibrate. A text had just come through from Brett. **How are you today?** Nothing too exciting, but she dialed his number rather than return his text. She wanted to tell him about tomorrow's service for Nancy.

He sounded surprised when he answered. "I just sent you a quick note while I was having lunch. I'm running behind today. Cassie called first thing and said she wasn't feeling well."

"Oh no, that's too bad. I won't keep you long, but I wanted to let you that there's going to be a memorial service for Nancy tomorrow afternoon."

"Already? That sounds awfully fast, considering her body hasn't been released. Or has it?"

"I don't think so. Mom is the one who told me, and she made it sound like this was a last minute deal."

"What a shame. Nancy deserved more than to have her husband rush what should be a tribute to her life, just so he can get on with his own life."

Kristen was taken aback at Brett's vehemence, though she agreed with him. "I know. I can't believe it."

"Would you like me to go with you?"

"Well, yeah, that would be great, but I didn't think you could get off work in the middle of the day."

"It's not a problem. I have some time saved up, so I'll just take the afternoon off."

"It'll be nice to have you go along with me. These things are never easy." And it meant so much for Brett to offer to go. She felt it was a step forward in their relationship.

"I'll have to figure out what to do with Cassie, since she'll be working with me…unless she calls in sick again."

"I'm sure you'll figure out something for her to do on her own. I'm just glad you're able to go with me."

"I thought Nancy was a nice lady, and I feel pretty close to the situation since we're the ones who saw her right after she died."

"I know what you mean!"

He sighed. "Well, I'd better finish my lunch and get back to work. I'll probably be working late tonight, so I'll just talk to you tomorrow. If I'm off the whole the afternoon, maybe we can do something after the service."

It felt odd to make plans for after a funeral, but their relationship had started off after one murder and continued with a second one. She'd make do with whatever time she could have with Brett. "Sure. We'll probably close the Nature Station at noon anyway."

"I'll pick you up at your house around twelve-thirty."

She bit her tongue before she could reply *I'll look forward to it.* "Sure, I'll be ready."

Kristen turned back to Hope, who was still squinting at the computer screen. "Did you see anyone else of note?"

"I'm still looking, but not so far. Same old thing. Either we already know the people in the pictures, or we don't know the people well enough for you to have recognized them if they were at Barney's Saturday night. Either way, no one's jumping out at me."

Kristen sat down again, sharing the screen with Hope. "You know, maybe the answer is right in front of us."

Hope looked at her curiously. "You think this elderly lady with the straw hat and red shorts is the one who murdered Nancy?"

Kristen cracked up at Hope's sarcasm. "No, I don't mean literally. We know for a fact that Ted, Patricia, Barney, and Robert have been to Nature Station events, and they were also at Barney's the night Nancy died."

"So what do you think? Should we focus on them and quit looking for anyone else?"

"We're not recognizing others who could have been at both places."

"Just because we haven't seen pictures of others doesn't mean they weren't at the Nature Station. And there were probably dozens of people you either didn't notice or recognize at Barney's."

"I know that," said Kristen stubbornly. "But what else do we have to go on? We can't try to root out information on everyone who attended one of our events."

"We've already checked on the main players."

"You're right, but we were pumping them for general information. In Barney's case we weren't targeting him as a suspect."

"That's because neither of us consider him as a suspect." Hope shivered. "I have to admit the atmosphere there was creepy yesterday."

"I felt the same way."

"Let's not forget what happened in the park afterwards. To be honest, it sounds like Sheriff Miller considers *you* a suspect!"

Kristen couldn't help but feel alarmed at that prospect. "I thought he was just bluffing."

"Try to look at it from his side, which I know is hard, considering your feelings for the man." Hope gave her a weak smile. "To him, you're a plant expert. He probably doesn't understand that you aren't an authority on poisonous plants. He just thinks you're a 'plant person.' After all, he thought one of the prairie plants in the floral arrangements could have killed Nancy. That points right to the Nature Station, especially since you were there that evening."

Kristen sighed and continued with Hope's reasoning. "To make matters worse, I was the one who discovered Nancy. For all he knew, I could have poisoned her while we were in the bathroom."

"That's right, though I can't imagine she would react so quickly to the poison. But from his point of view he *has* to consider you a suspect."

Kristen's stomach fluttered. Being accused of murder was not a good feeling. "I've been running around town trying to hunt down Nancy's killer to bring about justice on her behalf, but you're suggesting I should be doing it just to clear my name." A horrible thought crept into Kristen's head. "Do you know from Todd what they're doing to rule me out as the murderer? They'd better be looking into the suspects we've noted, not to mention others we haven't even considered."

"Calm down, Kristen," said Hope reassuringly. "I didn't mean to alarm you. I was only pointing out that though there are some people we wouldn't believe capable of murder, such as Barney killing one of his longest and best customers, the sheriff's department looks at them differently."

"And you're saying we should do the same."

"Exactly. We need to be objective, just like Sheriff Miller, even if he has a funny way of showing it. By the way, you know you have Todd in your corner. But that doesn't mean he and the others on the force don't have to work through the process to disqualify you as a suspect and then find the real culprit."

"It's time to get back to work, though the sheriff discouraged me from interfering with the investigation."

"You can hardly blame him for that, can you? He's concerned for our safety. Our snooping around may not only put the person who did it on guard, but he may also not think twice about killing again to protect himself."

Kristen's stomach grumbled. "I think we should reconvene after lunch."

"That's a great idea. We'll get some fresh perspective on the situation." Hope started straightening papers on her desk.

"In fact," said Kristen, "let's give Ruth Ann a call to see if she's learned anything new."

"I'll do that right now, though it's my guess she would have already contacted us if she had. Still, it won't hurt to check in with her."

"Let's put the 'Out to Lunch' sign up on the office door and see if she can meet us somewhere to talk."

"Sounds good to me. There are only a few hikers on the trails, and we shouldn't be gone longer than an hour or so."

"Unless we run smack dab into the murderer." Kristen chuckled, though it was no laughing matter. She felt more urgency than ever to resolve Nancy's murder. Besides the fact that no one would feel content with a murderer on the prowl, her own life was on the line. In order to clear her own name, she needed to figure out who had actually performed the nasty deed. No matter how she looked at it, it was a big job to tackle, and not one she wanted to attempt on an empty stomach.

CHAPTER 19

The women had called Ruth Ann to make arrangements to meet in town for lunch, but instead she graciously invited them to eat a quick bite at her house. When Kristen and Hope walked through the back door into her cozy kitchen, the older woman had ham and Swiss sandwiches on hearty whole grain buns and fresh fruit already waiting on dainty dishes on the table. Kristen assumed the leafy green lettuce was probably straight out of Ruth Ann's garden. There were glasses of fresh lemonade at each place setting.

"I thought it would be nice to eat lunch here, so we could talk in peace," said Ruth Ann.

"Good thinking," said Hope. "You never know who might be listening to our conversations if we were talking in public."

"Whatever the reason, I'm happy for the invitation. Not only does everything look delicious, but you have everything arranged so beautifully," said Kristen as she popped a crispy potato chip in her mouth.

"Are you closing in on Nancy's killer?" Ruth Ann looked at them expectantly.

"Not exactly," said Hope. "But we're hoping to regroup while we eat."

"At least I have some interesting tidbits to pass along," said Ruth Ann with a smug look on her face.

"Oh? Do tell!" teased Kristen. "And by the way, just because we aren't much closer to tracing the person who murdered Nancy doesn't mean we don't have information to share as well."

"That's right," agreed Hope. "Plus we have some new directions to pursue."

"Sounds like the two of you have been busy, which doesn't surprise me at all," said Ruth Ann as she squirted mustard onto her sandwich.

Her two visitors explained what had transpired since they'd been together the day before—Ted's new younger woman, the registration sheets from Nature Station events, and all the photos they'd reviewed. Kristen finished up by telling about her disastrous encounter with the sheriff earlier that morning.

"Just as I suspected, you've accomplished quite a bit this morning."

"I guess more than we realized," said Hope with a sigh.

"Including irritating the sheriff when he already suspects me of killing Nancy," said Kristen dramatically.

"Now dear, he can't possibly believe you'd poison Nancy. That's ridiculous!" Ruth Ann patted Kristen's hand. "But because you were there that evening and have plant knowledge, he does need to fully check into your possible motive, plant expertise, and other factors, so he can rule you out."

Hope grinned. "Yeah, he doesn't know you only know enough about poisonous plants and their medicinal uses to be dangerous."

"That could be said for all three of us." Ruth Ann shooed away their concern with a wave of her hand. "Don't worry about a thing. We'll have this mess cleared up in no time. You'll see, especially when you hear what I have to tell you."

Kristen felt reassured by her friend's support and optimism. "Don't keep us in suspense any longer!"

"It pays to be patient." The older woman paused dramatically, reveling in the spotlight. "I was at the salon this morning."

"Do you mean Betty's Clip 'N Color?" Kristen couldn't resist asking.

"Why, yes, of course. I agree that 'salon' is a lofty name for a small town beauty shop."

"Oh, Ruth Ann, I meant to mention it earlier, you look gorgeous. The color and cut are perfect for summer," said Hope.

"Thank you, dear." She smiled amiably. "But let's not get sidetracked."

"Please continue, Ruth Ann," said Kristen with an encouraging grin. "We're anxious to hear what you have to say."

Ruth Ann patted her perfectly done hair. "I wanted to see if I could dig up anything on red-haired women, so I made an appointment at Betty's. She was able to squeeze me in this morning. She probably thought it a bit strange, since I normally only schedule my regular monthly appointment, unless it's for a special occasion."

"Don't you consider preparing lunch for two friends on a Tuesday a special occasion?" asked Kristen.

"My, aren't you feeling your oats today!" Ruth Ann laughed. "Since I had just heard about the memorial service, I told her I wanted to look nice for it. Hearing that, she treated me to a few interesting morsels of information."

Hope leaned in more closely. "Such as?"

"You'll never believe this." The younger women looked at her questioningly. "It was quiet at the salon, since I was the first client of the day, so Betty spoke freely. She had dinner at Barney's earlier in the evening on Saturday. They like to take advantage of the early bird specials, so she was leaving just as Nancy and Ted were arriving."

"I had no idea Betty was there." Kristen frowned. "I suppose there were several diners I don't remember seeing or never saw in the first place."

"Which is why having the list from Barney's is so vital," chimed in Hope. "I wish I could have Todd sneak me a copy, but he's really having to toe the line."

"Don't worry about that," said Ruth Ann smugly. "I'll see if I can talk Barney into providing us with another list. But please let me finish. Betty was surprised to see Nancy and Ted together, since she'd recently seen him around town with other women."

"In all the years I've known Nancy, I never knew about Ted's philandering tendencies," said Kristen. "She never mentioned they were having problems."

"It's not the way of our generation to open up to the outside world about marital issues. However Ted seemed to be more flagrant recently. He used to be more discreet."

"So you've known about it for some time?" asked Hope.

"Yes, Nancy was a saint to look the other way for so long. I can't believe she wouldn't have suspected him of infidelity if he was currently having an affair," Ruth Ann said matter of factly.

"But was she really a saint?" asked Kristen. "Don't get me wrong, I thought the world of Nancy, but the fact is, someone killed her. Why?"

"Given the circumstances and murder method, it wasn't a spur of the moment attack," said Hope. "Someone was planning to do this for a specific reason."

"It's doubtful Nancy was in the wrong place at the wrong time," agreed Ruth Ann.

"So maybe she was in someone's way," said Kristen. "Which leads us back to Ted's women."

"There seem to be so many, it's hard to narrow the list down to one particular woman." Hope popped the last bite of her sandwich into her mouth and moaned in pleasure.

"Why don't we make a list of all his women. Betty can shed some light on that subject, I'm sure." Ruth Ann drained her glass of lemonade. "For starters, you'll be interested to know that she colored a few women's hair with red tones in the past month."

"Did you tell her why you were interested in redheads?" asked Kristen. "And did she give you their names?"

"I normally don't gossip when I'm getting my hair done," said Ruth Ann primly. "But in this case, I felt justified. I explained the gist of the situation to Betty, telling her that Monty had recently seen Nancy eating lunch there with a redhead he didn't recognize."

"And they were deep in conversation," added Hope.

"Betty rattled off a few names of redheads, but I didn't know all of them. However, Betty said she did her regular dye job on Marty from Swede's, since some of her gray was starting to show through, and she also added reddish highlights to Patricia's hair—you know, the new hostess at Barney's."

"The woman who started the new reservation system at the restaurant and was there when we discovered Nancy in the restroom," added Kristen.

"Wouldn't Marty have recognized Patricia?" asked Hope.

"Not if she's a new employee at Barney's and just moved to Eklund," reasoned Ruth Ann.

"We shouldn't jump to conclusions. Just because Patricia has red highlights, which I didn't even notice in the restaurant's subtle lighting—I thought her hair was a chestnut brown—doesn't mean she had anything to do with Nancy's death or was the one to meet her for lunch."

"I understand the need for caution," agreed Ruth Ann. "But we have so little to go on. Besides, she was also at a Nature Station event, so she is a likely candidate, or suspect rather."

Kristen remembered Patricia's reaction the night of the murder. She behaved calmly and efficiently. She hadn't seemed anxious or jumpy, given the fact they'd discovered a dead woman in the ladies room. "Do you think she and Ted are having a fling?"

"If she moved to town recently, would Ted have had time to start something with her so quickly?" asked Hope.

"If so he's a real fast mover." Ruth Ann shook her head in disapproval before muttering, "He'd better not try anything on me."

"Maybe the murder motive has nothing to do with Ted's womanizing abilities," suggested Kristen.

"Then what in the world could it be?" asked Hope.

Ruth Ann eyed the clock. "I have no idea, but I think as soon as you ladies leave, I'll pay another visit to the salon to pick Betty's brain for a list of Ted's conquests. And I'll see if I can drum up another list from Barney."

"If we find someone who comes up on all the lists, we'll have some viable suspects." Kristen rose from her chair and started clearing the table.

"We already know Patricia's name appears everywhere," said Hope practically. "So we already have one suspect."

"Let's not forget Barney and Ted." Ruth Ann started putting leftovers into the refrigerator.

"It keeps going back to them," said Kristen. "Thanks for lunch, Ruth Ann. It was delicious and a nice break from our normal lunch of sandwiches eaten in the office."

"No problem. I'm glad we had a chance to put our heads together. I'll be in touch."

The women left and walked toward Kristen's truck. After they'd climbed in, Hope asked, "How are you doing on gas?"

Kristen looked momentarily confused. "I guess I'll be fine once I've had a chance to use the bathroom."

"No silly, though I appreciate the warning," Hope snickered. "I meant, if you need some gas, now might be a good time to fill up."

The light bulb went on in Kristen's head and she blushed. "Sorry, I guess my mind was elsewhere."

"Apparently so," said Hope with a smile. "Don't you think it would be a good idea to check in with the gas station coffee crew?"

"I agree, but we'd probably have better luck first thing in the morning."

"It seems like there are always a few old timers clustered around the coffee pot no matter what time of the day—or night! Besides, the younger crowd will be filling up on soda to get them through this hot afternoon."

"It won't hurt to drop by and see what we can discover, though we shouldn't be away from the Nature Station for much longer." Kristen pulled up to the gas pump and topped off her tank, after which she parked her truck at the side of the busy convenience store.

Kristen went to pay for her gas while Hope meandered over to the fountain drinks and coffee pot. Sure enough, there were plenty of people milling around at this time of the day. While Hope worked her magic, Kristen waited patiently in line while people purchased their midday lottery tickets, beer, and cigarettes. No one was in line behind her when it came to her turn. As she slid her card out of her wallet, she noticed that the same clerk who had spoken with her about Johnny Thomas was working behind the counter today.

The clerk eyed Kristen curiously. "Aren't you the gal who runs the Nature Station? From what I've been hearing, you've been involved in another murder."

"Unfortunately that's the case. You probably already know I was the one who found Nancy."

"Yeah, I heard that. That must have been awful!"

"Definitely not pretty. Now I'm trying to figure out what happened." She sighed. "Nancy was a volunteer at the Nature Station."

"That's not a good track record for the people who work there."

"Tell me about it. That bad track record includes me being the one to find the two bodies and then searching for answers."

"So you're doing some snooping again? If I know the sheriff, he's probably not too keen on that."

"You've got that right. But since I am, is there anything you've noticed working here that seems out of the ordinary? I know the gas station is a hub of activity. Just about everyone in town passes through here on a regular basis."

The clerk looked thoughtful as she handed Kristen a receipt for her gas. "You're right. We see some real characters pass through here. Now that you mention it, there have been a few odd things recently. They didn't mean much at the time, but now that Nancy Meyers is dead, who knows? They could be important details."

Excitement washed over Kristen. Everything they'd heard so far had been wishy-washy. They hadn't discovered much tangible evidence, working on only a few hunches because they didn't know what direction to turn. "Go on."

The clerk didn't need further prompting. "I see Ted in here almost every morning when he coffees up."

Good, maybe Hope would learn something interesting from the stragglers. "It seems to be a popular place to drink coffee and catch up on the latest news."

The clerk rolled her eyes. "It always amazes me how often people come in here to do just that."

"Did Ted come in here alone or with someone else?"

"I was getting to that. Normally when he came for his morning coffee he was alone, but if he came in at other times of the day, he sometimes was with other people."

"Such as…" Kristen figured he probably had one of his many extra-marital fling women in tow.

"Some I recognized, and some I didn't. Most recently I've seen him with the new woman who works at Barney's."

Bingo! "Do you mean Patricia?"

"I guess. She has brownish-red hair."

"That's probably her." *But what does it mean?*

"I saw him with plenty of other women, but hardly ever his wife, poor thing." She paused to swipe the card of a customer who had just purchased gas. When he turned to leave, the clerk continued, "Of course, Nancy was in here with other men, so maybe it didn't matter much."

"I know she had some friends who were men. Is that what you mean?'

"Could be. It's not for me to say."

"Did you know any men in particular?"

"She hung out quite a bit with Robert who used to work at the bank and sometimes Barney."

"Barney…you mean the restaurant owner?" *This was news!*

"Well, sure. It's not a very common name, is it?" The clerk chortled at her own joke. "I could tell she was probably just friends with Robert, but I'm not so sure about Barney."

Kristen digested this crumb. She was uncomfortable knowing there could have been some sort of romantic relationship between the two. "Can you think of anything else?"

The clerk shook her head. "If you leave me your card, I'll let you know if I remember something or notice anything unusual."

Kristen whipped out her business card and thanked the helpful woman, then meandered to the back where Hope had set up camp. She was holding a soda and talking to several locals. The group broke into laughter just as Kristen joined them.

"Is this your friend?" one of the men asked Hope.

"Yep. This is Kristen." Hope raised her eyebrows. "Are you ready to go?"

"I am if you are." She smiled at the men and waved as she headed toward the door.

Once outside the women started chattering at the same time. "Wait until you hear what I found out," said Kristen, just as Hope said something similar.

"You first," said Hope as she hopped into the hot truck.

Kristen relayed what she'd learned about Ted and Patricia and Nancy and Barney. "Do you think there was some sort of love triangle—or love square, rather—going on among them?"

Hope shuddered. "I had no idea Eklund was filled with such sordid affairs."

"Maybe someone got jealous and decided to kill Nancy."

"It's a possible motive, but it seems awfully drastic." Hope shook her head in disgust. "It wasn't a heat of the moment murder."

"That's true. Planning was involved, and I would guess well in advance, given the method. Pokeweed could be gathered quickly and easily if the murderer knew what to do with it, but no one keeps it on hand." Kristen pulled the truck into the driveway. Fortunately, the parking lot hadn't filled with new vehicles during their absence. But there was one that looked familiar, and Kristen felt her lunch settle heavily to the bottom of her stomach.

Sheriff Miller had emerged from his cruiser when he saw them pull into the driveway, and he didn't look happy.

CHAPTER 20

Kristen swallowed hard. She had no idea what Sheriff Miller was doing at the Nature Station, but she had a feeling he wasn't planning to take a hike in the woods. Things hadn't gone well during their morning chat. Noting the tense stance of the lawman, she doubted this encounter would be an improvement. Of course, he was uptight every time she interacted with him. However, she should cut him some slack since she only talked to him during murder investigations. Timing was everything. All these thoughts raced through her head as she walked slowly to where he stood waiting impatiently.

He cut to the chase. "Ms. Matthews, I'd like to have a word with you."

"Sure. Let's talk in my office." She threw a helpless look in Hope's direction while she unlocked the building and opened the door. She willed herself to calm down, hoping he wasn't there to either drill her with questions or condemn her detective work. She felt sure it wasn't a social call, so chances were good it was one of those two reasons.

She ushered him into her office, uncertain whether to shut the door. The sheriff solved her dilemma and shut it himself.

Oh great. This can't be good. "What can I do for you?" She plastered a smile on her face and looked at him with her innocent blue eyes, which wasn't a stretch, since she actually was innocent.

"For starters, you can explain to me why you continue to snoop around town." He paused briefly. "Then we can discuss a few items relating to your involvement in Nancy's murder."

So he was going to tackle both topics—worse than I expected. She felt her stomach lurch. "Where would you like to begin?"

"At the beginning, of course!" he bellowed.

So much for the man in charge remaining calm. She had a better chance of being unruffled, and *she* was the one on the hot seat. "If you have something to ask me, go ahead and do so. I have no idea why you're here, so if you're expecting me to lead off with something, you'll be sadly disappointed." Okay, maybe she should work on *her* state of tranquility.

"I want to know why you've been running around town asking more questions when I distinctly told you not to!"

"After I left you this morning, I came back here. Hope and I worked all morning in the office until it was time to break for lunch."

"Working on what, exactly?"

"I don't see how that's your business." She pointed to the piles of papers and files on her desk. "As you can see, I have plenty of work waiting for me. I've been spending time outdoors as of late, so I've fallen behind on paperwork."

"I can see that, and you'll probably fall farther behind if you don't get busy on it rather than sticking your nose into a murder investigation. Did I not make myself clear this morning?"

"Oh, you made yourself crystal clear! You had no intention of following up on the information I brought you. What choice did I have but to act on it myself?"

"What choice did you have? You could have let trained people on the county payroll handle the situation."

Kristen smiled sweetly. "Is much progress being made?"

"As a matter of fact, we've accomplished a lot, though this time, it's none of *your* business."

"Why are you here again?" Kristen cleared her throat to cover her shock over saying such a thing to the powerful man.

His face bright red, he exhaled heavily. "I'm here to warn you yet again to mind your own business, or I'll shut yours down."

"I'm pretty sure you can't do that." *Or could he?*

"If I locked you up for interfering with an investigation, that would put a damper on your business."

Kristen refused to let him see how his remark had shaken her. "I trust Hope to manage things."

The sheriff's face grew even redder. "That woman should know better than to continue meddling. Her fiancé is on the force. His job is at stake."

Hope and Todd were engaged? This was news to Kristen, but she wisely chose not to dispute the fact and rile Miller further. "I find it hard to believe you'd fire one of your best men." He had to be bluffing.

The sheriff sighed. "Okay, you've got me. But you need to let us do our job."

"I thought I was. As I started to explain, we had lunch at Ruth Ann Swanson's house. She knew how hard we've been working and invited us in for a bite to eat."

"Of course she did." He rolled his eyes upward. "I'm positive your lunch was a harmless little tea party."

"We're just three friends having lunch together. Besides, have you tasted Ruth Ann's home cooking? Hope would be happy to testify to its tastiness. It was a welcome change from our normal lunchtime ritual." Kristen cut off her babbling.

"And it's likely no discussion of the case took place during this delightful meal?" The sheriff's voice dripped with sarcasm.

"It's on everyone's mind, isn't it? Besides, if you had given me any indication you were going to pursue the information I delivered this morning, all this could have been avoided."

He switched subjects. "What about your foray into the gas station?"

Boy, he had eyes—or ears—everywhere! "What about it? My truck is an older model. It doesn't get great gas mileage. It was due for a fill-up."

"And you and Hope managed to fill up with plenty of local gossip too, didn't you?" he said accusingly.

"Isn't that what everyone else does when they stop by? It seems to me they fill up on gas, coffee, and whatever information they can glean while they're there. Welcome to small town, U.S.A."

"I don't appreciate your tone, Ms. Matthews." Miller was fuming.

"And I don't appreciate yours either." She spat out the words, her earlier vow to remain calm long forgotten.

"Let's quit arguing and get back on track. You know my feelings on sticking your nose into this murder investigation. If I want your help, I'll ask for it." He wiped his brow with his handkerchief. "And believe it or not, I'm asking now."

Kristen suppressed a smug smile. "I'd be happy to assist."

"Something has been puzzling me, and all the deputies as well."

Her curiosity aroused, she raised her blond brows at him, silently prodding him to continue.

"One thing that led us to believe Mrs. Meyers was poisoned in the first place were the flowers in the centerpiece."

Oh no, not again. "What about them? I thought we went over this already."

"Our attention was diverted from the wildflowers when pokeweed entered the picture."

"Then why are wildflowers on your mind again?" They were always on Kristen's mind, but she couldn't picture the formidable sheriff giving them even a passing thought.

"Explain to me why the flowers appeared to be tampered with." He looked her directly in the eye. "Do you remember?"

"It's hard to forget. When you questioned me about them, I thought you were accusing me of murder."

"You're not off the hook yet, and don't forget it." He smiled, probably hoping to butter her up. "If pokeweed was used as the murder weapon, and I'm not confirming it was, mind you, why were the flowers disturbed?"

Good question. She was surprised she hadn't questioned it herself. Though she knew pokeweed was indeed the substance that had killed Nancy, she was smart enough not to reveal that information to the sheriff or their fragile truce would be wrecked. "Now that you mention it, something is odd."

"Can you explain it?"

"I can't very well put myself into the mind of a murderer," she said, looking at him shrewdly. "Besides, you didn't give me much to go on when you initially mentioned the tampered flowers."

"Our investigation had only begun at that point, and then it went in other directions. The flowers still have me stumped.

"I understand how you feel because now they're bugging me too." She flashed him a smile, glad they were cooperating. It sure beat yelling at each other. "I can't picture Nancy messing with the flowers. For one thing, she would appreciate their beauty and at the most touch them delicately, like you would any pretty flower you're admiring."

The sheriff wore a blank look on his face. She felt sorry for his wife—she probably didn't receive too many "just because" flowers from the staid lawman.

"There's also the fact that spiderwort can cause a minor skin irritation in some people. Nancy was aware of that and even sensitive to it, just like me. It can produce dreadful blistery sores if you're not careful when handling it."

"So it's not likely she's the one who disturbed them."

"No doubt at all. She would have probably gotten after her husband if he touched them."

"Would he have listened?"

"What do you mean?" She probed, knowing he wouldn't give much away.

"If you've been canvassing the town asking questions, you know the Meyers had a rocky marriage of late."

"Yes, we've heard the rumors." Kristen shook her head. "It sounds like Ted's infidelity has been going on for some time."

"Maybe Nancy had her own affair recently just to get back at Ted." The sheriff was staring into space, probably not aware he had given away a useful tip.

"I heard that from one source, but nothing definite." Now was the time to come clean on what all they'd learned that morning, so she enlightened him with the details. He took notes and asked for clarification on some items. At least he seemed to take her seriously this time.

"Barney? Are you sure?" He scribbled another line in his notebook. "And Patricia? How in the world did you get people to name names? This sheds a whole new light on the investigation."

"I'll feel better knowing you're going to pursue them as suspects. I'd feel very uncomfortable doing so. After all, they were with me when we found Nancy. I had no reason to think one of them could have harmed her."

"I'm glad there are boundaries to your investigative capabilities," said the sheriff dryly.

Kristen chuckled, not believing she'd made mention of questioning suspects. "I'm still wondering about the flowers. If the murderer is the one who tampered with them, that's strange. After all, the vase of flowers is what made you realize Nancy's death may not have been due to natural causes. Why would the murderer want you to make the connection that poisonous plants were used, even if it was possibly pokeweed and not one of the flowers in the centerpieces? It doesn't make sense."

He shook his head. "No, it doesn't, unless they were trying to pin the blame on wildflowers being the murder method—and you being the murderer!"

Kristen jumped out of her chair. "That's utterly ridiculous!"

"Calm down, I know that. You may be ornery and stubborn, but we've fully checked you out and are satisfied you probably didn't poison Nancy."

"Probably? So you were only trying to strong arm me earlier?" she scoffed. "What possible motive could I have?"

"Maybe you were one of Ted's lovers."

Even though Kristen knew he was only saying it to get her goat, she felt the urge to gag.

"No, I suppose you're too happy with your forester friend to want to have a torrid affair with a married man." He actually winked at her.

She was amazed at the man's mood swings. They'd practically been swinging punches at each other a few minutes ago, and now they were joking around. "I'm glad you can see the best in me," she said wryly. "I was fully occupied with Brett that evening, so I didn't have time to poison a good friend during appetizers or even notice anything unusual. By the way, do you know when she was actually poisoned?"

"We're still researching how long it takes for pokeweed to do its damage."

225

"So pokeweed was pinpointed as the cause?" She'd finally nabbed him and was gloating. "I thought you weren't sure." She vowed to search online for more information about the toxic plant. If Nancy had ingested pokeweed earlier in the day, that would alter the focus of the investigation.

"We're still waiting on the official results," he said vaguely. "And timing could be key."

"Exactly. I just assumed she was poisoned at Barney's. If she was poisoned beforehand, that would change the suspect list." She looked at him and smiled engagingly. "You wouldn't mind sharing the list of suspects, would you?"

"No, that's off limits. Surely you know that."

"I thought it might be worth a shot."

Sheriff Miller stood to leave. "I appreciate your time. I know how busy you are between running your business here and sticking your nose into the murder case. But now that I've officially told you to stop interfering, I know you'll heed the warning."

"Certainly, Sheriff." She was already pondering what to do next, but this time she'd make sure he didn't find out about it.

He left, nodding at Hope before exiting the building. Hope watched him go before stepping into Kristen's office. "That must have been quite a conversation."

"It sure was, but thankfully we parted on good terms." Kristen was clicking onto the internet to study up on pokeweed. She'd been so busy checking out background information and suspects that she hadn't finished her research on the murder method. Her search didn't glean much more than what she'd learned previously. Evidentially most deaths caused by this plant were accidental. Most people wouldn't think to use the plant as a method for murder, she reasoned.

She skimmed through the pages listed on the search site. She found it interesting that the toxins were more powerful if injected into the body cavity, rather than taken orally. "Do they know how Nancy received the poison?" she asked Hope, who was peering at the pages over Kristen's shoulder.

"No, but I can ask. We both assumed it was in her food or drink, but since many of her dishes were cleared away, I don't know if they were able to pinpoint the exact cause."

"And even if they did, we're not privy to that information." Kristen smiled. "Maybe the fiancée of one of the deputies would know."

Hope stared at her blankly, then reddened visibly and stammered. "Are you referring to me?"

Kristen had been teasing her friend, but there must be some truth in the statement. "Sheriff Miller let something slip, but I thought he misspoke." She looked Hope directly in the eyes. "Is it true?"

Hope's face got even redder, and she wasn't as prone to blushing as Kristen. "Believe it or not, we got engaged over the weekend. With everything that's been happening, I hadn't told you yet."

Though Kristen was ecstatic for her friend, she couldn't help but feel a little hurt that she'd learned the news from the sheriff. "But it's wonderful news!" She hugged her friend. "I only wish I'd heard it from you first!"

Hope looked guilty. "After what we've been through the past few days, I wanted things to calm down a bit first. Evidently Todd must have shared our engagement at work."

Kristen tried to lighten the moment. "Since Sheriff Miller is a top notch investigator, maybe he discovered it on his own."

"The way gossip spreads in this town," Hope said, rolling her eyes, "Todd could have only confided in one person, and it went from there."

"I understand why you wanted to wait before sharing the news, so no harm done."

Hope looked relieved. "I'm glad you feel that way. I wouldn't have wanted to upset my maid of honor."

Kristen squealed and hugged her friend again. "Oh, how exciting! I'll do whatever I can to help you! I think the world of you both, and I'm so happy for you!"

"Great, I was hoping you'd feel that way. We'd love to hold the reception here, in the Red Barn."

"Of course! Once we get this murder solved, we'll get busy planning the details."

"Which is exactly why I wanted to hold off telling you, though it's been really hard. I've been about to burst!"

"I'm glad I found out. Some good news is just what I needed today."

"Getting back to your original question, Todd didn't mention exactly how the poison was administered. I suppose the autopsy results would show an injection site if there was one."

"If it were injected, it would have to be someone extremely close to Nancy, like Ted. I can't picture him poisoning her at home, and then showing up for dinner afterwards. That's crazy."

"I agree. The poison was most likely added to the drinks or food she ate at Barney's. Didn't you say she was drinking red wine?"

"Yes, she had a glass on the table, and if she'd had a glass in the bar before they'd sat down to dinner, the poison would have had time to act sooner."

"Unless she started off with a cocktail at home," said Hope thoughtfully, "Which would again point to Ted being the one to kill her."

"Ted doesn't seem the type to kill his wife with a poison he extracted from a plant."

"You're right. It had to be someone with the knowledge to squeeze or grind up the plant parts to put them in her drink."

"I'm surprised she wouldn't have noticed a strange taste in her wine."

"If it was a heavy red like a cabernet or merlot, the wine flavor would help to mask the poison."

"Even so, I can't imagine she wouldn't have noticed plant chunks floating about." Kristen's mind was racing. "Maybe the plant was grated and mixed with her salad greens.

"I think you're onto something. Between all the veggies, shredded cheese, croutons, and salad dressing, it would be simple to mask the sight and flavor of the pokeweed."

"I read that the roots are the most poisonous part of the plant. Besides, the berries aren't even ripe yet, so their juice couldn't be squeezed into her wine," Kristen reasoned aloud. "It makes most sense that someone working at Barney's did it. I can't imagine someone stopping by their table and adding poison to her salad."

Hope nodded in agreement. "Surely someone would have noticed, unless someone else was distracting Nancy. Ted could have even known about it. It's too bad her salad plate was already cleared away."

"If the person who did it worked at Barney's, he would have been keeping an eye on her so he could get rid of the evidence as soon as she finished eating." Kristen shuddered. "The whole thing makes me nauseous."

"Which is why we need to discover who made Nancy sick as soon as possible."

"Unfortunately, I have no idea how to do that, but it's becoming increasingly obvious that someone working at Barney's that night was responsible. We let ourselves get carried away asking questions all around town when the answer is staring us in the face.

"I don't think our background work was a waste of time," reasoned Hope. "I bet Barney and his crew must be pretty nervous right now."

"I wouldn't want to be in their shoes." Kristen felt a sudden urge to get outdoors and sweat off her frustrations. It would do her some good to check the trails for hikers and routine maintenance. "Listen, I'm headed outside for a little while. Do you think it would be a good idea to contact Amber and Olivia to see if one of them can man the shop tomorrow afternoon while we're attending Nancy's memorial service? By the way, did I mention Brett is going too? We're going to spend the rest of the afternoon together, so I won't be coming back here." She couldn't help but feel giddy at the prospect, despite the situation.

Hope picked up the phone to call the two teenaged sisters who volunteered at the Nature Station as often as their busy schedules would allow. "I'll ask them right now if they're free. I'm sure we can work something out. If not, we'll just close for the afternoon. We don't have anything scheduled other than prep work for Thursday's Nature Camp. Most of the hikers will probably be gone by noon anyway if it stays this hot. Besides, I'd guess half the town of Eklund will attend Nancy's service. Whatever we do, I want you and Brett to enjoy your time together."

"Do you think the killer will show up?"

"It's a possibility. The thought of it gives me the shivers, though I know nothing bad will happen in a church full of mourners."

"Who would have thought something bad would happen in a restaurant full of diners?"

"That's true, but it's not a comforting thought."

"By the way, shouldn't we order flowers or a plant to be delivered to the church on behalf of the Nature Station?"

"You're right. After all, we told Robert we were ordering something when we asked him for a contribution. We should follow through on that."

"Bringing her killer to light would have been more important to her than remembering to order flowers. Still, it will be a nice touch."

"Don't worry, I'll take care of it."

"I'd appreciate it. If everything's in order here, I'm heading out to the prairie to check if the trails need to be mowed after last night's rain. Then I'll head into the forest. I'll be back in a bit." She hurried out the door, anxious to be outside to work off some of her nervous energy. With all the comfort food she'd been indulging in during the murder investigation, burning calories while working wouldn't be a bad idea either. She hadn't taken time to exercise that morning, and it felt good to stretch her limbs.

She strolled along the trail on the perimeter of the prairie, more interested in walking among the plants that had been the topic of discussion in recent days than checking the mowing situation. She hoped something would jump out at her if she were in the thick of things. She noted all three of the flowers that had been in the vase blooming right along the trail. Spiderwort, butterfly milkweed, and foxglove beardtongue growing together, their vivid colors and unusual blossoms mingling with the grasses growing behind them. She stared at them, not so much mesmerized by their beauty, but pondering all the factors they'd discovered relating to Nancy's murder case.

As the sheriff had pointed out, why had someone disturbed the flowers in the vase on Ted and Nancy's table? Was someone trying to pin the blame on her? If so, thank goodness it wasn't working. The sheriff seemed satisfied she hadn't done it. In fact, drawing attention to the wildflowers was a stupid move that only pointed to the fact that a plant had been used to poison Nancy. She couldn't believe a normal autopsy or related tests would be on the lookout for an obscure poison like pokeweed.

She was deep in thought as she walked the edge of the prairie. The plants seemed to have grown several inches overnight. Between last night's shower and the days of high humidity, the plants were thriving. Soon the flowers in bloom would be finished for the season, and others would take their place. She looked around, trying to decide which plants to select for the weekend fresh-cut wildflower order she provided to Barney. She speculated whether he would even want to continue his standing order, given the circumstances.

Before she forgot about it, she pulled her phone out of her shorts pocket and dialed the restaurant's number. A woman answered, sounding out of breath and anxious.

"Hello, Barney's. How may I help you?"

"Um, hello. This is Kristen Matthews at the Nature Station. May I please speak with Barney?"

The woman paused. "I'm afraid you can't."

"Oh, why not?" She was puzzled and starting to feel anxious herself. "Who am I speaking to?"

"It's Patricia. He's busy right now…talking again with Sheriff Miller. I wish he'd leave us alone."

"We'll all be glad to have this matter settled."

"They just keep bugging us. I'm sure you know what I mean."

"Yeah, I do." *How did Patricia know that? Was she the one who set me up?* "As a matter of fact, I talked to the sheriff earlier this afternoon. After all, we were all there when it happened."

"I guess. Did you want me to have Barney call you back?"

"That'd be great. I was calling to see if he wanted me to fill his order for centerpiece flowers for the weekend."

Patricia was still for a second. "Oh. Sure. Last week's arrangements were really pretty. I know the diners appreciated them."

Kristen pondered the significance of Patricia's remark. "I hope so, even if they're probably long forgotten in the big scheme of things."

Patricia cleared her throat and ended the call abruptly. "I'll let him know you called."

Kristen stared at the now silent phone curiously. What an odd conversation. The sooner this chaos was put in order, the better for everyone involved.

CHAPTER 21

After a busy morning at the Nature Station, Kristen rushed home at noon on Wednesday to change into something more suitable for Nancy's memorial service than her ratty old shorts and t-shirt. She pulled a slim black skirt and a sleeveless black and rose colored floral blouse from her closet She hopped in the shower to let the water wash away the grime of her morning's work. She and Hope had been bustling around preparing for the Nature Camp they were holding the next day. Feeling refreshed, she hurried through her routine, knowing Brett was due to pick her up soon.

She'd spent the previous evening alone, contemplating the case while she prepared food for the meal that would follow Nancy's service. She had dropped her contributions off at the church bright and early before work.

Her solitude had helped her achieve a clearer picture of the situation. She knew she was still missing some vital piece of information. She'd heard back from both her dad and Ruth Ann, but neither of them could contribute anything new; what they'd discovered only supported everything she'd learned so far. Ruth Ann had struck out in her quest to ask Barney for his staff and reservation list. Evidently he'd been warned by the sheriff not to share the information with the nature loving gals. Despite her disappointment, she had a hunch they were close to discovering the truth. With the information she had at her disposal, she felt Ted, Barney, and Patricia were the prime suspects. They had easier access to Nancy's food and drink and all knew she was planning to dine there that evening. They had all attended Nature Station events and perhaps gotten the idea to use pokeweed as the murder method afterwards. Kristen cringed at the thought. The goal of their events was to educate people about nature, not murder methods.

When it came to motive, she had to admit she was perplexed. She'd come to the conclusion that if Ted had done it, he merely wanted Nancy out of the way, or maybe access to the money she'd inherited. But what had provoked him to make such a drastic move after he'd been fooling around with other women for decades? And what about Barney? If he actually *were* having an affair with Nancy, it must have been some sort of jealousy provoked act—unless the intended victim was Ted, which made more sense. As far as Patricia, if she were the woman who met Nancy on Friday for lunch at Monty's, she could have killed Nancy, depending on the topic and outcome of their conversation. Patricia could have easily been one of Ted's many women. But why would she be more jealous of Ted's wife than any of Ted's other women? Kristen felt certain she was missing something key to the case.

She was determined to get to the bottom of it, and intended to keep her eyes peeled at the memorial service. Who knew what might happen there? She heard Brett's truck pull into the driveway just as she fastened her necklace. She felt her heart flutter in excitement. He was early.

She ran down the stairs as fast as her skirt would allow, careful not to trip on her heels. She met him at the back door, vowing to grab something to eat before they left.

"Hi," he said.

Boy, did he look handsome in his dress clothes. "Hello. Are you hungry?"

"Yeah, I am a little. I started work early so I could take off this afternoon. Then I had to drop Cassie off at the office and run home and change." He smiled engagingly. "I didn't take time to eat anything. Besides, I knew there was going to be a meal after the funeral."

Kristen was already rummaging in the refrigerator but paused at the mention of Cassie's name. "I've been rushing around too. Let's see if there's something in here to munch on before we leave. Otherwise, you'll be hearing my stomach grumble."

He laughed. "That's preferable to sitting through Nancy's service. I have to tell you, I'm not looking forward to it."

"Me either, but maybe we'll learn something new," she said, trying to be positive.

"Learn something? What kind of service is this going to be?"

"Oh, I meant learn something about Nancy's killer."

"Aren't you supposed to leave the detective work up to the sheriff and his crew?" His charming smile from earlier was replaced with a frown. "Haven't you done enough to help with the investigation? I can't imagine what you've been up to recently if you still have more leads to follow."

"That's just it. There *are* no leads. I'm just planning to pay attention to details, that's all. Normal people act strangely at these events. If the killer shows up, he or she is bound to stand out, wouldn't you think?"

"I wouldn't think the killer would dare to attend."

"It's been known to happen before." At least it did in the mysteries Kristen read. "And I plan to be on alert just in case it happens today." To change the subject, she handed him a block of cheese and some fruit. "Here, let me find some crackers and something to drink to go with those."

Soon they were scarfing down their lite lunch. "I'm sorry I gave you a hard time about working on this case," said Brett. "I know how important finding closure—and the killer—are to you."

"I appreciate it. Let's not discuss it any further, and I won't bring up Cassie."

"What does *she* have to do with anything?"

Oops. "Never mind. I didn't mean anything by that remark."

"I didn't think you minded when I talked about work."

"Of course I don't." She paused, suddenly at a loss for words.

Brett put his hand on her arm and pulled her close to him. "Then what's wrong?"

"Nothing. This is stupid, but you spend a lot of time with her."

He looked in her eyes. "Don't tell me you're jealous? You shouldn't be. She's just a co-worker. We get along well, but that's it."

Kristen felt a wave of embarrassment, then relief, wash over her. "I told you it was stupid, but that didn't stop me from worrying about it. Our relationship is still in the early stages, and you talk about her all the time," she stammered. "I thought you might really like her."

"I do like her, but not the way I like you," he said reassuringly. "So quit stressing about it!"

Kristen forced a smile. "Okay, I won't. Now let's finish up and get to the church. I have a feeling it will fill up fast."

"You're probably right." He touched her hair. "By the way, I didn't tell you how pretty you look today."

She blushed. "Thank you. You look rather dashing yourself." Whatever awkwardness they'd felt earlier was brushed away by the steamy kiss they shared, leaving them both breathless.

"We'd better get moving." Brett helped clear away what was left of their meal before escorting Kristen out the door.

Their lighthearted chatter made the drive into town pass quickly. However, they were both dreading the service. They arrived at the church several minutes early to find the street sides lined with cars and the parking lot full. Brett dropped her off at the entrance so she could secure them a seat while he tried to find a parking place.

Kristen entered the church and signed the guestbook, then scanned the sanctuary for a place to sit, preferring a spot near the back where she could keep an eye on any potentially suspicious activity. She had a feeling by the time the service started, it would be close quarters in the pews. She hoped Pastor Mike and the other people speaking didn't get long winded. The church was more than a hundred years old, and though the congregation had managed to raise funds for central air conditioning, it probably wouldn't be able to keep up today. Sure enough, it was already warm in the upper story of the old church. She fanned herself with the program, keeping a lookout for Brett as the place continued to fill. She could hear the low buzz of conversations all around her and spotted several people she knew. Her family was located several pews ahead of her, but she didn't approach them, not wanting to give up her seat. She also wanted to make the most of her time alone to scope out the situation.

Several dazzling floral arrangements stood at the front of the church along with a table covered with snapshots and mementos of Nancy. She felt her eyes grow misty. Nancy was full of life only a few days ago, and she lived her life to the fullest. Someone had cut her life short. That person must pay, she vowed to herself.

She craned her neck for a better view of Barney and Patricia, who sat two pews ahead with their heads close together. She was curious to know what her two prime suspects were discussing. She recognized other employees of the restaurant sitting near them. Ruth Ann sat with the Nature Station volunteers; Robert Wellington, David Steward, Shirley Larson, Carol Burnside, and even the younger Sara Martin were together.

She felt a hand on her shoulder and looked up to see Brett standing there. So much for being on the lookout for him, she thought as she scooted to the right to give him room to sit. People continued to file in, and soon the organist began to play.

She watched as Ted and the rest of Nancy's family filed slowly down the center aisle, their eyes cast downward and their expressions solemn. Kristen felt certain Nancy's children were deeply saddened by her death, but she wasn't so sure about her husband. Though his face was somber, she couldn't help but believe he was involved either directly or indirectly with his wife's death. He disgusted her, even more so after she'd seen him with the young chick coming out of Amy's on the previous day.

Kristen was surprised to see Marty from Swede's seated toward the front of the church. There had been no love lost between Nancy and Marty, but judging from the location of where she sat, she must have even arrived early to sit in the area normally reserved for family and close friends. Perhaps the murder had changed Marty's perspective on things, and she'd buried the hatchet, though there was no body available for burial, thought Kristen wryly. She saw Amy sitting a few rows ahead and wondered whether some of the downtown businesses had closed for the afternoon since half the town seemed to be in attendance. She hadn't paid any attention on the drive in; they'd been too intent on finding a parking place.

She felt the odd sensation of eyes boring into the back of her head, so she glanced around one last time before the service got underway. She about slid off the pew when she spotted Ted's latest conquest sitting in a row on the opposite aisle and a little behind her. She stared in shock at the girl, whose eyes also widened in recognition. Since they'd made eye contact, Kristen gave her a polite nod, though she wasn't feeling very polite. *Of all the nerve!* Something didn't sit right, and it wasn't just Kristen's rear end almost hitting the floor. She couldn't believe one of Ted's young hussies would dare to attend his wife's funeral. Then again, for all she knew, half the women here could have been romantically involved with the womanizing man, but at least they had the discretion not to flaunt themselves. She fumed inwardly for a few seconds then exhaled loudly in an attempt to bring some peace to her burdened mind. She wanted to focus her thoughts on the life of the woman she'd called her friend.

Pastor Mike led off with an opening prayer then started reciting the highlights of Nancy's life. Kristen had concentrated so hard on finding Nancy's killer she hadn't allowed herself to grieve for her friend. She felt tears glistening in her eyes and didn't care who saw them. She could hear the sniffles of others with the same emotions overcoming them, and felt Brett's arm go around her shoulders. Despite the heat and closeness inside the church, she welcomed his consoling touch. She leaned against his strong body, needing his comfort to make it through this difficult time.

Because Ted had rushed into holding this service, not only was everyone, or most everyone, grieving the loss of a prominent woman in the community, but there was still a murderer at large. Good grief, Nancy's body hadn't even been released. Kristen sniffed loudly at the thought, and Brett handed her his handkerchief and squeezed her shoulder. She smiled at him gratefully before turning her attention to the minister's soothing words.

They sat through the moving service for almost an hour, nearly sweltering in the increasingly warm church where the people were packed into pews like sardines. Kristen stood as soon as it was proper, lining up to exit the sanctuary and go down to the basement for the lunch that followed. She searched for the young woman who she'd seen right before the service started, wanting to point her out to Brett, but she wasn't to be seen, probably having slipped out earlier when the heat and emotionally charged eulogies became too much for her to bear.

Brett and Kristen filed into the crowded fellowship hall, which was thankfully cooler, trying to find a place to sit together. Everywhere they looked, small groups of people were huddled together, talking quietly and waiting for Pastor Mike to arrive and give the blessing so they could start eating. Kristen felt her stomach rumble, her quick lunchtime snack long forgotten. The stress of funerals made her even hungrier than usual, and the home-cooked food waiting on the serving tables was sure to provide not only sustenance but comfort to the mourners.

They found two chairs next to each other at a relatively empty corner table and hurried to claim them. Though she'd been sitting for the last hour, Kristen found herself drained of all energy. It felt good to rest on the normally uncomfortable folding chair while Brett sought out the drinks station with its pitchers of iced tea. He hadn't been gone but a moment when Barney, Patricia, and a couple of other restaurant employees approached the table.

"You don't mind if we sit here, do you?" asked Barney.

"Of course not." Kristen gestured for them to take the chairs across from her. "I've been wanting to talk to you anyway."

"Oh, that's right. I forgot to call you back. You left a message about flowers for this weekend."

"Yes, I did. I was wondering if you still wanted to continue your standing order."

"Why wouldn't I?" he said in a matter of fact manner.

Kristen shrugged her shoulders. "Since the centerpieces seem to be a focal point of the investigation, I thought you might want to discontinue buying wildflowers from us."

"Is there something I should know? Your plants didn't kill Nancy; something else did." He sounded adamant when replying.

"Okay, I'll plan on delivering them Friday afternoon, as usual."

"Sounds good. As you can imagine, we're trying to get back to business as usual at the restaurant."

"I know it must have been a rough week for you," Kristen said sympathetically. "For all of us, actually. And then we were shocked they decided to move ahead with Nancy's service so quickly.

Patricia jumped into the conversation with a prim retort. "I'm sure he had his reasons. It's not for us to judge."

Touchy, thought Kristen to herself, though she merely murmured, "Yes, I'm sure he did." She thought of the women who were probably already lining up for an opportunity to spend time with Ted. It appeared he'd gotten around plenty while he was married. Hard telling what he'd be like now that he didn't have marriage holding him back.

She spied him across the room. He stood next to Pastor Mike, looking around nervously while he waited for the meal to begin. When his shrewd eyes landed on Kristen's, she shuddered and looked away quickly. In that moment she could believe him capable of murdering his own wife.

Meanwhile, back at her own table, she sat with two other strong suspects; she planned to make the most of the situation. She turned her attention to Patricia, who had seemed friendly the night of Nancy's death, but had come across pricklier in the conversations they'd had since then. She supposed everyone was on edge, and if she'd had anything to do with the murder, it was only logical she wouldn't be acting very pleasantly to someone trying to root out answers.

"You're relatively new to Eklund, aren't you?"

Patricia stared at her suspiciously before answering with one simple word. "Yes."

"Where are you originally from?"

"I lived in the Quad City area for the past twenty years."

Kristen speculated as to why the woman would move from the metropolitan area that spanned both the Illinois and Iowa sides of the Mississippi River to the small town of Eklund. She continued her probing under the guise of making small talk with her tablemate. "Really, what did you do there?"

Patricia seemed to let her guard down a little and expanded more on Kristen's question. "I worked in a few places during the time I lived there. My most recent job was at a health food store, one of those shops in the revamped River District."

Kristen nodded, knowing there were several eclectic shops in that area. She contemplated why Patricia would decide to move to a town where its inhabitants drove an hour away to the Quad Cities for additional shopping and cultural options. "Do you like it here?"

"Oh, yes! I grew up in a small town, so I'm used to the dynamics. Since I'm getting close to retirement, I decided to sell my house and move here. I bought a smaller home and still had some money left over to invest."

"I'm sure the cost of living is quite a bit cheaper here." Kristen wondered why Patricia chose Eklund and not some other town. She hadn't said where she grew up.

"Much cheaper. And thank goodness I found a great job at Barneys that pays pretty well." She smiled at her boss.

Was something going on between them? Kristen couldn't imagine Patricia would earn a huge salary in her hostess position, but Kristen hadn't been in the work force for a few years. She couldn't believe how suspicious she had become. She was discovering that when tracking down a murderer, she couldn't afford to be too naïve. She'd had her eyes opened about the people who lived in what she had once considered the perfect town of Eklund.

"Well, I'm glad you like it here. We're proud of our town."

Just then Brett returned holding two glasses of iced tea, with Hope and Todd trailing behind him. Kristen's face lit up with a broad smile when she saw her friends. "Glad you could join us."

"Are you sure there's enough room?" asked Hope.

"Sure, we'll scoot a little closer and grab an extra chair," said Brett.

Kristen glanced over at Todd, who was dressed in his deputy uniform. She wondered whether he was attending in an official capacity, checking out the behavior of those who had come to pay their last respects. "I hear congratulations are in order!" She noticed Brett looking at her questionably.

Todd also noticed Brett's expression. "Didn't Kristen tell you we're engaged?"

"I only found out yesterday," Kristen reminded them while looking meaningfully at Hope. "And by accident, actually." She told them how the sheriff had inadvertently informed her, and the group laughed.

"I'll be happy to offer you a bid to hold the rehearsal dinner." Barney was always trying to drum up new business.

"We'd appreciate that," said Hope. "We haven't even set a date yet. Todd's been pretty busy the past few days."

"Yes, I've had the pleasure of talking with him and his colleagues a few times," said Barney smoothly. "I have an idea. Why don't the four of you stop by afterwards for a drink, on the house, of course!"

"Unfortunately, Todd needs to get back to work," said Hope. "Perhaps another time? We can discuss menu and price options then."

"We'll schedule something soon." He looked at Kristen and Brett. "Why don't you two come on over? I'd like to make it up to you after your disastrous meal on Saturday night."

Brett raised his eyebrows at Kristen. She guessed he didn't care whether they went or not and was leaving it up to her. "That's not necessary, Barney. What happened the other night wasn't any fault of yours." *Actually, maybe it was, or maybe it was the fault of someone who worked for him.*

"No, I insist. I'd love to have you back again for a complimentary dinner, but I'll bet you won't be hungry after this meal." He looked toward the food tables, which by now had lines of people filling their plates along both sides.

"No, probably not, but if you insist, we'll stop by for a quick drink." She figured she could take a look at the restaurant again and maybe remember something important about that fateful night. Besides, a glass of wine would hit the spot after this action packed day.

"Perfect. Come on over as soon as we're done here. It looks like it's our turn to get in line."

Kristen and the others stood to walk toward the serving tables. She noticed Sheriff Miller standing in the corner, holding a plastic drink cup. His expression was dour, and she wondered if it was intended for her as a reminder to discontinue her involvement in the case—or for one of her suspicious tablemates. Whoever he was directing it at, she didn't like the way he looked.

CHAPTER 22

Even tottering along in her dressy heels, Barney's was within easy walking distance from the church for Kristen. She and Brett took their time, wanting to talk alone before being on public display at the restaurant, which was sure to be crowded with those stopping by after work for a drink. They'd chatted briefly with her family and a few other friends who also attended the funeral. After such an emotional afternoon, she preferred to go straight home, or somewhere else not connected with Nancy's murder, but she felt obligated to drop by Barney's. She also felt something else, but she couldn't quite describe it. Even though she wanted to take a closer look at the place where Nancy had died, she had a terrible feeling about returning to the crime scene.

"Why don't we just make an appearance, have a drink, and then head for home," she said. "I'm dying to get out of this skirt and heels and into something more comfortable." Brett wiggled his eyebrows at her, and she responded with a giggle, playfully slapping him on the arm.

"Sorry, I wasn't exactly sure what you meant by that remark," he said and laughed good-naturedly.

"If you'd ever worn a tight skirt and high heels on a hot and humid day, you'd know *exactly* what I'm talking about."

"Fortunately for both of us, that's never happened."

"That's a relief. I've been thinking. If we have to go to Barney's, we may as well make the most of it. I plan to take a peek in the ladies room and see if I can remember anything."

"I'm sure whatever may have been there when Nancy died is long gone." He grimaced, probably remembering the state Nancy was in when they found her body.

"You're probably right, but I'm hoping if I take another look, a memory or something I've overlooked will be triggered."

"You know it's not up to you. The sheriff is taking care of the investigation. The look he gave you earlier said it all."

"Yeah, it said to 'back off,' didn't it?"

"Pretty much. You should heed his advice." He sighed. "It's pointless for me to tell you that."

"It's taken you long enough to figure that out," she said and chuckled.

By the time they reached Barney's, the parking lot was already half full, even though the eatery had only just opened upon Barney's return. They walked in from the bright sunlight to the dimly lit restaurant and lounge. Kristen paused a moment to let her eyes adjust as she turned toward Brett.

"Can you please order me a glass of wine? I need to freshen up in the ladies room."

He shook his head at her. "I'll order your drink, but you're wasting your time."

"No, I'm not. I really do need to reapply my lipstick, and do other things women don't mention when they say they're 'freshening up,'" she said with an impish grin.

She sauntered off toward the ladies room, trying to ignore the negative vibes radiating from its direction. Despite her offhand remark to Brett, she was worried she would remember something from that awful night. But if something helpful came from the memory, it would be worthwhile. She told herself to stop being so silly. Besides, if something bad happened to her, she knew she could count on Brett to come check on her, unlike Ted, who had neglected Nancy in her time of need, and probably throughout their entire marriage.

She took a deep breath and entered the brightly lit bathroom. She smelled the characteristic disinfectant smell, covered with a more pleasantly scented air freshener. She paused to check her hair and make-up, then took another breath before entering the stall where Nancy had died. She flung open the door, surprised to see it looked just like a normal stall in a business restroom. What had she expected? To find a wineglass containing poison residue or a note of confession from the killer?

She scanned the bathroom one last time and scrubbed her hands and arms vigorously with hot, soapy water. Feeling physically and emotionally cleansed, she left the restroom and walked toward the lounge where Brett was waiting for her at a low table with two comfortable armchairs. Their drinks had already been delivered, and Kristen took a bracing sip of wine.

"Ah, much better." She looked around to see if Barney was in the vicinity and lowered her voice. "After the way Barney and Patricia were acting earlier, maybe I should have sniffed the wine or checked it out more thoroughly before knocking back a swig so quickly."

"Don't worry, I made sure it was kosher while I was waiting for you." He winked. "Now don't keep me in suspense. What happened?"

"Nothing, which is fine with me," she said, though she couldn't help but be disappointed. She'd had a strong feeling something would click today.

"Let's just relax. That's what we'd planned on doing this afternoon, even if we didn't plan on ending up here."

"You're right." She leaned back in her chair and was tempted to kick off her heels and prop her feet up on the table. She swirled the wine in her glass and willed herself to unwind and enjoy a rare afternoon off with Brett. She looked around the room and noticed Patricia scurrying about seating guests and doing other jobs that were required of her hostess position. All at once it struck her, Patricia reminded her of someone. She couldn't pinpoint exactly who. Patricia had opened up somewhat about her past, but Kristen still sensed she was holding something back. Could that something pertain to Nancy's death?

"What's on your mind?" asked Brett, following her gaze.

"She reminds me of someone, but I have no idea whom."

"I almost hate to encourage your sleuthing, but it's funny you should mention it. I got the same feeling."

Kristen chose to ignore his jab about her sleuthing, knowing he just wanted her to remain safe. "Do you mean you recognize her from somewhere, or does she remind you of someone?"

"I don't know," he said, glancing again at the older woman.

"I'm afraid if I ask her more about her background she'd only clam up, and since she's new in town, not many know her."

"Except for her co-workers…" His voice trailed off as he watched Patricia speak with a woman who had just entered the front door. "What in the world is Cassie doing here?"

Kristen swiveled around to look at the hostess station where Patricia was posted. She couldn't believe her eyes. She was talking to Ted's mysterious young woman. "That's Cassie…your summer intern?" she stammered.

"Yeah. I'll introduce you as soon as she's finished." His face didn't show anything other than curiosity. "I wonder what she's doing here. I gave her some work to do at the office."

"There's no need for an introduction. She's the woman I saw Ted with yesterday morning." She paused for effect. "And, she was sitting behind us in the church. I looked for her afterwards, but I couldn't find her."

"You're kidding me." Brett was silent for a moment, letting Kristen's words soak in. "She called in sick yesterday, which is when you saw her the first time, right?"

Kristen nodded and was amazed to witness the normally mild mannered man become irritated with his intern. She felt satisfaction wash over her when she realized there really *was* nothing romantic going on between them. She should have taken Brett's word for it, but it was better to witness it with her own eyes. Putting those feelings aside, she wondered why Cassie was talking to Patricia, and then it hit her full force—there was a remarkable resemblance between the two women. Were they related?

She continued to watch them, not caring whether she was being rude. Why would Cassie lie to Brett? He'd been impressed with the woman's work ethics, and then she skipped out of work two days in a row. What was Cassie's relationship to Ted, and more importantly, to Patricia? It looked as if Cassie and Patricia were wrapping up their conversation, which is what Brett had been waiting for before he made his move. He stalked over to the entryway in an attempt to confront Cassie before she left the building. *This wasn't going to be pretty.*

Not one to cause a scene in public, Brett took hold of Cassie's elbow and steered her outdoors. Kristen was dying to eavesdrop on their conversation, but she knew she could rely on Brett to fill her in on the details. She'd wait patiently indoors and finish her drink in the cool comfort of the lounge. She let her gaze wander around the dining area, where a few people who were crowded out of the busy bar area were sitting at tables with drinks and appetizers. The early bird diners would soon be arriving. It appeared business was brisk at Barneys. Not bad for a restaurant where a suspicious death by poison took place only a few days ago. Customers were either extremely loyal or perhaps a bit nosey. She recognized several people who had been at the funeral. She supposed many people thought a stiff drink was in order after such an emotional memorial service. She looked at her own glass that was almost empty. She agreed.

As if anticipating her thoughts, a waitress delivered a fresh glass of the crisp white wine and a frosty bottle of beer for Brett. "We didn't order another round."

The young waitress smiled. "Barney told me to keep an eye on you and make sure your glass was full."

"I appreciate that, but this had better be my last glass." She wondered why Barney was so keen on making sure she had enough to drink. Was he hoping to loosen her tongue, or was his reason more sinister? All joking aside, perhaps she should be cautious. She leaned closer to the woman and lowered her voice. "Were you working here on Saturday night?"

"Yes, I had the misfortune to be scheduled for the dinner shift. But then we all were on call Saturday night."

"Were you Ted and Nancy's server?" She nodded toward the table where the couple had eaten their last meal together.

"No, they weren't seated at one of my tables, but I did refill their water glasses as a courtesy."

"Did you notice anything peculiar?"

"Not really, it was so hectic in here. It was all I could do to keep up with my tables. It was a good thing we had some extra help that night."

"Extra help? You mean someone not on Barney's regular payroll?"

"Yeah, one of the other waitress's boyfriend stopped by to see her on her break and ended up helping wash dishes, and Patricia's daughter was here working too."

Patricia had a daughter? *Was it Cassie?* "I'm sure Barney told Sheriff Miller everyone who was working here that night, including the extras."

The waitress shrugged. "I would hope so, but you never know with Barney."

What was that remark supposed to mean? Before Kristen could ask, the waitress flitted off to take an order at another table. She was still digesting the fact that Cassie, formerly known as Curly Q, could have been there that night.

She seemed to be popping up everywhere, which was disturbing.

Just then, Brett strode in through the front door with a grim look on his face. He sunk in the chair next to Kristen and sighed. "That was pleasant."

She leaned over and patted him on the arm. "Here's an ice cold beer, compliments of Barney. Now tell me what happened."

"I'm going to have to file a report on her, which is a real bummer. Besides the fact that I've enjoyed working with Cassie and having some extra help, I don't have time to mess with the paperwork involved."

"I can understand that. Your regular paperwork is bad enough."

"That's right. I questioned her on what she was doing here this afternoon, and she spilled the beans that she was talking to her mom." He nodded in the direction of the hostess station. "Patricia."

"I figured that out while you were outside." She smiled smugly.

"How in the world?" He took a long swig of beer. "Never mind. I know how you operate. Did you also hear that she was here Saturday night? She was helping in the kitchen."

That correlated with what the waitress had just let slip. "Why didn't she reveal that tidbit to you earlier?"

"I have no idea. We've been talking about the murder all week. I think it's strange she never mentioned she was here."

Kristen also thought it odd. "It sounds like she's been acting strange. Playing hooky from work, being seen with the widower of Nancy, showing up at her funeral, and now we learn she was here that night. Something doesn't smell right." Kristen's mood had reverted to disliking Cassie, now for a different reason than her being after Brett.

"Maybe she's trying not to draw attention to her mother's possible role in Nancy's death."

Kristen chewed on that for a moment. She could only hope Barney had passed on the entire list of people who were here that evening. She could picture him supplying only the partial list to appease the sheriff, probably in an effort to brush those he considered inconsequential under the carpet to avoid having them undergo questioning. He was a nice guy who probably thought that was the right thing to do. In Kristen's mind, when a murder took place, the definitions of right and wrong differed from their usual meanings. It wouldn't hurt to alert the sheriff to the fact that other people were on site who may not have been accounted for. Oh, how she dreaded that conversation. Still, it needed to be done.

She noticed a glare of bright light, signifying the front door had opened. Sure enough, someone else had entered the busy restaurant, and lo and behold, it was the widower himself, Ted Meyers. As he stood in the foyer, waiting to be seated, he looked at the same time younger than his years and older than his true age. Standing alone, his face emitted vulnerability and bewilderment, which was understandable after everything he'd been through the past few days. Kristen was struck by an earthshattering thought. Somehow his expression reminded her of another person she'd seen just moments ago.

CHAPTER 23

"Come on, Brett. We need to get out of here."

He stared at her incredulously. "What's the matter with you? You look like you've seen a ghost!"

"Actually, I think I have!" She stood to leave. "I've had a revelation."

"Oh?" He threw some money on the table for their waitress. "Then we'd better get out of here right away."

She waited until they were outside before she spoke. "Brett, I'm serious."

"Okay, sorry. I didn't mean to make light of the situation. It's just when you said 'revelation' you sounded a bit like a drama queen, which is not your usual persona, you'll have to admit."

"I know, but I'm not normally in the habit of chasing down potential murderers."

"I think it's quickly becoming a habit," he countered dryly.

She was growing exasperated with his joking manner, which normally enthralled her, when she suddenly felt ill at what she realized was a very important missing link. "Listen. I'm not trying to be a drama queen. It's just that something important finally clicked, and we need to get to Sheriff Miller right away."

He sobered quickly. "What's going on inside that pretty head of yours?"

They were walking through the crowded parking lot behind the building to reach the sidewalk that led back to where Brett's truck was parked, via a shortcut to the Sheriff's Department first. "You aren't going to believe this, but I think Ted Meyers is..."

Just then a voice spoke up from behind a parked SUV. "Ted Meyers is *what*?"

Kristen felt her heels sink into the fine, cushy gravel, and she almost toppled over. The infamous Cassie was standing before them with an evil look marring her pretty features. Kristen stumbled for the right words as she nearly fell into Cassie. "Ted is not a nice person," she said rather feebly.

"Really? I think that's a matter of opinion."

"I'm sure you're bound to have one about him, considering he's your *father*!"

Brett put his arm around her in an effort to show his support. "Kristen, what's come over you? You're not acting like your normal cheery self." He looked questioningly at Cassie. "And neither are you!"

"I'm not feeling very cheerful at the moment, that's all. This woman"—Kristen pointed her finger directly at Cassie—"is not only related to Patricia, but also to Ted."

"How in the world do you know that?" He looked at her incredulously, while at the same time pulling her even closer to him, sensing an element of danger to the situation.

"I saw the resemblance."

"That's all you're going on? You have no proof." Cassie spat out the words. "Besides, even if we are related, what difference does it make? It's nobody's business in this town full of busybodies."

Kristen's mind was busy processing the new information. What did it mean? If Ted was Cassie's father, and Patricia was her mother, any one of the three of them could have killed Nancy to get her out of the way. The big question was, which of them actually committed the horrible act? From the hostility radiating from Cassie, either she'd been the one to poison Nancy, or she knew who had done it and was protecting that person. Either way, Kristen had a hunch Cassie wasn't about to let the couple traipse off to tell the sheriff. How were they going to get out of this mess before things got ugly?

"You're right, it's none of our business, and we wouldn't be busybodies if we didn't have a dead one on our hands. By the way, I don't believe we've formally met." Kristen held out her hand, willing it not to shake as she reached for Cassie's hand. "I'm Kristen Matthews."

Cassie ignored her attempt at politeness. "I know who you are, you fool."

Brett put a restraining hand on Cassie's arm, although the action did little to calm the volatile and increasingly un-balanced girl. "Cassie, we're not here to hurt you. Let's just talk this out. Or you don't have to tell us a thing. If that's the case, we'll just be leaving."

"Get your hands off me! I thought you weren't like all the other men I've known. I trusted you, and now you're ready to turn me in for missing a few hours of work."

"It's not that simple. I'm your supervisor, and you're an intern. I'm accountable to my boss for your actions."

Kristen stood watching the situation unfold. From the remark she'd just made to Brett, she wondered if Cassie was resentful of how Ted had possibly treated her and Patricia, or was trying to protect him. Either way, she didn't want to tangle with her. While Brett tried to reason with Cassie, Kristen slowly reached into her purse, trying to slide her phone out far enough to dial 911. If they couldn't reach the department to talk to the sheriff, she'd try her darnedest to bring the law to them.

Cassie spotted Kristen's attempted maneuver. "Don't even think about it. I know what you're up to. You're probably trying to reach one of your multiple police contacts. I've heard about you." She glared again at Brett. "You're all he ever talks about."

Kristen filed away that scrap of information for future reference. She'd enjoy mulling the remark over once they were clear of this mess. "That's good to know."

"It's disgusting how he prattles on about how golden you are." This time she glowered at Kristen. "And I don't mean your hair. You can do no wrong in his eyes. How could I stand a chance compared to you?"

Golden? This was new to her. She had plenty of faults, but it was good to know Brett was able to look past them. "I didn't realize you'd set your sights on your boss. That's probably not a wise career move." And probably not wise to mention it to the unstable young woman, although Kristen couldn't resist prodding her.

"Oh, shut up. I know how you've been snooping around, sticking your nose into places it shouldn't be, just because you were friends with Nancy." She spat out the name with a contemptuous sneer.

"To tell you the truth, I'd be curious about any dead body I happened to find in the bathroom. But yes, Nancy was a friend."

"And now I suppose you think you have it all figured out."

Kristen bluffed the best she knew how. "No, I don't understand any of it."

Brett tugged Kristen by the arm. "I think it's time we go."

"Hold on. You're not going anywhere."

"You're right. This is getting us *nowhere*," said Kristen heatedly. She linked her arm in Brett's and started to walk away from the enraged girl who'd looked so sweet and guileless the other times they'd run into each other. To emphasize her true demeanor, Cassie yanked hard on Kristen's free arm. Taken by surprise, Kristen stumbled once again in the cursed heels. She vowed never to wear the wretched contraptions again. In the meantime, she wasn't going to let this ill-mannered woman overpower two strong adults. Neither was Brett. Before she could react, he lunged toward Cassie, who managed to pull a knife out of nowhere.

Perfect. Now what? They may be two capable adults, but they were unarmed against the spiteful Cassie, who was wielding what appeared to be a knife she probably used for field work. The crude knife was not designed to kill anyone; nevertheless, it could do some serious damage. Kristen still didn't know what the truth was, but she was determined to find out and put Cassie in her place. Brett appeared stunned for a second before making an unsuccessful move to grab the knife. He dropped his hold on Kristen, who then twisted her ankle and fell to the ground.

She couldn't believe this was happening in broad daylight in a parking lot full of vehicles. It's not like they were attacked in a dark, big city back alley. Though the entire confrontation had so far consumed mere minutes, and they were in the more deserted section of the lot, odds were good they would be spotted soon. What was Cassie thinking? She must have gone off the deep end. Kristen still hadn't figured out who had killed Nancy, but it was obvious Cassie knew.

Since Brett and his intern were still battling over the knife, Kristen hoped Cassie wouldn't notice as she tried once again to pull her phone out of her purse to call 911. Just as she did so, Cassie jabbed the weapon into Brett's upper arm. Blood gushed from the wound; the sleeve of Brett's crisp white shirt quickly became soaked with the sticky red fluid. Kristen prayed the gash was only superficial as she watched her boyfriend struggle to subdue Cassie. After an initial wince from the pain, he fought even harder to free the knife from her hands.

Finally he landed a blow to her wrist that catapulted the knife underneath a nearby car that hugged the pavement. There was no way Cassie could wiggle her plump body beneath the car, but she headed that direction anyway. Brett pounced on her in a tackle worthy of an NFL player, not caring one iota if he injured his intern as he brought her to the ground.

Kristen scrambled to join in the game, adding her weight to Brett's by sitting on top of Cassie's still struggling body. She grabbed her phone and rapidly punched in the numbers that would send them help. The dispatcher had just answered when Ted burst on the scene, a horrified look on his haggard face.

"What on earth is going on here? Leave her alone."

"She just tried to kill us!" Kristen shouted indignantly while still on line with the operator. "Thank goodness help is on its way."

Ted froze, looking confused. Cassie had quit fighting long enough to allow Brett time to strip off his shirt and wind it tightly around his wounded arm. Ted's eyes widened at the sight of the bloody gash. He took a step back just as the wail of sirens filled the air.

Because the sheriff's department was only a couple of blocks away, two squad cars roared into the lot within a minute of Kristen's call, braking just a few feet away from the group. An ambulance arrived right behind them. Medical personnel jumped out, quickly surveyed the situation, and went to work on Brett's arm as soon as the police had Cassie under control.

"What's going on here?" bellowed Sheriff Miller, his gun drawn and aimed directly at Cassie. He assumed Kristen and Brett were in the right for once, which was a relief.

Kristen scowled in Cassie's direction. "We were on our way to tell you that we'd learned how this woman is related to two prime suspects."

"How do you know who our prime suspects are?" The sheriff kept talking while his officers worked to secure Cassie.

"Anyone with reasonable deduction abilities could figure that out," Kristen countered, her confidence returning now that law enforcement had arrived on the scene. She gave him a brief rundown on what she and Brett had learned during their afternoon cocktail hour at Barney's.

"We'll determine what happened." He nodded at Ted. "I'm afraid you'll have to come along with us." He spoke quietly to Todd, who left the lot and walked swiftly toward the restaurant.

Kristen assumed he was on an errand to seek out Patricia, and they'd sort out the entire matter back at the department. She was dying with curiosity since she'd been in on the investigation from the start. She suspected the situation which led to Nancy's brutal murder started around twenty years ago. With all the information she had contributed, she felt she'd earned the right to know the entire story.

Kristen's attention was drawn back to Cassie, who was muttering as she was escorted to the sheriff's cruiser. "But I just wanted us to be a family," she heard Cassie say. She felt a lump rise in her throat and almost conjured up pity for the girl. Nancy didn't deserve to die, but everyone deserved a chance to have a complete and happy family life.

Once Cassie was safely inside the cruiser, the sheriff turned to them. "Why don't you both join us at the station? We'll take your statements there and then send you on your way."

Kristen glanced at Brett, who by now had a heavy bandage wrapped around his arm. "Are you okay?"

"Yeah, they patched me up well enough to make a statement. Luckily, the knife only grazed the surface, even if it bled like crazy. I'd prefer to get the statement out of the way as soon as possible."

"Me, too." She threw her arms around him, avoiding his wound, but hanging on for dear life. She rejoiced in the fact that they were both safe, and she felt satisfied to know they'd helped catch the killer. Though she didn't understand the details, or who had been the one to actually poison Nancy, the full story would come to light soon. That was good enough for now.

* * *

By the time they finally left the sheriff's department, the sun was sinking low in the sky. Beautiful shades of gold and orange mixed with traces of reds and purples. After being inside the stuffy and drab interior of the department for hours, Kristen relaxed and felt ecstatic as she stared at the beautiful sunset and enjoyed the gentle breeze. The mystery had been solved. They could enjoy the beautiful evening as they strolled to Brett's truck and then drove to Kristen's house. She couldn't wait to change into her coolest and most comfortable clothes and sit barefooted on the porch rehashing the recent events with the man she was growing to love.

From what they had pieced together about Ted, Patricia, and Cassie, along with information Sheriff Miller had let slip and comments from Todd, Kristen figured Ted's wild and crazy days had finally caught up with him when Patricia moved to Eklund. Patricia's motives were simple. She wanted Ted back after a romantic liaison they had shared twenty years ago resulted in a child—Cassie. After Patricia's affair ended with Ted, she'd moved away from the area to the Quad Cities, where it was easier to hide. She never told Ted about his illegitimate child since he'd already been married to Nancy and had his own children.

Once Cassie started college, though, she began to grow curious about her background and begged Patricia to shed some light on the sketchy details of her past. Patricia relented and even unburied her feelings for the father, Ted. She decided to stir the pot and move to Ted's home town of Eklund, where it was hard to avoid running into not only her past lover, but also his current wife, Nancy.

When Patricia contacted Ted to break the news about his long lost daughter, he took the news fairly well, but didn't want to commit to meeting Cassie, let alone have a relationship with her. It was one thing to flaunt his extra-marital affairs in public, but something else to recognize his illegitimate child. Not acknowledging his child worked until Cassie moved home for the summer after being away at college for the school year. It was only a matter of time before they met on their own. Ted decided he'd better explain the uncomfortable situation to Nancy. She took matters into her own hands and met Patricia at Monty's the day before she died. Hard telling what their discussion had entailed.

Patricia had no intention of harming Nancy. If she wanted a relationship with Ted, she already knew from past experience she didn't need to get Nancy out of the way to do so. However, once Cassie found out her birth father didn't want to recognize her, she was livid. Her mother told her the couple dined at Barney's regularly, and Cassie even went as far as to sneak a peek at the reservation list to learn when they were planning to eat there next. She put her classes in forestry and ecology to good use and cooked up a scheme to poison Nancy using a common nuisance plant. Knowing how busy weekends were at the bustling restaurant, she offered to help out that fateful Saturday night.

Kristen wasn't sure how Cassie had gotten her hands on Nancy's food or if she had been the one to disturb the wildflower arrangement. After witnessing Cassie's attitude toward her firsthand, Kristen suspected the intern had tried to divert attention to her, initially casting suspicions on the centerpieces the Nature Station had supplied. That act backfired, since it only encouraged Kristen to do her own research and ultimately help pinpoint the poison used. Besides, Cassie couldn't predict Kristen would be the one to discover the body, further spurring her interest in the murder.

Kristen and Brett had discussed the parking lot scene at great length while waiting their turn at the sheriff's office.

They both felt Cassie wanted Nancy out of the way so her parents could reunite and they could become a true family.

"I wonder how Cassie ended up hooking up with Ted yesterday morning." They sat together on a settee on Kristen's front porch.

"I have no idea. I can't believe I ever thought they were romantically involved."

"You had no way of knowing they were related," Brett reasoned. "I can't believe I worked with her and never suspected how evil she was."

"What's sad is, she only wanted to experience a complete and loving family life."

"And a lack of what she craved apparently warped her."

Kristen snuggled closer to Brett. "I'm just glad no harm came to you when you were working together, not to mention the scuffle in the parking lot. You worked together in some out of the way places, and she seemed to be obsessed with you…and me."

"It freaks me out to think about it. After all, she could have poisoned one of us just as easily as she did Nancy."

"Luckily she didn't, and now that this nasty business is settled, we can focus on us." She leaned in for a kiss that was as warm as the summer evening.

"That's what I want, too," he said, then kissed her again. He looked at her earnestly. "Do you think I should request another summer intern to replace Cassie?"

He sounded serious, but Kristen knew he was trying to be jovial about the loss of an employee he had considered top notch only a few days earlier. She punched him playfully on the arm, his healthy one, and said. "Not on your life!"

Soil Painting Activity

Nature Station programs offer something for everyone. Believe it or not, there are thousands of types of soil, all with different colors and properties. Try using one of nature's most basic resources to create a fun arts and crafts project. Here's an activity for youth and adults alike.

Materials:

Heavy duty sketch paper, cardstock, or blank notecards

Different types of dry soil ground into fine powder using mortar and pestle or other method

Small containers (cups or bowls)

Popsicle sticks or spoons

Colored pencils or crayons

Craft paint brushes

Newspaper or washable surface

Spread newspaper over work area. Add small amount of each soil type to a separate containers. Add water, and stir well. This mixture will be used as soil paint. Add more water for a watercolor consistency, and add less water to achieve a thicker paint consistency.

Use the paintbrush to dab a small amount of soil paint on the paper surface, and spread around as desired. If more than one type of soil is used, shades can be applied in different areas or mixed to create your painting. If you'd like to add color to your picture, use crayons or colored pencils to outline the objects to be painted. Allow the paint to dry.

Use a variety of soil types and paper styles to create a natural art masterpiece.

Acknowledgements

Writing mystery novels is a dream come true. I love mixing creative writing with my biology and conservation background. Writing *An Unnatural Selection* allowed me to branch out and explore new possibilities.

I supplemented my knowledge on poisonous and medicinal plants with information obtained from plant fact sheets produced by the USDA Natural Resources Conservation Service.

I thank my family for their patience, support and help when I squeezed valuable time into our busy, daily lives for writing and editing.

I thank my business partner at Progressive Rising Phoenix Press, Amanda M. Thrasher. Her ideas, encouragement, and positive outlook mean so much.

I am grateful to my editor, Mary Welk, for her insightful, practical suggestions.

Thanks to my colleague and friend, Sherrill Cannon, for giving *An Unnatural Selection* a final proofread.

I appreciate my co-workers, who provided me with valuable input.

Thanks to loyal Rachel Raccoon and Sammy Skunk book readers – they have inspired me to continue writing about nature, but this time for adults.

Lastly, thanks to all you readers! I hope you enjoy the second book in the Nature Station Mystery Series, *An Unnatural Selection*. It's been a delight to write and a true growing experience.

About the Author

Photo By: Alexandra Powelson

Born and raised on a farm in Northwestern Illinois, Jannifer Powelson's interest in writing, conservation, and the natural world was sparked at an early age. Books in the Nature Station Mystery Series encompass her passions of writing, photography, nature, and reading mysteries.

Powelson is also the author of four books in the Rachel Raccoon and Sammy Skunk series. These books use entertaining storylines, colorful and realistic illustrations, and photos taken by Powelson, to educate children about nature.

Jannifer is employed as a conservationist and resides in northwestern Illinois with her husband and two daughters. In 2012, she co-founded Progressive Rising Phoenix Press. Ms. Powelson is currently working on *Freak of Nature*, the third book in the Nature Station Mystery Series.

Other Books

When Nature Calls – A Nature Station Mystery
Rachel and Sammy Visit the Prairie
Rachel and Sammy Visit the Forest – A Guide to Spring Woodland Wildflowers
Rachel and Sammy Learn About Trees
Rachel and Sammy Learn to Conserve

www.janniferpowelson.com

CPSIA information can be obtained
at www.ICGtesting.com
Printed in the USA
LVHW111536310519
619751LV00001BA/12/P

9 781940 834672